GI

Barbara Anderson is t
Portrait of the Artist's Wife (winner of the 1992 W
Award), *All the Nice Girls*, *The House Guest* and *Proud
Garments*, and a collection of stories, *I think we should
go into the jungle.*

BY BARBARA ANDERSON

I think we should go into the jungle
Girls High
Portrait of the Artist's Wife
All the Nice Girls
The House Guest
Proud Garments

Barbara Anderson

GIRLS HIGH

VINTAGE

Published by Vintage 1998

2 4 6 8 10 9 7 5 3 1

Copyright © Barbara Anderson 1990

The right of Barbara Anderson to be identified as the author of
this work has been asserted by her in accordance with the Copyright, Designs and Patents Act, 1988

Lines on pages 192 and 231 from *Mother Courage and her
Children* by Bertolt Brecht, translated by John Willett (Eyre
Methuen, 1980) are © Stefan Brecht and used by permission.

Some sections of this book have been previously published in
Sport, the *Listener*, the *Dominion Sunday Times*, *Metro*, *More*
and *London Magazine*

First published in Great Britain by
Martin Secker & Warburg Ltd 1991

Vintage
Random House, 20 Vauxhall Bridge Road, London SW1V 2SA

Random House Australia (Pty) Limited
20 Alfred Street, Milsons Point, Sydney
New South Wales 2061, Australia

Random House New Zealand Limited
18 Poland Road, Glenfield, Auckland 10, New Zealand

Random House South Africa (Pty) Limited
Endulini, 5A Jubilee Road, Parktown 2193, South Africa

Random House UK Limited Reg. No. 954009

A CIP catalogue record for this book
is available from the British Library

ISBN 0 7493 9149 9

Printed and bound in Great Britain by
Cox & Wyman, Reading, Berkshire

For Jeremy and Heather

Contents

Staff Meeting

The Staff Room is on the first floor of the Administration Block. Sooze (Ms Powdrell, Science) stares down at the dusty bobbles of the plane tree as she waits for the first Staff Meeting of the year. Sooze has not settled into her teaching life though they have been back a month. Her heart sinks each morning. Her bowels turn to ashes. All is not well in the pit of her stomach. All clichés are true which is why they are clichés which is probably another cliché. Sooze sighs and clenches her lower face muscles to smile at Miss Franklin (First Assistant and French) who beams back at her, her cheeks pink, the crest of her white cockatoo hair rampant.

—Tell me, Miss Franklin, says Sooze, —when a new year starts do you think, Oh God, or ho hum, or what.

—I think my real life is beginning again. Miss Franklin's hands are busy, her head is down as she sorts, aligns, stacks her lists.

Sooze nods her head slowly. —Yes, she says. Yes.

—Hi, says Carmen (Ms Doyle, Phys Ed). Carmen was discarded by her lover last year and almost raped by the ex-Art Master. Sooze and Margot (Ms Murchison, Home Economics) supported her, loved her, talked her through. After endless discussions both have decided the worst thing they could do would be to go on about it any more, or to treat Carmen in any way differently. However Sooze finds to her shame that this is not a completely natural reaction. Woman as victim is out, rage is the thing she knows, and she has plenty of this, but somehow . . . And if she feels like this, what about Carmen? —Hi, she says, hugging her.

Carmen stands in front of Sooze in her tracksuit. She moves rhythmically from the ball of one foot to the other. —Keep it moving, keep it moving, she chants in her aerobics voice. Rays of energy leap from her as from an ad for an Art Deco wireless.

Sooze watches in silence. Her heart is in her boots.

Carmen is now feinting, ducking, her plait leaps from side to side as she knocks the new year into shape.

Sooze has thought of something else. She doesn't get enough exercise.

Margot enters and flings her class list on the table. —I've now got three more! I've now got forty-one in last year's 4F. Look!

Why should they doubt it. There it is. Forty-one. In last year's 4F.

Miss Tamp (Head) enters with her arms full of papers. She kicks the door shut with her black cuban. She has a new perm. Not bad in front. Frizzed at the back where they didn't neutralise thoroughly enough. An old lady's perm. Her jersey suit is meant to mix and match three ways but she always wears the same two bits together. Taupe on taupe. Blue nylon blouse. Margot gives a tiny unconscious shake of her head.

Miss Tamp's smile is firm. Incisiveness is the name of the game. —Sit down please ladies. Miss Franklin sits on Miss Tamp's right and stares straight in front of her. The more experienced members of the staff, Mrs Toon, Miss Hobbs, Mrs Benchley, Mrs Hopere, Mrs Stillburn and Mrs Vaughan the librarian take their places according to unwritten protocol which is so much more difficult to grasp than the written variety. Mrs Sinclair (Secretary) sits on Miss Tamp's left, her shorthand pad at the ready. The less experienced members of the staff as Miss Tamp calls them, Carmen, Sooze, Margot, and Jenni Murphy who is vegan, sit at the other end of the table. It is a large kauri table donated by Mr Smythe, the Chairman of the Board of Trustees, when the kids flew the nest and Grace and I moved into the penthouse. Miss Franklin calls it Le Nid.

Cliff Marden who has replaced the sacked Alec Tysler as Art doesn't know where to sit but he has been teaching long enough to know he could get it wrong. Jenni Murphy (Social Studies and Audiovisual Equipment) pats the chair beside her. He is grateful for this small gesture and sits.

Miss Tamp greets them formally then begins.

—I hope you all had good holidays, she says, tugging at the left-hand side of her collar which has a tendency to ride up. Margot knows it's the stiffening. Too heavy. And the whole thing is badly cut. Mrs Sinclair, who is relieved to get away from almost three months close proximity to her teenagers Ben and Fred, stares at an aerial photograph of the school on the wall opposite and smiles so broadly her gums show. Jenni Murphy also smiles. She has not been listening as she is thinking about her sexuality, but she gets the feeling something is expected of her at this point. No one else smiles at all. They are not paying attention to the preliminaries which they have heard before, even Mr Marden recognises them from Dannevirke High.

The staff are thinking.

Miss Franklin sniffs. —Who's got pepper? she mutters.

—Could be me, replies Una Benchley who has been thinking about David Hockney. She demonstrates, hunting down the small pottle of cracked pepper pâté in her bag labelled Loot.

Miss Franklin has a sudden glimpse of her father's pink hands on the dining room table in 1978. She sniffs again. Pepper. She remembers the conversation.

Sooze thinks about Bryce's job in the morgue.

Carmen notices that Cliff Marden's hair is thick and heavy and hangs across his forehead. Stuff him. She thinks about the pink flatty outside The Trinket Box.

Margot thinks about last Saturday night after they'd all gone. She smiles.

Miss Hobbs (Music) sits with her little girl's strapped shoes wide apart. She thinks about the peonies near the Kamikaze pilots' Memorial in Etajima.

Mrs Hopere (History) thinks about 4F.

Mrs Vaughan wonders why it all went wrong.

Mr Marden thinks that Carmen is the most beautiful woman he has ever seen in his life and what a clown he was last Saturday night. She is looking down. He stares at the two dark cusps of lashes against her cheeks. She glances up, glares at him. He moves quickly and converts the action into a search for his pen. Jesus.

Mrs Toon (Maths) thinks about her youngest.

Mrs Stillburn (Typing and Keyboard Skills and Guidance Counsellor) thinks that life is so sad. She worries about the girls at risk. And what more can she do about Armenia, Afghanistan, the famine in Ethiopia or is it Eritrea, except money which is not enough. She can scarcely bear to watch the news.

—As I was saying, says Miss Tamp. She has now moved onto the probable effects, as she sees them, of the Government's policy document *Tomorrow's Schools* on the day-to-day running of the school. —The success of *Tomorrow's Schools*, as I see it, she says, —will depend on good relationships between principals, staff, the community and the Boards of Trustees.

Miss Franklin tugs the edges of her cardigan together and grunts. —Hh.

—How many have read it? The Report? continues Miss Tamp. She glances at the uplifted hands: Miss Franklin, Mrs Benchley, Mrs Hopere, Mrs Stillburn, Susan Powdrell. Typical. And not enough. —There are two copies in the library (Mrs Vaughan nods) and any staff member is welcome to borrow my copy.

They do care. All of them. Miss Tamp knows that.

—'Scribble, scribble, scribble, Mr Gibbon', mutters Miss Franklin to Mr Marden.

Mr Marden's pen stops for a moment. —What?

—Doodling, says Miss Franklin.

—Picasso, says Ms Murphy, touching the face Mr Marden has drawn inside an elaborate cartouche.

Mr Marden nods and keeps drawing.

—I estimate that about five per cent of the girls are at risk due to parental neglect, says Mrs Stillburn out of nowhere.

—I'm not sure about the morality of the staff spending ninety-five per cent of their emotional energy and time on five per cent of the girls, says Miss Franklin.

—It's because that five per cent have no one else, says Mrs

Stillburn. —You can't tell me every bruised face we get has walked
into a door.

—I would like to bring up the matter of last year's 4F, says Mrs
Hopere.

—Certainly, says Miss Tamp. —Yes indeed. Perhaps you'd
like to discuss the matter with me later, Mrs Hopere. We have a
very full agenda today, don't we Mrs Sinclair?

Mrs Sinclair nods. —Yes, Miss Tamp.

—It's a matter of peer pressure, says Mrs Hopere.

—The worrying thing as I see it . . . , says Sooze. —About the
parent involvement recommendations in *Tomorrow's Schools*.

—Yes Susan?

—Well, parent involvement. Great. But the parents who get
involved won't be the parents whose kids need remedial reading,
say. Sooze blushes with anger at blushing.

—No, says Miss Franklin.

—We don't *know* that, says Miss Tamp.

—Yes we do, replies Miss Franklin, still staring straight ahead
at a faded reproduction of Cezanne's *Lake Annecy* donated to the
Staff Room by Lorraine Steel who just missed a University Scholarship in 1973.

The Staff Meeting goes on far too long. There is little conversation
when Miss Tamp declares the meeting closed. People move to their
lockers in silence. They want to get home, especially Sooze who
has to pick up Jared from Day Care.

Carmen runs after her as she leaves the Staff Room. —Hang
on, Sooze. I want to ask you something. She laughs, scrubs a hand
across her face. —To do something for me.

—It won't take a minute, she says. —Last Saturday night . . .
on the way home . . .

The new term, year, life, has begun.

Single shoes lie cheek by jowl outside The Trinket Box. A bull-nosed black leans against a grey suede, a beat-up sandal nudges a pink flatty. There are two baby boots, one red, one white scuffed. If you want to try a pair you take the shoe inside and find its mate.

At the Aces High café next door two young men sit side-by-side at a table near ours. Each has a cappuccino and a filled roll, one of which leaks alfalfa, the other ham. They gaze into each other's eyes as the older one with the moustache chants German numerals, —eins, zwei, drei, vier, fünf, then gets stuck and they laugh, how they laugh. The fingers of one right and one left hand almost touch as they lean their elbows on the back of the pseudo-rustic bench on which they sit. They are gentle, the younger one's newly-washed hair is soft and straight. They smile with shy excitement. They have found each other.

Think how lucky they are, for finding is all.

We sit at our pseudo-rustic table beneath the octagonal wall-clock with bronze rays which goes bong on the hour, and I jump and Barry smiles involuntarily, because I am a girl and he has nerves of chrome vanadium. I look at him stowing away his lasagne. Well grown larvae are quite capable of devouring their own kind. I watched them at it in *World Alive* last night as I ate my fettucini sitting cross-legged on the mattress in front of the TV I insisted on taking, because who paid the rental month after month after month. Whenever I eat food in front of the TV animals devour, especially insects. Crunching, munching, spitting out the carapace, nothing can stop them. Or toads. I shut my eyes when the giant tadpoles of the Spade Footed Toad ingest their weaker siblings. Sometimes there is a news clip of the sheep-meat chain at some sad and beleaguered freezing works. The camera lingers on bluish membranes, stalactites of waxy fat, the rip of entrails.

I shove my Savoury Chicken aside and scrabble in my Indian mirror-bag for a cigarette. I don't often smoke and it will make me feel worse. Barry pulls my plate towards him with a lift of an eyebrow. I nod. I can deny him nothing. He lifts his fork and shovels the stuff in between his beard and moustache. There is silence at our table except for gustation noises. The young men next door are gazing into each other's eyes again, or perhaps they never stopped. Denim inches to denim. The older man strokes the leather fringe of his friend's shoulder bag. I look away, blinking.

Barry pushes my ex-chicken plate away, not to one side, straight in front of him; the gesture of a replete child. —Well, he says, emptying two sugar sachets into his coffee. —That's the situation.

I have always been beautiful. You do know. Most little girls are attractive, then it thins out. Some, like me, just move on. I don't remember greasy hair, spots, puppy fat, any of that. My mother was terrified of vanity. —Don't mention the *hair* she used to hiss at her friends. Wendy Mahon told me that when we marched into chapel the light from the lancet windows turned mine into spun gold, that's what she said. I think of that when I see a sheep outlined, haloed by late afternoon sun. The hair was a lovely colour. Still is, though darker.

I was good at sport, especially diving. I began training with Eddy Bates when I was about twelve. He was a good coach, he never bullied. He never said, —Go up again, tight-lipped like some of them, when you've landed smack on your back from three metres attempting a one-and-a-half somersault, say. He'd send me off for a hot shower then explain again what I'd done wrong, more control, you need more consolidation, forget it for a while. After the shower I trotted up again and did the dive OK.

I lived at the Teps; toes curved over the end of the board, knees bent, arms out, the water moving way below then rushing to meet me with hardly a splash, the thrust and power of my body hooshing up again, two strokes, then heave onto the side, the water streaming back into the pool as I checked with Eddy. You need a coach, you can't train yourself in diving. There's a world of difference between what a diver thinks she's doing and what she is. Once you're launched you can't deflect your flight path, you've only got marginal control. And you have to equate perfection of execution (which only the coach can see) with the tariff value of the dive.

—You're coming along very nicely, said Eddy. —Nice, and slow, and gentle.

The guys at the pool liked the shape and the boobs, but my life was the push for perfection, and I didn't mind winning either. I jogged in green satin shorts with Eddy, who was older.

—I've got a thing going with your gluteus maximus, he said.

—Huh?

—It winks at me beneath your shorts, left right, left right. It's killing me.

—Run in front.

—You're joking.

I gave up diving when I went South. There weren't enough deep pools.

One of the books we handed around under the desks at the convent was *I Leap Over The Wall*, by an ex-nun. She said she had always been what she called easy on the eye and used to admiring glances, and when she left the convent years later this no longer happened and she was surprised which I think is a really honest statement. Ingrid Bergman said she supposed her perfect face would collapse one day, but she died before it did, if you follow me. You get used to wolf whistles and all that crap but if you're not fussed it's just irrelevant, pathetic.

Your self image is behind the eyes, the place where you hear rock music when there's nothing on. I can understand anorexia. I can understand people being confident when there is no apparent reason for their self regard. Maybe their mothers worshipped them.

I don't blame Mum. Shit, I wouldn't want five daughters and two sons, and I was the last. All I'm saying is I got my confidence another way. We all did, boys and girls. Theresa and I were pretty fronty ladies as well as beautiful and the boys were OK too. The dinkum Doyles my jokey father called us. The nuns went on about vanity and vanitas but I don't reckon the Doyles knew what they were talking about.

So what I'm on about is that knowing you're special leaves you unprepared for being dumped. It's a real shock, not the faint surprise of the ex-nun. If you've always had a queue you get used to it. If every time you lift a finger it starts a stampede, then it's a shock.

My sister Theresa is now a nun in a closed order in Melbourne. I write to her though it's getting more difficult to think of things to say and she's not allowed to answer except at Christmas. Saint Theresa we called her. When we were about fourteen she equipped us all with Durex Gossamers supplied by her boyfriend Manny. It was quite a little ceremony. She was way ahead of her time. She would put one on her finger and demonstrate the little bobble and explain quite pragmatically so we weren't shy. The Pommie Aids prevention films years later were old hat to me. After the demonstration she told each of us that we were never never never to come to her with any excuses.

Theresa and I were the only ones with our own rooms. I can feel the breeze from the window, see the faded curtains fanning across the Sacred Heart above her bed, her Dire Straits poster; the toes of her right foot moving incessantly against her jandal as she speaks. She was the most beautiful of all the Doyles. Her eyebrows were dark strokes, her eyes green, and I mean green, fringed with thick dark lashes. Manny said they were like lagoons surrounded by rushes. There was something wrong with his description though we liked him too much to mention it. Her eyes were clear, translucent.

She wasn't religious then, obviously, though Catholics are

always informed. Conviction came later. I suppose our Theresa of the Sacred Name makes endless penances. I don't know. She told me that she loved Manny like a hole in the heart, but that nothing less than a closed order would do. He runs a trucking firm now, on the North Shore.

So when I was sixteen and Eddy and I were rolling around on the tray of Kia Ora Metal Industries' truck at the pre-Christmas wind up of the Swimming Club and he kept grabbing my hand and trying to wrap it around his solid mushroom-capped penis and moaning, —Carmen, Carmen for God's sake, I said, —I'll do it if you like but I'm not going to do that.

I liked Eddy. He had one of those narrow, hope of the seminary faces; pale with dark jowls and rimless glasses. He had an honest mind and he knew about training. He was amazed that I would ever smoke, but two or three a week what the hell. One night at the Western Park Tavern a year or so later he was getting maudlin and mumbling, —Carmen, Carmen, into my neck, and I put down my lime-and-soda and said, —Look Eddy let's get this straight. I like you a lot but I don't love you. He sat bolt upright at the sloshy table and said, —Good God no, and we laughed so much I nearly did. He's dead now.

I won a Scholarship to Dunedin for Phys Ed. It's not so hot teaching it, but at least you're still moving which is what I'm good at, and most of the kids are OK. I can't imagine life without Margot and Sooze either, but then I used to feel that about Theresa.

They had a thing in the Capping Mag the first year I was in Dunedin. 'Bizet's had nothing on this one,' it said, underneath a photo of me at the Freshers' Hop with about six guys draped about. I look pretty weird but the men look worse. Sort of loose.

And it went on like that.

In second year I moved in with Ken. He was a fourth-year dental and the flat was full of casts and pink latex moulds and false teeth grinning at you. They marched along the mantelpiece, leered from the fridge, booed from the broom cupboard where he'd hidden a set beneath a feather duster.

He had a golden retriever called Chubb who ran with me, pounding up Maori Hill into the Town Belt, his chestnut hair streaming in the wind, his tongue flopping against his frilled gums and my gluteus maximus bouncing I suppose, but safe with Chubb who was tougher than he looked and jumped barking at any hoon in a trailing car. Obscene gestures I dealt with by return.

Ken loved the rolling about, panting and squelching night after night in some sort of ecstasy. We both did. He liked me to dress up. He bought me a pair of black leather pants in Christchurch which I never knew how to clean. He preferred an old red satin shirt Theresa had discarded to my T-shirts. He begged me to grow my hair. I didn't mind. It grows quickly, my hair, and was soon long enough to plait. But he didn't sit about gaping with wonder, that was what was so restful. I was beautiful, he was gorgeous, and he was too and funny with it.

He was quick, glancing, a picador from Balclutha practising to become a fully paid-up eccentric. About the only thing he was serious about was flossing. —You've got to floss, he said. —It's the only way. A trip to the Supermarket could be heaven or hell as he camped it up imitating TV advertisements, his favourite viewing after the Muppets. He sidled in the door like the beautiful woman in the Omo ad, he was the old man with the pack of Mainland cheese in his hand, he discarded mythical Brand Xs at the feet of professional housewives. We went to a winter wedding in Gore and he walked through a creek to pick me a dandelion. He wasn't stoned either.

Everything with Ken and Chubb and the teeth made me laugh until one morning I took a long look at the dentures on the cistern and realised they weren't funny. Just large and shiny and not real.

My love life is like the toy weather-house Gran McCormack had on the wall of her glassed-in sunporch in Hokitika. Set fair the little lady swings out, the little guy has a sense of humour and lives inside laughing, and life is a breeze read. The rains come and the winds blow and beat upon that house. The little man swings out from the shadows. I see him in the cold light of intimacy. He has no sense of humour at all. What I thought at a distance was wit, is ha-ha at cartoons. He is po-faced and pompous and up himself. I ditch him. I am well rid of him, yes indeed.

I depend too much on laughs. It is addictive. And not very clever.

So that Barry who is the light of my life, the ache in the gut and below, was a surprise. No jokes here. He is a systems analyst. He analyses systems. Concepts. Not nuts and bolts.

He lives inside me. He is a slow fuse to the interior, two tongues in the mouth. He touches Delia's cheek and I, who belong to a women's group, grind her foot beneath mine. He lights Morgan's cigarette. Sorry, I mutter, as I drag her canvas bag through deep beer. I despise women. All women. Me.

Lovers who are on the skids have no redress. They should leave the sod/bitch immediately. With dignity. Like adults so help me God. When people feel suspicious and threatened they behave like threatened and suspicious people. They nag. They pry. They bitch. The slide steepens to a whirlaway crash and they are sunk, without trace.

The mating of the ladybird may take as long as four hours.
   —You're sure she's pregnant, I say.
   —Yeah.
   I have seen the other other woman. She has huge haunted eyes, so anguished she made *me* feel guilty as I peered through the window of the New Vision Bookshop. Small cervix I bet. She wears Indian muslin skirts. She has one purple and one saffron. The saffron one is tight about her hips, then gathered. It hangs to her ankles. The rhythm of her rolling buttocks is orchestrated—right, left, reroll, repeat, right, left etc. It is hypnotic like kinetic sculpture and knocks my gluteus maximus into a cocked hat as she drifts with slow steps about the New Vision where she works. I didn't go in. I could see well enough to kill through the gap between the Jeffrey

Archer and Janet Frame hardbacks. The cat on Jeffrey Archer's cover has a dollar sign in one eye and scales of justice in the other. I believe the prostitute.

The palm of my right hand has deep nail marks. I squeeze my legs together.

—Is she going to keep it I say, casually, casually like the end of the world and Mars, which is the one the colour of serum tinted with blood cells.

His beard needs a trim. Some men, not Barry never Barry, can't leave them alone, they like the silky feel, like me. I blow my nose.

—Yeah.

—Stop saying yeah, can't you.

—Sorry.

Barry the clench, the necessity, is never sorry.

I force myself. —Where does that leave me?

I look away quickly from the silence.

Two grey-haired ladies, overweight, elderly—the lot—each carrying two laden trays, totter to a nearby table. Each plate has a filled croissant which I know from experience is disgusting, slabs of cheesecake, stuff, I don't care. Two men glance up and extend hands in silence to receive a tray each. One man is cadaverous, the other pudgy and pallid. No one smiles, thanks, kisses a foot. —Tt, says one of the ladies, flinging forgetful hands into the air. She scuttles back to the counter, nods to the proprietor and returns with a teaspoon. —Sorry she says, smiling as she places it on the zombie's saucer. He raises pinched shoulders. He has black sideburns. No one has told him they are finished.

—Why'd you have to tell me in this dump! I yell. The two young men look up, startled, then drop their eyes quickly. Gentle so gentle.

Because you thought I wouldn't yell and scream and refuse to abandon shit.

—Fuck you, I scream, again and again and again. Even the proprietor looks up from his safety zone. I seize my pretty bag and hit my lover about the shoulders, then grab the straps tight for more purchase and slam it against his head again and again and again. He sits there. I run out bawling.

The back of my Kung Fu has come off. I lean against the steamy window of the Aces High—blind, drunk, reeling. —Theresa, I gasp, sobbing it out to Australia. My head weaves from side to side. —Theresa.

I pull up the back of my shoe as the shelves outside The Trinket Box swing into focus. My snorting self-loathing changes to a lower key as I stare at the pink flatty. I hiccup as the door swings open. The four people from the table near ours trail past in ordered silence: zombie, pallid, the two ladies. The larger one in the beige pudding hat knocks against me. She laughs. She knows it is her fault. —Oops, dear, she gasps, patting her stomach in rueful apology. —Pardon me, she says.

Una Benchley thinks about
David Hockney

Una Benchley sits opposite Carmen at the April Staff Meeting. Rays of sun from the high clerestory windows fall on Carmen's blonde hair illuminating it. The effect is dazzling as Mr Marden who sits beside Una has also noticed. Una thinks of David Hockney at fifty-one and is sad. There he is dyeing his hair every Thursday night just like a girl. He saw a Clairol ad the first time he was in New York which told him that blondes have more fun and believed it. And who's to say he's wrong unless they've tried, which Una hasn't.

Years ago she saw a Hockney self-portrait, drawn when the artist was still at school. It was a plate from a French pottery museum. The authority of the few lines which sketched the owlish face knocked her socks off. What a future.

'If ever I stopped dyeing it,' he says, 'people would interpret it as a statement.' Una can understand that. He is trapped inside his own cult figure, turned to gold by his own Midas touch. He is deaf and wears a double hearing aid and doesn't go to parties because of the background buzz they call it. He has a problem, perhaps, with consonants. Ps and Ts. Is love a big ship or shit following him? Is the *Dame aux Camellias* requesting police or priest at her deathbed? He must make snap decisions through fog as he watches television most evenings alone with his beloved dachsund called Stanley, after Stan Laurel, and wasn't there something funny about him or was that the other one.

Una folds the paper. She will cut out the Hockney article and put it in a pink folder where she stows things she can't bear to throw out and never looks at again.

She also discovered Richard Burton before he was famous or rich or married or dead. Instead of finding out whether it's true

what they say about blondes Una stood in theatre queues surrounded by incompetent buskers throwing balls about and fought
vertigo in the terraced gods. She saw Richard Burton in a small part
in *The Lady's Not for Burning*. She couldn't take her eyes off him as
he sat downstage left and smouldered.

None of what followed was a surprise to her.

Una came back from her OE bringing gifts from swinging London:
a tin tray and tea towels printed with the Union Jack which
offended her father as the flag meant a great deal to him; a mug with
Kitchener pointing at her; Beatles memorabilia. She resumed
teaching at Girls High and met Brock who taught at Boys High, and
was a friend of a friend as is so often the case.

Slim as a bluebell Una hops behind Brock on his Matchless and they
are up up and away, her arms tight about him as they lean helmetless
into the well-cambered curves of the Bay. Her hair flies, sweeps
salty into her mouth as she laughs, is spat out when they reach
Westshore and her hands are free. Brock tells her she doesn't lean
far enough. Go with me all the way, he tells her. Don't be a dead
weight.

Brock stopped short of total immersion in valves and chains.
He had other interests. Amateur theatrical rehearsals were held in
the dusty Scout Den by the Park, surrounded by pennants and
photographs of Akelas and Leaders now defunct, including a signed
one of Lord Baden Powell in long shorts holding a staff. B.P.'s wife
was thirty years younger. He fell in love with her springing
confident stride as she walked the dogs in Hyde Park and they lived
happily ever after. Una knows this because she has found, spread-
eagled beneath a bench, an autobiography by Lady Baden Powell,
and is reading it surreptitiously while prompting for *The Importance
of Being Earnest* by Oscar Wilde. Brock plays Jack.

—'Oh, she gets around very little,' he declaims from the dais,
his head and script held high.

—'Goes about very little,' mutters Una from the floor, a finger guarding her place in the true love story.

Brock juts his pelvis forward, his hands on his hips. His beard points. She is at eye-level with his zip. —Must you pick me up on every single solitary . . . ?

—Going about is not the same as getting around, says Una.

—True, says Vince the director.

—This is a *run* through!

—If you get it wrong now you'll get stuck in it, says Una.

Gwendolyn pokes her parasol at the stage. She insists on having it even though it is a run through so she can get the feel of it.

—'Don't get *around* much any more,' belts Canon Chasuble.

—Why are we doing this crap anyway? asks Brock, flinging his script on the chair which represents a tea table. —Why couldn't we have a crack at *Waiting for Godot*? He turns upstage to check his zip.

—Because we've got to fill the fucken Muni, says Vince the director tugging at his eye-shade.

—You don't have to fill it, says Brock.

—You'd have two men, says Vince, and . . .

—Fifteen women, says Una.

Brock swings like a machine gunner at Una who smiles at him, her heart beating pocketa, pocketa, pocketa.

Gwendolyn has found a knot in the stage to dig at. —What about *South Pacific*? she says.

Vince leaps to his feet, skinny and outraged. —We've been through this a thousand times! *The Importance of Being Earnest*. In three weeks. Right!

Una swings well into the curves on the way home and the wind blows.

'John is displeased by my person' wrote Effie Ruskin to her parents. He had never seen a naked woman before, only nudes, and was repelled by her pubic hair. Brock kept the lights off and his eyes shut and moved to the sunporch after a few weeks of marriage because he didn't want to keep Una awake with his snores.

Una screwed her trousseau nightie between her hands, pressing its faint mustiness against her face. His mind was made up. He was fine out there.

The sunporch was male as a sergeant's billet. A Royal Stuart rug given them as a wedding present covered the low bed. An alarm clock, a small Swiss army knife, a yellow Gollancz murder, a blue plastic glass of water shared the kitchen chair alongside. Una lay awake each night listening for his snores.

He asked boys from school home in the weekends. Jimmy the Captain of the 1st XV ate six melting-moments and Brock christened them Jimmys and Bill and Terry and Vince laughed, flinging back their heads, haw haw haw. They sunbathed, sweating on beach towels beside the toolshed on the back lawn, their shy white backs and brown necks anointed with oil, their knees and forearms tanned and hairy. Their faces were hidden, cradled in their arms. Brock took photographs with his Canon as they hammed it up in Mr Universe poses. —Bit more biceps there Bill, cried Brock. Bill clenched his fists, his face contorted with the effort of the joke. He had the head of a young Picasso, wide mouth, neat ears, hair clipped close to his head above intent eyes. Una stood laughing, loving them all, her hands on the railing of the deck. Brock took the boys out to Blackbridge for a swim, happy to ferry them in turns on the Matchless.

Brock is now a dramaturg and lives with his lover Clive in downtown Los Angeles. They have a good life and Brock has nothing against Una. Nothing at all. He tells her so. He sends her photos of himself taken by Clive. The last ones were at a picnic in the smog. Brock is solid, even his gut is muscular as he leans against the Lincoln convertible with its roof down, his ankles crossed, one white Reebok sideways on top of the other. He wears tracksuit trousers, the cord hangs below his red T-shirt which says HARVARD in black. He has a suntanned bald head and a well-trimmed curly grey beard and an enthusiasm for life like David Hockney had, and Una hopes still has. Brock squints into the smog-bound sun and squeezes her heart.

Una had never stopped teaching and her superannuation was unaffected by two years' matrimony. Una is a conscientious teacher. She keeps up with her own reading and hacks her way through prescribed English explaining the syllabus musts, though nowadays there is a lot about communication skills. Levels of discourse.

—Fucken wimp, says Ella of 3C, bending to retie her Charlie Browns.

—Who? says her friend Tracey, her hands flat on the concrete of the lab steps.

—Tampax.

—Tamp? Yeah. Fuckwit.

Their gym skirts are heaved above their pants, their legs stick straight in front of them, smooth, hairless and brown.

—I don't mind Benchley, says Ella, wrapping the remains of her muesli bar in a tissue dragged from her pocket.

—What!

—Well she's, you know . . . Not a bitch, sort of.

—Her old man's a queer.

—Yeah. Ella stows the package down her front. —In LA.

—Gay in LA.

—Yeah. Ella hides her face on her knees to laugh. The sun is warm on her neck.

Una did not discover Andy Warhol herself but she admires him nevertheless. His writing more than his pictures though she accepts them as Art because they make her see, especially the one of the electric chair, its straps hanging. Andy Warhol used to wear leathers but went back to bluejeans because it is their nature to be washed. He was obsessed with cleanliness. He said that God lurks in the detail. He said that everyone's sense of beauty is different from everyone else's. When he saw people dressed in maroon polyester waffle iron pants he tried to imagine what went off in their heads when they bought them. Did they say, 'This is great. I like it. I'll take it.' What did they reject as not beautiful. It worried him. He also bleached his hair though Una does not know whether David Hockney or he did it first.

Una stares across the kauri table donated to the staff room by the Chairman of the Board of Trustees, at Carmen's hair. It is the colour they strive for but natural. Perhaps though they prefer the stark bleached effect rather than Carmen's multiplicity of shades which range from fresh-picked to darker corn-silk. Probably they do. The artificial is desired, the real rejected. Carmen turns her head. Tendrils of pale gold drift against her neck. She wears a silver chain, one silver ball lies at the base of her throat. She is infinitely desirable. Una can see that. It's not that she can't understand Brock. Una sees Mr Marden's eyes on Carmen yet again.

> In such a night,
> Troilus methinks mounted the Troyan walls,
> And sigh'd his soul toward the Grecian tents,
> Where Cressid lay that night

In such a night . . .

Una's quotes are a great help to her. They are her talisman. She clutches them to her. They see her through.

Carmen, my dear. It will be all right. I promise. Attempted rape is a violation. It is worse than rejection. Much worse. I do know that. But remember Andy Warhol's philosophy—the So what philosophy. 'My mother didn't love me as a child. So what. My husband doesn't ball me anymore. So what.' Let the dead past bury its dead though he doesn't say that. It's now that matters. Una's left hand tightens on her handkerchief. But remember, Carmen. Donne was wrong in one sense. Every man woman and dog is an island. Seventeen children, three husbands. So what. We are all on our Pat Malone, Carmen. So what, so what. I promise.

Carmen lifts her head and grins at Bench baby who is a good sort. Mr Marden moves from one buttock to the other. Una smiles.

Una was sad when Andy Warhol died. His death seemed

mishandled and unnecessary. And now there's that sale of his effects. Effects. An odd word.

Una puts down *From A to B and Back Again: The philosophy of Andy Warhol* which she is rereading in her sunporch at Eastbourne and walks out to check the letter box. She is neurotic about mail on Saturdays, often making several trips God knows why. She moves heavily in her yellow hand-knit between the borders of Mrs Sinkin dianthus which line the straight concrete path. Mrs Sinkin is a good doer with a long floraceous period but splits badly, the frilled white petals exploding from sprung calyxes.

There is a letter from Brock. He and Clive are coming out on another trip and will look forward to catching up with Una about the twenty-fifth. A week from now. They can take in some local theatre together. Will Una make bookings for three so they can see what's on. Brock will be interested to hear her views on indigenous New Zealand drama. Where it's at at the moment. Improvisation is the name of the game, the state of the art on the West Coast he writes. There is so much more scope for spontaneous input, for genuine creativity, when bouncing ideas off other people. You don't get locked in.

Una stands at the front gate and reads the letter twice, one hand clutching the wrought iron curlicue which decorates the aluminium cuckoo-clock letter box.

Brock sits crumpled on Una's sun porch. There is a divan covered with a blue and red woven rug where his bed used to be and comfortable seagrass chairs Una has painted a rather good blueish purple. You can see a sliver of sea beyond the carpark across the road. There is a Norfolk Pine which her mother called a monkey puzzle when Una was little but never explained why.

Brock leans forward in the seagrass, his head in his hands, his shoulders slumped in despair beneath his pink sweat shirt. Clive has left him.

—I'm so desperately unhappy, he says, lifting his head to gaze into her eyes. He means it. There is nothing left. Nothing. Sometimes he feels there is no point in going on. Brock hangs his head again, his eyes scarcely see the striped offcut-rug below them. He reaches in the pocket of his Calvin Kleins and pulls out a handkerchief.

Una stares at him and wonders what on earth he thinks she can do about it, or would do about it, and why should she. Who in the name of all that's merciful does he think he is. Or think *she* is, but this she knows. You wouldn't read about it. The astonishment of life. There is always something to behave about.

Brock says that when he thinks. He says that Clive was a ribbon clerk (rhyming it with dirk) when they met, and look at his lifestyle now. He says that life is so fucking unfair.

Una agrees, her eyes on the monkey puzzle outside the window.

Brock says there is nothing left in his life. Nothing.

Una rearranges a limp cushion behind her, tucking it into the small of her back with a firm hand. She leans forward.

David Hockney leaps to her mind. His blond head. His Thursday nights.

—Have you ever thought of . . . ? she says and stops.

Brock's arms hang helpless. His dark eyes lift to hers, wounded as a bushbaby's.

—What?

—Nothing, says Una. —Just something I thought of. Nothing.

—I've been rereading Brecht, she says after a long pause. —Have you seen any interesting productions of his stuff lately?

Brock's eyes are on the carpet once more. His head moves slowly from side to side.

He covers his face with his hands.

Cam and Margot lead separate lives during the day like most people. This is all right by them. They are content with the mornings which separate, the evenings, the weekends which are precious.

Margot doesn't ask Cam about his working life now. When she did he told her. He told her about soffits and dwangs and uprights and things which mean nothing to her, though she knew to take an interest because her mother told her. Her mother believed in taking an interest. —How did your day go? she asked Margot's father each evening as his hand reached for the paper after a rough day in Industrial Laminates.

Now Margot says, —Cam, how're things at work, don't tell me, and he grins and Margot walks into his arms. Rock of ages. Her feeling for Cam is archaic, Margot knows this, though of course she doesn't go on about it.

Cam also knows not to go on too much about Girls High, though he does ask occasionally because he is courteous.

—How're things in the Clothing Room?

—We had a blackout.

Cam's forehead is creased like that TV news announcer who looks so worried he makes Margot feel worse. —Why? he asks.

One of her hands flings in the air. —Phht! I don't know. Overloaded maybe.

—It shouldn't do that.

—Well it did. Phht!

—Someone'd better have a look at it.

—Mr Gilchrist's meant to fix it. Cam has met Mr Gilchrist. A shy weasel of a man in check shorts.

—Yeah but . . . Why's it overloading?

—I don't know. I just teach Textiles.

—I could have a look.

—It won't stop doing it just because you have a look. Remember Milan. Cam electrocuted himself in Milan, or is that only dying. A major shock anyway.

—I could get Charlie to check it out. Charlie is an electrician with marital problems whose hourly rate is off the clock high compared with Cam's. —How often does it go?

—Phht?

—Yeah.

Margot shrugs. —Forget it. I'll get Mr Gilchrist.

Margot and Cam rent a dilapidated flat in Oriental Bay, one of the last left among the high-rises. The rent is too much but they like the area; they enjoy the daily cruise of tourists in Ultrasuede, the tight-faced joggers, ambling locals, the occasional bum poking about with a stick. There are always children, usually dogs.

The flat is cold though. Margot pulls on a pink sweat shirt which used to belong to her sister Michelle who played in a social softball club which had the shirts printed. *Funky funky Epsom* is printed on the front and a telephone number, *674-501*, on the back but Margot doesn't know whose it is. Not Michelle's, who is now in Caracas with Dominique, a urologist with a special interest in renal tumours. The club had two teams. They played once a year. On New Year's Day.

—Cam, says Margot.

—Mmn.

—I think we should have Sooze and Bryce and Carmen and that new guy at school over on Saturday.

—Why?

—He's in a grotty bed-sit in Willis Street. The new guy.

Cam turns from the window. The areas beneath his cheek-bones are faintly shadowed, his eyes are deep set. —Saturday? he says.

—They won't stay all night. Margot laughs up at him, wriggling her behind into the hooked rug she made last year. She sits cross-legged, a child at kindergarten waiting for the story on the mat. Her hair is dark, well cut, shiny as a buffed shoe. —You're getting paranoid about Saturday nights, she says.

—I like Saturday nights because of Sundays. And anyway, Bryce's a pain in the ass.

—It's our turn to have them.

—We never *had* people at home. People just came and ate. Uncles mostly, Larry, Harry, Syd.

—Carmen's last guy was called Barry.

—The shit?

—Mmn. Margot dips her head to her left knee then to her right, then to the floor between.

—The new guy's Cliff Marden, she says straightening.

Cam's face sags. —Cliff?

—And it's just Bryce's way. I mean he's OK really.

—I never get that. If it's his way it's him, for Godsake. Cam stretches. —The Children's Session guy in Invercargill, he says, —was Uncle Clarrie.

—How're your four-by-twos Cam? asks Bryce on Saturday night.

Cam smiles. —Hundred-by-fifties now, he says. He pats Bryce's hand which lies on the table. —Still thick as two planks though.

Bryce snatches the hand away. He shoves it into his pocket in search of his handkerchief but Sooze's round blue eyes hold his. Bryce describes Sooze as my partner. She wears a grey shirt and black trousers tucked into calf-length boots. She looks work-personlike, a sexual helpmeet with her sleeves rolled up.

Bryce removes his hand from his pocket and studies it.

Sooze shifts on the hard chair. —When I was a child there was a cartoon. One rook was saying to the other, Bred any good rooks lately?

Bryce leans back. —What was the answer?

—Nyer, says Margot. She lifts a large spoon and ducks her head slightly to peer beneath the lampshade. Her eyes move from face to face around the table. The lampshade is apricot and mauve silk, an imitation Tiffany which she bought last payday. When she hung it she forgot to make allowance for the depth of the silk fringe.

—More? asks Margot, her spoon hovering above the oxtail with olives. Carmen's olives lie black and succulent with juices, abandoned on her white plate. Bryce takes one with an outstretched hand, puts it in his mouth and nods at her.

Carmen smiles at Margot and shakes her head. She puts her hands on her shoulder to adjust her wide scarf of pink and orange silk. Cliff Marden puts out a hand to help her. Carmen snatches hers away. Hands are moving around the table. Sooze clasps hers together, Bryce's are now polishing his glasses. He doesn't need them now, just for long distance. He puts them back in their case and rubs it with his middle finger.

Margot and Sooze can never understand how Carmen, like some other women too beautiful for this world, can be such a bad picker. —Wouldn't you think, Margot shouted at Sooze above the running water in the staff cloakroom just last week, —Wouldn't you think that someone like *Carmen* would've learnt by now?

Margot glances at Cliff. He sits straight-backed as a short man though he is above average height. His head is high, his shoulders back as he looks the world and Margot in the eye. She smiles at him, her eyebrows raised. —No thanks Margot, he says. —Great.

Cam passes his plate up Carmen's side of the table. —We had *E.T.* last night, he says.

—On video? asks Sooze.

—Yeah. Cam smiles, remembering the kids' faces as their bikes took off across the moon.

—You lose a lot on the small screen, says Bryce.

—Mention video, says Carmen, —and someone'll bang on about the wide screen.

Bryce leans forward across his oxtail bones. —Yeah. Because it makes a difference.

—Sure it makes a difference. OK, so it makes a difference.

Carmen tugs at her vibrant shawl. She is all in black otherwise. Her skin is creamy.

Cliff's eyes are on the silver ball which lies at the base of Carmen's throat.

—They say it's Christian, he says.

—What's Christian? says Bryce. He blows his nose, takes a quick peek at his handkerchief and replaces it.

—The light in that shed, say. When Elliot first meets E.T. It's like the manger, says Cliff.

Cam is interested. He picks up a vertebra for a last suck. —I hadn't thought of that he says, scrubbing his hands with a checked cotton napkin before giving them a final rub on his jeans.

Sooze dips around the lampshade fringe at Cam then at Cliff. —Tell us more, she asks, leaning her breasts on her arms as she bends across the table.

—Well at the beginning everyone's fighting, right, all those kids yelling . . .

—4F, mutters Carmen pleating her napkin into a fan.

Margot's large spoon is arrested in midair. —I couldn't stand that triangular table, she says.

—Table? says Cam.

Longing for Cam—sudden, unexpected as a hammer from scaffolding—crashes on Margot. Why did she ask all these people. Margot sees herself and Cam lying naked and entwined, the silent television blinking with a voyeur's shame, mouthing and gesturing to itself at the end of the disordered bed. The vision is so bright she blinks.

Cam catches her smile. He shifts his behind slightly, his hand strokes the table which he made himself and is proud of. It is pine, a beautiful job. —What table? he says.

—Just a table Cambo, says Sooze, touching his hand. —It was triangular. The kids were all sitting round it fighting. You know. At the beginning.

—Oh yeah. Mmn. I liked the way the bad guys didn't have

faces. The teacher even with those millions of frogs. You just saw his legs. Cam goes back to the oxtail.

—The back of the Headmistress's chair's got a neck like E.T. says Carmen. —Coiled and grey and retractable.

Margot pulls a tissue from her sleeve and scrubs at her nose. —Hay fever's the pits, she says.

—I'd need more than the light in the shed, says Carmen, —to convince me.

—I'll get out the video, says Cliff. —Come round. Give you a demo.

—Some people'd say anything's Christian, says Carmen lifting her glass. She sips and replaces it. Her finger traces a circle around its base. —Nice, she says. Bryce leans across the table and turns the bottle so that the label is towards Carmen. They smile at each other through the fringe.

—Go on, says Sooze to Cliff. —Tell us more.

—Well it's pretty obvious isn't it, he says. Cliff sits taller than ever, his eyes fixed on Sooze. —It's all there. Arrival from on high, Redemption by suffering, Ascension to heaven at the end.

—What about Atonement? says Cam.

—Well that's Redemption isn't it. The back of Cliff's hand flicks against the end of his nose.

—No, says Carmen.

—You get it too? says Margot.

—What? says Cliff.

—Hay fever. Margot repeats his gesture. —The allergic child's salute. They smile at each other. They are sympathetic, pleased with their bonding.

—What was redeemed? says Cam.

—Oh at the end, cries Sooze, her hands now clasped in supplication. —The bad kids turn into good kids, the siblings love each other. There's that man beside the mother . . .

—Great, says Carmen. —So everything's peachy.

Bryce switches tack. —Still got your backpack? he says.

Carmen pounces swift as a cheetah across the table. —Unlike you.

Bryce leans back. He runs a hand through his tough springy hair. —Rock's theory's crap.

—Cliff.

—Little joke there.

—Pudding, cries Margot, leaping up to stack the plates on the divider, her thumb supporting tail-bones against the slope.

They have knocked off the Gisborne Chardonnay long ago and are now onto the cardboard cask. It is two am. No one will move. No one will go.

—Why don't they *go*, hisses Cam in the kitchen, his hand on Margot's rump. She is on her knees, her head in the cupboard beneath the sink, searching for a cloth to mop up Carmen's spilt wine. She lifts her head. —What?

—Go!

—You tell them. She turns to scrabble deeper. It is behind the bucket.

Cam follows Margot back to the living room which was originally a sunporch. The floor has a slight seawards slope. Cam slaps both hands hard against his thighs. —Well! he says.

—Give it to me, says Carmen, her hand reaching for the cloth.

—Forget it, don't worry about it. Margot is scrubbing at the navy blue weave of the sofa cover. —White's OK.

Carmen turns to stare out the window at the dark night. The city lights cast long reflections, rainbow strips curve around the harbour. She leans her head on her arms. —No wind, she says. —They can hang straight. Ribbons at sea.

I want to hold your hand. Like a fucken Beatle. Just your hand for now. What the fuck's wrong with you anyhow.

No one has told Cliff that the man he replaced nearly raped Carmen last year. It's not a secret. Nor is it information which is easy to let slip casually.

Bryce sits on the floor leaning against the sofa, his dark head alongside Carmen's thigh. —The morgue's all right, he tells Cam.

—Approached? were you, says Cam, pouring himself more wine. —Asked to join?

—Makes a change from the money market though. I was kicked out of Futures. Bryce laughs. —Did y'hear that. No future for Brycey. He is expansive. Relaxed.

—Pas de Futures, he says, lifting his empty glass high. —Thanks. You look like a Desert Road pylon from this level, Cambo. Thirty metres high and shoulders like an ox.

Cam's voice is gentle. —Not Cambo, he says.

—My, burp, my partner calls you Cambo.

—But I like your partner.

—So do I. So do I. Too thin though. Not enough fat. Sooze, yells Bryce, flapping his hand at her. —Cambo says he likes you.

—I know. Sooze stands. —Come on, she says. —Time we went home.

Carmen is also on her feet. She picks up her scarf and drags it around her. She is swathed in colour. —I'm going for a swim.

—Great. Bryce crawls up from the floor. —Carmen and I, he says one arm round her shoulders as he leans against her, —are going for a swim.

—Don't be so bloody stupid, says Sooze shoving her left arm into her old blue jacket with force.

—I'm coming, says Cliff.

—No. Bryce shakes his head sadly. —No togs. No more persons. E.T. can bugger off home.

—Can I borrow a towel? says Cliff.

—Sure, says Margot.

—We'll have to go too, she hisses at Cam as they stand by the linen cupboard in the hall. —Otherwise they'll all come thundering back. She loads his arms with towels.

—OK. Cam likes swimming at night. He floats on his back and checks out the Southern Cross, the false Cross, Betelgeuse and Bellatrix, Orion's belt. Sometimes there is phosphorescence, the last time on Margot's left buttock. He walks a few steps along the hall then stops. —They'll have to come back anyway, to get dressed and that.

Margot nods. —Yes, but it'll wake them up. They'll go.

—They'll want nightcaps and stuff.

—They won't get them.

—No. Cam smiles as he pads up the hall. There are no stars though. Not tonight.

But still they don't go. They lie about talking, the stereo is silent. Carmen is leaning forward to discuss street-kids with Cliff and Sooze. She has pulled on Margot's sweatshirt to keep out the draught from the ill-fitting windows. *Funky funky Epsom* is printed across her in black. She lifts her eyebrows to Margot. —OK? she asks, meaning can she borrow it. Margot nods. She hadn't realised it looked quite like that. —It's yours, she says. Carmen shakes her head smiling.

—What about the swim? says Cam.

—It's got a bit cold, says Carmen, looking out the window as though someone out there had told her. —Any more wine, Cam?

Cam places the pile of towels on the floor and fills her glass from the cardboard cask which no longer gushes. —When are you lot going home, he asks.

—Thanks, says Carmen. Both her palms are upwards as she offers Sooze and Cliff the interrupted conversation. —You can see them any day of the week sniffing. Manners Mall, the beach below here. What can the cops do?

Sooze has now got her second wind. She is kneeling on a large cushion made from an old piece of carpet. She is overworked, she works too hard for comfort though she tries to hide it. She sits very still, her hands in her lap, her back as straight as Cliff's as they gaze up at Carmen. —That's just it, she says. —I get sick of the Government, the Council, Churches, talking talking. How do you fix street-kids? Kids at risk.

—It should be possible, says Cliff.

Carmen leans forward to stare into his eyes. —I know what's weird about you. Your eyes and hair are the same colour.

—So they tell me.

—Let's have a look. Sooze puts out a hand and turns his unsmiling face towards her.

—Toffee, she says.

—It's not impossible, continues Cliff. —Everyone just keeps duck-shovelling, running for cover. Expecting the schools, the cops . . . His behind is inching nearer Carmen's legs. Carmen sits up and tugs at her skirt.

Bryce's head is still propped against the sofa beside her thighs. He opens his eyes. —It's Mae West's birthday, he says.

—She's dead, says Margot who has given up and replaced the towels in the cupboard.

Bryce yawns. —Someone then, he says rubbing his hands. The left one has gone numb. —Thank God your mother's got Jared.

—Some of the kids at school sleep rough occasionally, says Sooze.

—Well, occasionally, says Cliff.

Carmen wraps pink arms around herself and the scarf. —Still. Even in summer.

Bryce is past it. —What summer?

—That house in *E.T.* was interesting from a construction point of view, says Cam from the floor.

—Not the table. Margot is lying prone, her eyes closed like Cam's. His remain shut as he takes her hand and holds it against his chest. They are stone effigies on a medieval tomb.

Carmen turns to stare out the window.

—Home, says Sooze. She crosses her legs beneath her and stands, then bends to retuck a trouser leg in her boot. The car keys clipped to her belt swing forward, glinting in the light.

Bryce focuses on her face. —I like it here.

—I'm leaving. Sooze slaps her hands against her trousers. —Now.

Cam and Margot spring to their feet. Cam grasps Bryce by the

wrist and heaves. Bryce is yanked to his feet. —All right. All right.
He unhooks Cam's hand from his wrist, his hand fumbles as he
prises each finger. He looks at Sooze with surprise as though he was
expecting a different face. —Home, he says.

Cliff is squatting on his heels by Carmen. He holds out his
hand. —Where d'you live ?

Her hair moves as she turns to him. Her smile at Bryce's
plastered dignity remains.

—Near here.

—Got a car?

She shakes her head.

—Give you a lift home.

Carmen turns for a final look at the harbour. The reflections
still lie like crumpled ribbons. She props her face on one hand and
leans against the back of the sofa as she gazes out. —Oh shit, I don't
know, she says. —Why does everyone always have to go home.

Miss Franklin remembers the smell of pepper

Pepper. Miss Franklin sniffed again. It must be ten years since that conversation.

—She is my friend, she said, staring out the window at the collapsed hen house in the corner of the section. Who needs definitions. Names to stick. Labels to slap.

—People will talk, said her father, pink as a boiled sweet, his hands spread wide on the stained-oak table.

Kate Franklin replaced the salt and pepper in the sideboard cupboard and sniffed its hot pungent smell. As a child it had made her think of spice routes. Marco Polo.

'They say. What say they. Let them say.' Let them publish and be damned.

—They'd talk if the first assistant shared a house with a man, she said, coming up from the cupboard.

—You could be headmistress!

—Jean is headmistress.

—Somewhere else. He flapped a plump hand to indicate a waiting world.

—I like it here.

—Because of her!

—Her name is Jean Sargesson. And yes. I like it here. And, said Kate, —it's eight years since mother died. Remarry, she advised, her eyes on his harvest moon face, —before it's too late. She picked up her woven Cretan bag from the sideboard with her good hand. —That would be the best plan.

Miss Franklin glances at Carmen who is on her feet distributing rough paper around the table at the Staff Meeting. The way

Carmen moves still stabs Kate's heart. Why do people pay so little attention to the way people move, the particular grace of the few. Nothing lasts, but physical grace lasts longer than most things. Miss Franklin shudders and tugs the edges of her cardigan together with both hands.

Jean Sargesson was young to be Head, mid thirties at the most. 'Lithe' was the word that came to Kate Franklin's mind when the new Headmistress swept into the Staff Room. Each time Kate sees Miss Sargesson she thinks, —Ah good, there she is. She is here. Good.

Miss Franklin's heart, if not a singing bird, is no longer a dead duck. Miss Sargesson's presence enriches her life. The second time she appeared in the Staff Room calling, —Miss Franklin, may I have a word? Miss Franklin smiled. —Do call me Kate.

Miss Sargesson glanced up from her Timetable Options list. She ran a quick hand through her black feather-cut hair.

—Kate, she said. —I like that. It suits you. The thing is Kate, the thing is, she said, —as you've only got seven Scholarship French this year, including Amanda Greeson who may drop it at any moment, would you, could you, bear to use the small room behind the Main Lab until I get the Fourths sorted out? Just for a few weeks. I promise.

So Miss Franklin found herself and her brightest and best jammed into a sort of ante-room with an inadequate blackboard, a smell of formalin, and an axolotyl pickled upright in a bottle labelled *The Eternal Peter Pan*.

Kate stares at the headmistress (Do call me Jean) who is not a tall woman. The Head wears a heavy silver-buckled belt which accentuates the small waist between her white pleated shirt and black skirt. She is arrayed as a headmistress. Soft black leather encases her feet. Her ankles are worth watching. She shakes her head at Thea Sinclair's proffered plate. —No thank you, she says. —Fate has placed too many bran muffins in my path recently.

—But Miss Barclay made them herself, says Thea Sinclair, hefting the plate up and down slightly to emphasise the fact. —For her Shout on leaving.

—I knew a woman who made the asparagus rolls for her own funeral, says Kate, reaching across the Head for a muffin. —She put them in the deep freeze. Miss Sargesson glances away to hide her smile. —They can make their own rolls, continues Kate, biting deep into the mellow buttery thing, —when I set out to sea.

Miss Sargesson laughs. She turns to her secretary. —Yes, Thea, I do know that Miss Barclay is leaving today and where I'm to find another music teacher at this stage of the year is one of life's major mysteries. She waves, a quick amiable fling of one hand at Miss Barclay's anxious face across the room.

Miss Barclay had always wanted to teach. She gave up a secure job in Radio New Zealand Programmes to do so. She had loved the post-graduate training and done well both in theory and teaching skills. She had begun teaching at the beginning of the year and been scuppered in three months, reduced to a hulk by the wilder shores of Girls High. Her doctor insisted on her leaving. Collapse was imminent.

One of her mistakes had been to assume, to hope to assume that the girls might like her. —Fat chance, Tess Nation's aunt Ruby had said as she applied a second coat of black nail varnish in the back row during Assembly. The 4Fs of the day relit their wrecker's lamps. Miss Barclay, foundering, had attempted to appeal to their better natures. —I understand girls. Believe me, I know how you feel. She told them that she had been young herself not so long ago. She burst into tears in front of them. She was sunk. And now she leaves and nobody cares, except Miss Sargesson. —Does she think, she asks smiling, —that music teachers grow on trees.

Miss Franklin cannot help laughing. She doesn't mean to because she feels sorry for the unfortunate woman which is the ultimate insult, but the new Head has this effect on her.

Miss Sargesson is now talking to Miss Barclay. She takes both failed hands in hers and holds them gently as she smiles. Miss Barclay says that she hates to let the Head down and that she is so very very sorry . . . Her clouded eyes fill with tears.

—Don't give it a thought, says Miss Sargesson. —Perhaps I will have a bran muffin after all. She waves it in the air. —Good luck, she says and eats it. —Thea, where is that . . . you know.

After a brief friendly speech she presents Miss Barclay with a gift-wrapped copper bowl. —From us all, from all the staff, she says, taking the shiny parcel from Thea and handing it on to the waiting hands, —with all good wishes for the future. It is a generous present for only one term, but many of the staff feel slightly guilty. They feel perhaps they could have done more to help Miss Barclay though they can't think how. They feel that they have not, as it were, saved a suicide, and thus many have donated more towards the farewell gift than they might otherwise have done. Miss Barclay is overwhelmed.

All this Miss Franklin watches, smiling.

—Isn't life beautiful, says Jean as she greets Kate in the carpark next day. —A music teacher has dropped from the skies.

—What a bit of luck. Kate is concentrating. She holds the car door open against the gusting wind with one knee and bends to lift a pile of books from the back seat.

Jean acknowledges the comment with a quick downward dip of her chin. —A Miss Hobbs has appeared from Eastbourne. Oh ye of little faith, she adds, turning to lock her Toyota.

—I never doubted for a moment, says Kate. She now carries a large pile of open 5A *cahiers* which she took home last night to mark.

—I meant me, says the Head, picking up her black briefcase. —Come on. They walk quickly, stepping it out across the concrete path to the Administration Block.

—I see *Zorba the Greek*'s having a re-run at the Penthouse, says Jean. —I've never seen it.

—I have.

—As good as they say?

—Better, says Kate, remembering the deathbed scene. The stoning. —I'd be happy to see it again, she says.

—Good. Let's go.

—I saw it with a Cretan last time, says Kate. —It was very interesting.

—What did she think of it?

—It was a he.

—Oh. Jean turns at the foot of the stairs. —How about Tuesday?

Costa had wanted to marry her.

—It would never have happened like that, would it? she had asked him afterwards among the bright lights and shining plastic of the Acropolis restaurant in Courtenay Place. —The stoning?

Costa continued munching his dolmades. He shook his head. —No, he said eventually, placing his hand on hers. —Never. They would have waited till she had left the churchyard.

—I'll pick you up, said Kate. —Parking's impossible in Brooklyn.

—No, no, no, no, said Jean, one hand already on the banister. —I never have any trouble parking. About seven-thirty?

—Would you like to come for a meal first? I could find a pizza or something, said Kate, staring vaguely ahead to a pizza horizon beyond the glass panels of the stairwell.

—No, no, no, said Jean again, running up the stairs. —Let's make it seven-thirty. Food is such a bore.

A woman after my own heart.

—Have a look under your seat, said Kate as they settled in the front row of the dress circle. —There's a man who sometimes crawls along underneath them.

—What!

—He's quite harmless, said Kate, heaving up her coral corduroy skirt to peer between her legs. She came up, her hair fluffed above her pink face. —His name's Simon. He's quite well known.

—That's all very fine, said Jean, peering between her trim navy shoes, —but it makes my legs twitch. To kick. What does he do?

—Nothing, said Kate. —Just lies there.

Jean shrugged. —We all take our pleasures differently. Who met up with this character?

—Dulcie Barclay.

—A sitter if ever there was one!

They smiled at each other, united by secret flickers of malice. Jean winked. She lifted one hand and touched Kate's cheek.

—It was during *Christ Stopped at Eboli*, said Kate.

They lay back gasping with pleasure as the lights dimmed.

Funny, thinks Miss Franklin. I can't remember the shorts. Not one of them. It is only ten years ago and I am famous for my memory. She glances across the table at Mr Marden. There is something so irritating in the self-absorption of others. Concentration is one thing, doodling is another. She sighs. Tampo is beyond human redemption. Miss Franklin thinks of Miss Sargesson's control, her ability to delegate, her wit. She lifts her eyes to the clerestory windows from which comes no help at all. —Can't we get *on*, she begs.

Jean leapt to her feet as soon as the lights came on at the interval.

—Excuse me, she said, pushing past Kate. —I must ring someone.

—Now? said Kate, glancing up in surprise from the Tip Top Family Pack which filled the screen.

—Yes. Jean was already in the aisle.

—I don't think there's a telephone.

—They'll let me use the one in the box office. Excuse me. She ran down the stairs.

Kate followed slowly, placing each foot on the autumn toned treads of the carpet with care. Jean was standing beneath the overhead light in the box office, the telephone receiver clamped against her head, the other hand gesticulating above the head of a dark young man who sat on a stool beneath her, his face wooden.

Jean's face was animated, alive with joy, her body tense.

Kate stood in the small musty foyer and stared. Why did she have to ring now. Why is it essential to ring now, to communicate such radiant happiness.

She is talking to her lover. That is why. That is why she looks like that.

Jean replaced the receiver. She shook her head smiling, thanked the young man and patted his shoulder. He stared straight ahead, one hand manipulating a broken match between his front teeth.

—Well, said Jean, that's done. Sorry about that. Roll on Zorba. Come on, she said. —We'd better check on Simon.

—Frankly, she said afterwards as they walked to the car, —I think the whole thing was based on a false premise. It's all very well Alan Bates saying at the end 'Teach me how to dance.' Why would he want to dance, to be part of that primitive . . . she flung her hands apart in a quick dismissive gesture. —People are so soppy. One dance and they fall flat on their over-civilised backs and wave their legs in the air.

Soppy. Kate hadn't heard the word for years. —I don't agree, she said.

—Why not? Jean turned to stare, peering at her in the dim light of the street lamp.

—I think, said Kate striding ahead, —that we have lost a lot of the vigour of life, the joy.

—Certainly, certainly, said Jean, scurrying a little to catch up, —but how can you separate them? Which would you prefer?

—I don't think that they are mutually exclusive. I think, said Kate, —that that is muddled thinking.

—I am discussing a film. Jean stopped again, her dark hair blowing across her face. —What's the matter with you?

—Who were you talking to? On the telephone?

—What on earth has that to do with you?

—Nothing.

They drove home in silence to Kate's flat. —Would you like

to come in? said Kate from the pavement, one hand on the still open door.

—No, thank you.

—Well, good night then. Thank you for the lift.

—Good night.

Kate shut the door and stood watching as the car disappeared round the corner.

—I am thinking of walking the Milford Track, said Jean in the Staff Room three weeks later. She slipped into the chair beside Kate and placed her silver ballpoint on the kauri table. She picked it up, retracted the point and put it down again. —Next January, before school starts. Would you like to join me in this enterprise?

—Why on earth has she suddenly put a *grave* on *bouleversée*, said Kate, her eyes fixed on Elizabeth Toddington's Unseen Translation.

—I don't know.

—No. Kate lifted her eyes to Jean's. —What about your friend? she said.

—Which friend?

—The one you rang in the Interval.

Jean laughed. —Ah, Harriet. My friend Harriet. Harriet, said the Head, —has gone to Bologna.

—For how long?

—For ever. I don't know.

—Oh, said Kate. She wrote 15/20 in the margin of Beth's *cahier*, closed it and placed it on the marked pile. —I've always wanted to walk the Milford Track, she said.

—I'm not sure, said Jean, putting one booted foot onto the swing bridge and removing it, —that I like swing bridges.

Kate heaved her pack higher onto her shoulders. —Just look straight ahead. She adjusted the rubber pads beneath the straps of her pack. One of them had a tendency to slip.

—But . . . Jean turned. She looked like an anxious twelve year old in short shorts and T-shirt. A red cotton sunhat was planted on the back of her head. —Look at it for heaven's sake. She stared at the bridge which bounced and swayed beneath each tread of the tramping feet. A man in front of them turned, waved, moved on.

—Go on, said Kate. She glanced at Jean's face. —I'll go first. Focus between my shoulder blades. Don't look down.

—Nn, muttered Kate.

—That was easy, she said on arrival at the other side. —Come on.

The sun slanted through the trees as they strode along the spongy floor of the silver beech forest. In the clear pools of the river beside the track rainbow trout nosed upstream, their tails moving rhythmically from side to side. Small rapids splayed over black rocks. A fantail danced above flipping its tail, darting occasionally at invisible insects.

Jean slipped out of her pack two hours later. —Lunch. She slapped a hand against a giant beech trunk. —Nothofagus menziesii, she said, kicking a pile of leaves together before collapsing on them.

—Is that right? Kate peered at her rubber pads. They examined the lunch packs.

—This is like primary school, said Kate. —Discovering what a benevolent power has provided for lunch. They munched their corned beef and Chow Chow pickle staring at the shade patterns, the sunlit river, the dark cliffs beyond. It was very still. A riro riro called, was answered, called again. A South Island robin appeared hopping on long stiff legs to inspect their boots in silence, its head cocked on one side.

Kate lay back when they had finished their lunch. —This is the life, she said beneath her yellow towelling hat.

—Girls High is the other side of the moon, muttered Jean, her eyes closed. The next minute she was on her feet. —Come on. They'll have pinched all the hot water at Pompalona. That man in jandals. I don't trust him an inch.

Jean's berth in the women's bunk room was empty next

morning when Kate woke. She dressed with speed, leaning forward to drop her breasts into her bra, adjusting parity of nipple height with a quick flip of her thumb. She tugged on her cottontails and jeans, dragged her Charlie Chaplin shirt over her head and moved quickly outside, shutting the door behind her.

Jean was sitting on the verandah, her eyes on the silent bush. Mist rose, smoking from steep valleys into the pale grey sky. Jean glanced up. —Hullo. The dawn chorus was unbelievable, she said.

—Why didn't you wake me?

—You were sound asleep. Jean's hands lay side-by-side beneath her slanted head. Her eyes were shut. —A disciple fallen down on the job.

—Disciple? Kate's hands were stiff against her thighs.

—That woman snored all night, said Jean.

—Which one?

As if it mattered.

—The American in the polka dots. With the hair. The one who buys one good thing per country. Who's through buying junk.

—Oh. Her. Greenstone here, I suppose.

—I suppose. Jean's eyes were on the bush once more.

Kate sat down. The boards were cold. —Tell me about it.

—First one bellbird calls, or tui maybe, I never know the difference, Jean waved a hand across the valley, —over there anyway. Then another answers, then another and then all the other birds all join in. Unbelievable. A halleluiah chorus. She shook her head. —They shut up, she said, —as it gets light.

—Wake me tomorrow.

Jean's hand stroked the wooden planks of the verandah. She looked at the palm then brushed it against her other hand. —All right. If I wake up.

—Did anyone else come out?

—No. Not a soul. Jean shook her head again. —Amazing, she said.

*

The McKinnon Pass was not easy. Nobody said it would be. Andy, their tough young guide, his red Swanni completely hiding his minuscule shorts, briefed them. —It's over eleven hundred metres, mind. Keep a steady pace. Don't belt off with too much of a hiss and a roar at the start. He looked at a gnarled old man in an orange woolly hat. —One foot after the other, he advised. People adjusted their packs, tugged at their socks, practically shook hands before they set off. But the track was good, the gradient of the wide zig-zags gradual. Everybody reached the summit by lunchtime. —We made it, they said to each other. They lounged about identifying the surrounding mountain peaks with Andy's help, pointing out the silver thread of the airstrip far below. —It wasn't too bad, was it? they said as they ate their sandwiches.

—Piece of cake, said the man in jandals.

—How can you walk over mountains in those things? said Jean.

—No probs, he said. He leapt to his feet flapping his arms. —Bugger off, he roared at a kea whose curved beak was tugging at the straps of his Mountain Man pack. —Keaa! Keaa! screamed the bird, lifting and whirling away down the valley, a flash of scarlet visible beneath the olive-green of its outstretched wings. It circled back to perch on the ridge of Pass Hut roof then sidestepped briskly along to join a line of silent colleagues. It ruffled its feathers, stamped from one clawed foot to the other and settled, glaring straight ahead. —Keaa, it squawked.

Jean and Kate watched its progress with pleasure. Jean pulled off her hat and waved it. The kea dropped from the roof, snatched it from her hand in mid flight and departed to a nearby rock where it tore it to pieces, its talons clamping the limp red thing to the rock while the beak gouged and ripped.

—See! said the man in jandals.

—Do you mean I deliberately encouraged it, enquired Jean, her eyes snapping.

—I just mean they're bloody pests that's what I mean.

—They are keas and they behave like keas and that one is

welcome to my ex-hat. Jean shouldered her pack. —Come on, she said to Kate, striding down the rocky track.

The next day was hosing, absolutely hosing down. People gathered on the verandah of the Quinton Hut to tell each other so. They stood peering out through the sheets of water which cascaded from the overhang of the tin roof. —It's hosing down, they said. —Look at the *rain* for God's sake.

The party set off after breakfast calling and laughing to each other.

—We've had two good days, anyway, they cried. —Two beauts.

The rain fell, heavier than ever.

—It's raining chair legs, yelled Kate.

Jean's head was sleek as a drowned otter's. —*What!*

—They say that in Crete! The wind tugged the words from her mouth, flinging them down the valley.

—Say what!

Kate shook her head. —Forget it! she screamed into the mouth of the deafening storm. Billows of rain surged from right to left across the valley. Rain streamed down their parkas, they were blinded by horizontal gusts as they weaved down the track. Jean's knees were scarlet, shiny as polished fruit above her sodden socks. Kate's jeans were plastered to her legs.

Andy was tireless. He ran, literally ran, leaping up and down the track to swap his pack for a heavier one, to carry two packs, to exhort and encourage. —Look at the waterfalls! he yelled. —You don't see those when it's fine. Cataracts of water fell down the bush-clad mountains, spraying the trees with clouds of spume. —Lovely, gasped the walkers.

The American woman gave them a brief glance. —Just darling, she snorted and strode on, her head down, polka dots glued to her buttocks.

Chafing began after several hours. A small boy whimpered, raising his wet face to his mother's worried one. —Mum.

Kate peeled off her jeans and shoved them in her pack.

—Drop your strides if they're chafing, shouted Andy. —All y'gears. Walk in y'grunds like Kate. In the nuddy if y'like. What the hell. You're soaked anyway.

Kate and Jean laughed in each other's faces and slogged on.

The party came up all standing on the banks of what Andy assured them was normally a small stream. It was now a boiling torrent of white water, gushing, exploding, rocketing down tthe valley floor. Rocks and branches were flung momentarily to the surface, bucked and sank again. There was no sign of the bridge.

Andy gazed at it in silence, sheeted in his yellow rain cape. Everyone stared at him. The old man rung out his woolly hat, shook it once and replaced it. —I've never seen her like this, said Andy finally. —Sorry folks. We'll have to go back up to Quinton and double bunk for the night.

Everyone behaved beautifully. The strong helped the more enfeebled. Andy redoubled his efforts. A child was carried. Andy produced a walkie-talkie and radioed Quinton. God-like young men and women appeared when they were nearing the hut to heave packs from shoulders and disappear at speed up the track. The rain fell.

Kate was in front. She turned to help Jean up a long slide of small rocks loosened by the rain. Jean snatched upwards at the proffered hand. Kate lost her balance and fell heavily, crashing past Jean who clung to the rockface, her body flattened, her face hidden.

—I don't think it's broken, said the doctor at Quinton who had arrived with the next party, —but it's a very nasty sprain. His fingers pressed her right wrist gently, probing. Kate concentrated on the puffs of red hair above his forehead. —It'll be very painful for a while. The fingers pressed again. He looked up. —Does that hurt?

—Caramba, gasped Kate.

He shoved her head between her knees. —Ice packs, he said. —Frozen peas.

—Dear heart, said Jean later, placing Kate's heavy cardigan gently over the bad arm. —It's all my fault.

—Don't be nuts, said Kate, her eyes bright, her unbrushed hair a mess.

Jean brushed it for her. —You're going to be prematurely grey, she said. —Lucky old you. I love white hair.

The hut was bursting with people. The cooks were doing their best. There would have to be some doubling up in the bunks.

—Kate must have one to herself, insisted Jean, her head high. —Even if I have to sleep with two. She is in real pain.

Her father was shaking with rage. —And what about your mother then? What about poor Else? What would she say. I'm sorry for you. You know that. Sorry for you!

—You! Sorry for *me*. How dare you be sorry for me! Kate's fingers clenched about the soft cords of her bag.

A gleam of triumph snapped in his blue eyes. —What is this woman to you!

Kate opened her mouth to shout her answer then shut it again. Her shoulders sagged. What did it matter. What could anything he said or did matter. She was calm, relaxed, slack as emptied sails. A boat in harbour.

She stroked her grey and white bag with her good hand and looked into his eyes.

—She is my friend, she said. —We care for each other. She lifted her bandaged wrist from its sling for a second. —She helps me on with my cardigan.

We are walking down to my car from Cam and Margot's place. It is very dark, three o'clock in the morning. Very still. No stars, no wind, no sound except for the occasional swish of tyres along Oriental Parade.

Carmen walks in front of me encased in an orange and pink thing which trails behind her. I snatch it from the ground and hand it to her. She takes it without a word and drags it tightly about her. Something's out of kilter; there are fault-lines, tectonic plates slipping. She stands very still staring out at the harbour as I unlock the car. I can't see to get the key in the lock. I fumble about, trying to keep calm as though it is important, essential to get it right first time.

Carmen slips into the passenger seat. Every movement she makes is graceful. I try to imagine her being ungraceful, which isn't a good idea because I see it too clearly and she's still graceful all the ways I'm seeing her.

—I like Cam, she says as I turn on the ignition.

—Yeah, nice guy.

—A lovely man. She moves her head reverently from side to side.

I am waiting for her next comment, both hands clutching the wheel as I peer forward like some old guy in a hat driving up the Coast on a Sunday. I know she's going to say it.

—Bryce is OK really, she says.

—He's a prick.

—Most men think that.

I wipe the inside of the windscreen busily with my flattened hand. —Well, then.

She looks out the window. —No, she says.

54

—I like Sooze.

—Most men do. She tugs at the pink thing. —Like her. Loathe him. I've got an aunt like that. Slam. Bang. Off with his head. Bryce, says Carmen, —is having a tough time.

—I'm sure you're right, I say. The back of my neck pricks. My father used to say that when my mother wanted to fight. She rollicking, slack-breasted, wading about the hot afternoon kitchen; he very tight, controlled. A small man. —I'm sure you're right dear, he'd say. A non-combatant, refusing to let her in, denying her access. His moustache was two toothbrushes and a central parting. My hands tighten on the wheel. —Why? I ask, getting back to shitty old Bryce.

She tells me about Bryce's old job in the money market, his job as a cleaner, his new job in the morgue. Tough, I think happily. Carmen sits very straight, her fingers on the dash, her knees and feet together.

—What part of McFarlane Street? I ask, as we start climbing the hill.

—On the right. Sixty-four.

—Have you got a flat?

Her head turns. —I don't own it, if that's what you mean. How do I know what I mean. I stop the car and turn to her. She has one hand on the door-handle. —Thanks, she says. I grab her hand. —Carmen. She tugs it away and yanks at the door-handle. I lean across and lock it. I don't mean to. Christ I'm not going to. I didn't mean to. I just want to look at her, to hold her hand like some bloody Beatle, to talk. We're fighting, twisting and writhing, slithering about like eels in a tub. I'm on top of her, she's screaming, my hand's on her mouth. She bites. It's nothing at first, then the pain hits. Tears stream down her face as she kicks and punches. The gear lever twists in my bum as I roll back. —Shut up! I'm not going to rape you! I yell, sucking my hand.

She laughs. She laughs and laughs and laughs. I can see her teeth, her hair has come down, the pink scarf is tangled. She unlocks the door and sprints up the steps in the dark.

★

I doodle my way through the first Staff Meeting of the year. All Staff
Meetings are boring but some are more boring than others. The
Headmistress has the control and thrust of a knife through candy-
floss. Jenni Murphy sits beside me and admires the visuals. She is a
tiny woman, late twenties I suppose, her face round, mad orange
hair trapped in a pile on top of her head. She wears a red jersey four
times too big for her, a green miniskirt and heavy white stocking
things. Degas would have liked her compact body, her sturdy legs.
Her tiny hands rest on the edge of the table like placating paws
seeking nuts. I doodle so I can stare at Carmen without seeming to,
though I am getting quite interested in the curving forms and
patterns on the pad. Dürer was delighted by the sensual violence,
the sculptural forms of early South American art. He saw examples
in Germany in the fifteenth century. You forget things like that, or
rather you don't think such things could happen. This art, that art,
it's good when they collide. Like African and Picasso. Miss Franklin
makes a crack about doodlers so I doodle harder. I draw Picasso's
face inside a swirl.   —Picasso, whispers Jenni touching the face. I
stretch my legs under the table and stare at the fall of light across the
base of Carmen's throat. Someone is banging on about some form
called 4F. —What's wrong with them, I ask. For the first time since
last Saturday night Carmen's eyes flick in my direction. As I bend
back to Picasso Margot and Sooze's eyes meet. Something is
happening, going on, trickling underground. What is the matter
with Carmen who is tearing me apart, who hates me because I love
her and it's not only screwing. Carmen. I know I blew it.

They are now on to peer pressure.

—I think there is something you should know Cliff, says Sooze as
we walk to the car park after the meeting eventually finishes. It is
like any car park, flat, windy, bits of paper toss and rip in the air then
flatten themselves against the wire meshing of the fence. I tread on
one. It is a flyer for the New World. Their size six Tegels are

reduced to $5.98. I know Sooze is going to tell me something about Carmen so I keep my face blank. Most of the cars have gone by now, leaving empty blue-grey space, iridescent oil slicks in the puddles, white lines. People shoot through with speed after Staff Meetings; the young ones running to their cars, the older ones trotting briskly, their arms deep with marking. Carmen's red Nifty-Fifty is still there. The wind flattens Sooze's denim skirt against her stomach, tugs at her hair. I stare at her. I must paint her. *Sooze in the Car Park* I'd call it. Quite a lot of black in the shadows. Straight black. Hard edge.

—What is it? she says.

—I'd like to paint you.

—Listen, says Sooze. I unlock the clapped out old Datsun on her side. —Get in, I say.

Sooze folds into Carmen's seat. Her legs are longer. They come higher up. I like Sooze. I can't see what she sees in that muscle-bound shit in the morgue, but that's not what we're talking about.

Sooze turns to me. Her thin fingers are laced together like a kid playing 'Here's the Church and here's the Steeple'. Her tongue moves behind her lower lip, pushing it out. —I think you should know, she says, —that Carmen was almost raped last year by the previous Art guy. She is staring straight ahead now. —A weirdo.

An old woman bent almost double is creeping along the footpath outside the car park. I have seen her before.

—What's that got to do with me, I say, focusing on the shuffling effort, the slow pain.

Sooze is too. —Nothing, she says, —but Carmen's my friend, our friend. She is speaking quickly, her hands are still tight. —She was ditched last year by a guy called Barry, then she was raped and . . .

—I thought you said almost.

—What difference does it make?

—None.

How would I know.

—Yes, well. Anyway. Sooze's hand is on the door-handle. She

is getting the hell out of this.

—Thanks Sooze, I say. Carmen. Christ Almighty. Sooze turns to me, smiles, then looks away. There is something about the sharp chop of her hair which makes the back of her neck vulnerable. —Could I paint you? I ask.

—What? she says, meaning what a moment to ask. —When? I can't stop. —Anytime.

—Well, Jared's only six months. I mean the weekends are a bit . . . Her voice trails into silence.

I see her standing in the deserted car-park. Or leaning against the mudguard, arms by her sides like the young girl in that Edith Collier nude. I'd have the feet dorsi-flexed though. My tongue flicks my lips. I can feel it. Lots of black, or maybe strong blue. Side by side, flat pure colour laid on with the end of the knife.

—The weekends are a bit . . . Bryce'd have to mind Jared.

—So?

—Well, she says.

—I want to paint you nude.

She looks at me, not pleased. —I'm too thin.

—That's the whole point. Thin bodies are more interesting. My hands are demonstrating planes above the steering wheel, sliding under the ribs, slicing down to the hollow of her pelvic floor.

Sooze gives the little wriggle on her buttocks which I've noticed before. A regrouping gesture. —Look, Cliff, she says. —a) I've got to go now to pick up Jared from day-care and take him to my mother's. Bryce and I are going out tonight. b) The weekends are pretty busy, especially now, and I don't know that Bryce would be mad keen on the idea of me lying around naked. She laughs. She's got a good laugh, Sooze. Infectious. She really sounds as though she can't help it. —He'd think I was wasting time. She blinks. —c) He wouldn't like it.

—What's it got to do with him! Anger is thickening, clotting inside my head.

Sooze looks at me again and smiles. She shakes her head.

—Would you like it if Bryce painted Carmen with nothing on?

—Nothing *on*. God in heaven. Nothing *on!* And what's Carmen got to do with it! I can hear my spluttering rage. I take a deep breath. —If Bryce wants to paint Carmen nude, he has my full . . . I can't say it. My visual imagination locks.

—How did we get into this, bleats Sooze. She gives a quick glance at her watch. —Look at the time!

Once more I'm grabbing passengers, by the wrist this time. —Listen, I've got to paint you. It'll be great. I can see it. Ask the territorial shit if you have to.

Sooze's hair leaps as she swings to me. —He's not a territorial shit! And what do you mean *ask* him? What do you think I am! It's just that I see no reason why I should waste my time lying around . . .

I see it so clearly. —Standing.

. . . —naked for you or any other . . .

—You're not naked for me. You're nude for me to paint! I'm a good painter. Very good, you should be proud to be asked.

She is angry now. —If you're so shit hot why're you teaching.

—Because I am shit hot. Because I paint what's there!

—All right, all right. She is scrabbling at the door. —Don't you give a stuff? she cries. She leaps out and runs.

—Ask the shit! I yell at her heels. She doesn't run well, her legs are all over the place, sticking out sideways from her knees like an old ram with foot-rot. I fold my arms on the steering wheel but I don't put my head on them. I can see Carmen's red bike in the rear vision mirror but I don't stay. The old woman has gone.

The dreams are not good either. I have rented a well-used bed-sit in Willis Street till I find something. Nothing works, there's no TV, no telephone, the owners are very kind. —Oh dear, says Mrs Olsen, clutching the edge of the counter in greasy astonishment each time I trail along to the office with the bust jug, the bust heater, the eiderdown which smells of sick.

—We'll have to do something about that, won't we. Leave it

here, dear. Mont'll have a look at it.

I am learning.

But the dreams. I saw an old film at the Paramount a few weeks ago. A hundred years old. —If I had a thousand dreams, said the subtitle as a man all eyes and soul stared out the window at the curved terracotta roof tiles of Tuscany, —Angela della Bardi would be in every one of them. But it is worse than that, because Bryce is in mine as well. He is on top of Carmen, underneath Carmen, fucking Carmen all ways, slashing Carmen with paint. Miss Bickerstaff, my Primer One teacher, is driving the Stanley Bay launch. Carmen, minus Bryce now, flings the rope out, her breasts bouncing. I am five years old, flat on my belly on the haircord in Calliope Road, Devonport, popping bubble-gum as I copy each frame of Dennis the Menace and Jiggs which is how I learnt to draw.

I didn't realise you could draw the world until Miss Bickerstaff showed me amidst the sniffs and smells of the Primers' Room at Stanley Bay Primary. I thought you drew drawings. —Cliff has a remarkable visual memory, Miss Bickerstaff told Mum in her wash cotton at a PTA meeting. —A very good graphic line. None of us knew what she meant except it was drawing. I don't suppose Dad ever mentioned it in the Boiler Shop at the Dockyard, but it did help. I launched out. Mum stopped nagging so much about running outside to play. Dad pinned up some of the boat ones on the wall of the unlined shed out the back where he slept, and I kept drawing. I see Miss Bickerstaff whenever I go back. She is retired now and spends a lot of time whitebaiting at the ferry wharf, her white hair tossed to fluff about her red woolly hat. She doesn't know how much longer she can continue though because of the weight of the net. She is not getting any younger.

Sooze is talking to Carmen and Margot, propped against the table in the exact position I want for *Sooze in the Carpark* when I go into the staff room next morning. My arms are full of old School Certicate Art portfolios which I want to go through, so I have to

dump them on the table beside her. Sooze sits up straighter.
—Good morning, she says. Margot smiles at me. Carmen's eyes
give one flick to the large Band-Aid which I still need on the back
of my right hand, then look away. Margot's lipstick stays on, Sooze
doesn't wear it, Carmen's comes off. Perhaps she eats it.

—Thanks for Saturday, I say days too late to Margot. She
laughs. —Good to see you. You got home all right? Carmen's yawn
swallows the staff room. —Why wouldn't he? she asks Margot not
me.

Sooze's head is quite a bit lower than mine so she has to look
up at me. —Bryce thinks it's a great idea, she says.

I feel it in the groin. Stuff the shit. —Next Saturday? I ask
quickly.

—Oh. Sooze brushes chalk dust from her black leather
miniskirt. —No. Saturdays are hopeless. Say Sunday week.

—What time ?

—Afternoon. Not before one-thirty. I'm sorry not to ask you
for lunch but . . .

—No, no. Great. I'll be there.

Margot is opening a pottle of apricot yoghurt; she runs a
thumbnail around the foil, folds it back then gets busy with a plastic
spoon. —What's going on? she asks. Already I know that Margot
likes to know what's going on. I wonder why she didn't tell me
about Carmen. She would have liked it a lot more than Sooze.

—Cliff wants to paint me, says Sooze.

Carmen's head turns.

—With nothing on, continues Sooze.

—Nude for God's sake, I say.

Sooze shrugs. —Nude. Margot stops spooning for a second
then resumes her dip and lick with enthusiasm.

The buzzer goes for end of break. Margot writes Margot on the
lid of her yoghurt pottle with a felt pen and puts it in the staff fridge.
Carmen picks up a netball and departs with speed, her plait
bouncing. Sooze stretches to the roof. —Free periods are a sensual
experience, she says.

—Passionfruit please, said Rita Vaughan.

   —Topping? asked the young woman behind the counter.

   Rita leant forward. —Pardon?

   —Topping, said Molly. —Look! She pointed to a large sign on
the wall. *Cones:* Waffle or honey comb. *Toppings:* Cream; Jubes;
Cherries; Nuts.

   —Oh I don't think I want any *topping*, said Rita, glancing from
Molly's face to Fleur's blank one. She had always done that. Just
signed off. —I don't usually. Not topping.

   —You don't have to, said the young woman, one hand
adjusting the rake of her white cap.

   —Then I won't. Rita smiled. —I won't.

   —You pay for it anyway, said Molly. —I heard him say. She
indicated a vast man in a striped jersey who was concentrating on
a double scoop. —Rum and raisin please, she said. —Cream and
jubes.

   —Do I? asked Rita staring at her unembellished passionfruit,
naked beside the confections piled on Molly's Rum and Raisin.

   —It's the same price, yes. The young woman's cap dipped
again as she patted Fleur's plain chocolate into the cone. (—Are you
sure there's no coffee? I would've thought. I mean it is on the
board.)

   —That's $5.10 please.

   Fleur handed the exact change. She was good with money. —
You can pay me later she said. —$1.70 each.

   Rita held out her passionfruit, her arm extended. —I think I
will have topping after all, she said. —Cream please, and cherries.
As it's the same.

   The cap glanced at the queue forming behind them. —Oh you

can't have it now, she said. Not now it's licked and that.

Fleur's eyes shut briefly.

—Don't you know about Aids? laughed the man behind Fleur, both hands dragging his walkshorts above his belly. His wife smiled at Rita. —Norman, she said.

Rita had driven them up the Gold Coast the day before they left for their South Island trip. —For some carriage exercise. Remember Dad and his carriage exercise? They thought of Rita's dead father. A ratty little terrier of a man forever snapping at the heels of childhood. Stop mauling. Stop giggling. Outside. Out. Now.

Rita and Molly and Fleur sat on a bench in silence licking their passion fruit, rum, and chocolate, though Molly bit hers occasionally. They stared out over the man-made duckponds to the bush beyond. The breeze was soft, the sun gentle on their backs.

I am happy, thought Rita, her eyes straight ahead. Completely happy. I am with my friends.

They had been such tremendous friends. Inseparable. How long did it go back? Forty years? More. She lifted her cone and licked, operating damage control.

—I must introduce you tomorrow to three of the young staff, she said after a pause.

Fleur was watching Molly who was now chomping at her cone like an old horse put out to grass. —Why? she said.

—Carmen and Margot and Susan, continued Rita. —They're just like we were. Her tongue flicked out eliminating a dribble of passionfruit. —You know. Inseparable. The three of them.

—Hh, said Molly. She had nearly finished. Only a doll-sized cone remained.

—And so lovely, continued Rita. —There was an awful thing last year . . .

—What? asked Molly and Fleur

—No, she said after a pause. —It doesn't matter. Not what it was, I mean . . .

—Then why mention it, said Molly, standing to shake honey-comb fragments from her skirt.

—Yes, I shouldn't've. It's just that . . . They're so lovely. You'll see what I mean. I'll introduce you.

—It's nice here isn't it, she said between final chews of honeycomb. —And I can show you the Library tomorrow.

—Thank you, said Molly and Fleur after a pause.

—You've got cream on your nose Moll, said Fleur.

—We kicked the bottom out of each other's bassinettes, laughed Rita as she introduced Molly and Fleur to Miss Tamp after the Prize Giving which had gone on too long as usual.

—Hardly, murmured Fleur who was six months younger. She indicated an expansive man with silver hair. —Who's that man?

Miss Tamp touched his elbow. —Have you met Mr Smythe, the Chairman of the Board of Trustees. Mrs Rita Vaughan? And her friends. Mrs . . .

—You're Computer Science aren't you? bellowed Mr Smythe.

—No. I'm the Librarian, said Rita.

—I could've sworn. For a moment Rita thought he was going to insist, but someone lurched against him, splashing his coffee down Rita's green. —Excuse me. He laughed. —Bit of a scrum. Need the new hall, don't we?

It was very hot. Stifling in fact. —Who's that beautiful creature? pointed Molly.

—Carmen Doyle, said Rita. —She's one of the ones I was telling you about. Isn't she lovely.

Carmen's hair was pulled onto the top of her head and caught with a velvet ribbon from which curls leapt and tumbled. Rita thought of Leonardo da Vinci's water currents and whirlpools. The same curves and spirals. The same exuberance of plenty; the grace of natural forms. The book was called *Leonardo*, the reproductions were excellent.

Rita chewed her bottom lip.

—Irish, said Fleur. —Good bones.

—Bones are a help, said Molly. —Who's the little one yawning her head off?

—Margot Murchison? Home Economics. She's lovely too. And the other one's Susan Powdrell. Sad. Her husband's just been declared . . .

—I wonder if she meant to wear black with navy? said Fleur, her eyes fixed on Margot.

They stared at the conundrum.

—What do you think of my flowers? said Rita pointing to a huge red white and blue arrangement at the edge of the stage.

—Your what? The noise was deafening.

—My arrangement, shrieked Rita.

—Lovely! said Molly and Fleur.

—Pooch and Rup and me, said a large girl with round glasses into Molly's ear.

—What?

The girl glared at Molly, a large spot on her chin turgid and gleaming beneath the lights. —We're going to Whitianga if you must know, she said, turning her back to continue her conversation with some hidden midget.

—I'm afraid it's a little close, said Rita. Close. A Rita word.

Molly enlarged on Margot's yawn. —I suppose they'd frag me if I had a smoke, she said.

Fleur dipped her head at one of the several *Thank you for not smoking* signs. Her hair had gone from ash blonde to more ash blonde to platinum with no help from anyone or anything. For thirty years it had swept up and back and coiled neatly about her scalp. The only change she had had to make was to find paler hairpins.

Molly surged into the crowd, tacking from left to right around knots of staff, parents and prize-winners. (*Unfortunately as space is limited in the Hall only prize-winners' parents are able to attend Prize Giving. The Chairman and the Board apologise for this and hope that when the Centennial Fund allows work on the new hall to commence . . .*)

—How long've you been here Rita, murmured Fleur. She

moved slightly to allow the passage of an Indian woman in a pale
embroidered sari and black boots who was escorted by a slender
young girl. Mavis Kanji had topped 4C. She clutched *Wuthering
Heights* to her chest with pale hands and smiled.

—Twenty years, said Rita.

Fleur shook her head then turned to Mr Smythe who knew a
pretty woman when he saw one.

—And this is the library, said Rita flinging the door wide.

It was a huge space, a high-tech storehouse for books. The steel
beams were visible as well as the rafters, the bookshelves were
adjustable. —It's bigger than our local one, muttered Fleur. *No
jumping on the beanbags* said a notice above the four corduroy-
covered bags in an alcove. Molly's mother had never allowed
reading during the day. The sight of the things, inviting the young
to curl up, to lose themselves in ways not only condoned but
encouraged, made her hot with spite. —Do they appreciate it?

—Oh they love it, replied Rita. *Love* it.

—I'll bet they do. Molly indicated *The Undertaker's Gone
Bananas* which sat alongside *Sue Barton Staff Nurse* beneath the sign
entitled *Books for a Quick Read*.

—Honestly, she said.

Rita's face was pink. —But it doesn't matter . . . as long as they
read. Then they move on you see, and even if they don't . . . She
knew there was some unanswerable exposition which seemed to
have been harried from her by the spectre of taxpayers' money.

Fleur looked at the swirls of black hair trapped beneath Rita's
30 denier tights. 30 denier and unshaven legs. Probably Rita didn't
know the difference. The whole world, Fleur thought, one hand
resting on *I'm OK You're OK*, could be divided into those who
know and the rest.

—We just have to be completely open, Rita was saying.
—They learn different things. It doesn't mean . . . The other day,
for instance, I had a sixth former who'd never heard of Mary Queen
of Scots. At first I nearly said —Carla! But then I thought —No.

You just have to be *open*.

—Mnn, said Fleur.

Libraries, said the sign above the desk, *are for Life*.

Molly had a dream at the Snowgoose Lodge where Rita had booked them as there was no room in her humble abode. Buzzing flies were trapped in hot ovens, the outside of which was mottled grey ceramic. Darker smudged areas represented eyes and mouths. She blamed the dream on a fly spray advertisement on TV last night where flies died with their legs in the air; but blame was little help in the middle of the night when she lay drenched in sweat, staring into the dark, her mind on the unknown holiday. And those young women. Their faces. Their eyes. Carmen's eyes, thought Molly, groping blindly beneath the pillow for her handkerchief, looked as though they had been put in with a sooty finger. Irish. She sighed and rolled over to gaze at Fleur's shape humped in the opposite bed. Her expelled breath whistled faintly in the dark.

Two permed fluffs of girls hung over the rail of the ferry. One turned her head and laughed, her mouth a scramble of orthodontist's hardware. The other wore a pleated and padded leather jacket which reached to her crutch. Nothing else was visible above the lace-patterned black nylons, the sharp-pointed shoes.

—Do you remember stud frocks? asked Rita suddenly. They sat on deck eating her ham and mustard sandwiches beneath a large sign saying *No food to be consumed here*, gazing at the gleaming sea, the white foam creaming into a V below them.

—We might see a dolphin, said Fleur, giving a little wriggle at the thought.

Molly reached over for another sandwich. —These are good, she said. —Stud frocks?

Rita knew they were good. She nodded. —Stud frocks. She flung a closed hand against the midline of her blouse three times. —Mine was maroon.

Neck to knee, demure, the stud frocks of maidenhood

returned. Molly's Hush Puppies swung outwards from the bench in the small excitement of remembering. —Stud frocks. Mine was navy, she said.

—Yes, and yours was more of a wine, said Rita, turning to Fleur with the plastic box of sandwiches in her hand. Fleur shook her head. Her face was calm. —I never had one, she said.

—You did! cried Rita. —It was sort of winey. Not as dark as mine. More, you know, winey.

—I'd know whether I had one or not, said Fleur, snatching her petticoat from beneath her pleated skirt to polish her dark glasses.

—Not if you can't remember, you wouldn't. I can see it now. Not as dark as mine. More winey. With studs.

—Of course it had studs, said Molly. There was a bit too much mustard in this one. She tore off a crust, lifted the upper slice of bread, scraped off the excess and dropped the crust into the plastic bag with the eggshells. —It was a stud frock. Extraordinary. Just like sheep.

—We all had them.

—I didn't, said Fleur, her eyes on the high, wheeling gulls.

—You did.

—I didn't.

A Japanese woman with stiff cropped hair sat upright on the bench opposite them, her eyes closed behind pebble glasses. Her husband peeled a banana with slow careful fingers.

The seagulls dropped screaming into the wake, swooping on the contents of a gash bucket emptied far below.

—They have to be careful which side they empty them, said Rita, whose brother Geoffrey had joined Scheme B and served in the navy during the war. She licked her forefinger and held it upright. —Otherwise it would all blow back. Ashes too.

—Ashes? Molly's tongue flicked about her lips. There was still quite a lot of mustard.

—I did have an edge to edge coat, said Fleur.

—Navy blue wool georgette, cried Molly and Rita.

—Of course.

Navy blue edge to edge. They shook their heads slowly, hands suspended halfway to their mouths, their minds transfixed by memories.

When they were little Rita lived in Nelson Street and Molly lived in Church Street and Fleur lived in a two-storeyed house in Tomoana Road and they were all in Miss Royston's class who said she had eyes in the back of her head and they half believed it, because how else did she know. They sang 'There is a green hill far away without a city wall' and Rita wondered if it minded. She didn't ask Miss Royston because that would be sucking up and Molly and Fleur wouldn't know.

Molly and Fleur sometimes had secrets from Rita. Rita and Fleur once tried to have a secret from Molly but it didn't work as Molly didn't care. She tossed her carroty head and played knucklebones under the pepper tree with Audrey Wilkins as though nothing had happened, and Rita couldn't remember what the secret was when Fleur asked her. On April Fools' Day Fleur told Rita to bang on the caretaker's door and ask him for a straight hook, and Rita did although she knew it was an April Fool, because she'd rather have Mr Balcom growl at her than Fleur have secrets.

Miss Royston made Rita stand up and read to the whole class because she was good at it even though Rita said, —Please Miss Royston, oh please do I have to.

—Listen to Rita girls, said Miss Royston. —She is a girl who can read really well, she will read the story about pirates in the new Journal page eight.

—Oh Miss Royston, said Rita.

—Now Rita. Come along.

Rita left her desk and dragged her brown sandals to Miss Royston's table. —Turn around Rita, head up. The whole class wants to hear.

—The Captain's name was Captain Deadly, read Rita.

—Good, said Miss Royston touching the chain which kept her

glasses around her neck when they weren't on. —Notice girls. Deadly not deedly.

—The crew were rough and tough.

—Good. Rough and tough. This is a really hard story. Go on Rita.

—They had guns and knives and other weepons.

—Weepons! cried Fleur. —She said weepons. Ha ha ha.

Each morning Rita ran up Nelson Street and waited at the Park gates which were a-memorial-to-the-fallen. Molly ran down Braithwaite Street and they waited for Fleur to arrive in the Chevrolet with her father Mr Leckey, who was a dentist and had to keep his hands clean. Mr Leckey coudn't wait if they weren't there because his first patient was in the chair at eight-thirty sharp. —You know that girls, don't you, eight-thirty sharp. —Yes Mr Leckey, said Molly and Rita, wriggling their shoulders and shuddering at the thought of the patient and the chair and eight-thirty sharp. —Don't be silly you kids, said Fleur. Mr Leckey didn't say anything. His clean right hand rested on a little ball thing attached to the wheel. It made the steering easier for him.

Rita had lost her spelling words. She searched and searched all through the house.

—Miss Royston will tell me off, she said on her knees, her hands scratching and hunting beside the fridge.

—Don't fuss child, said her mother pouring herself another cup of coffee.

—She'll go butchers, gasped her daughter.

—Rita. Such a solid child, four-square above the Cleveland legs.

—She *will*. You don't know.

She knew nothing.

—Write a note Mum. *Please*.

Clutching her note, Rita ran down Nelson Street. They had gone. She knew they would've. Sniffing, she ran past Evans where the ginger corgi barked with sharp tilted head; past Crutchleys who baked bread at the back for sale; past the murder house where a baby with no arms was buried beneath the pergola which sloped to one side because of the baby.

She swung round the corner into the wind at Colchester's high brown fence and came face to face with a large Alsatian. —Hullo, said Rita putting out her hand to stroke its neck. The dog swung its head sideways to nip the sudden pink thing before its eyes, barked twice then trotted off, its tail stiff.

Tears slid down Rita's cheeks; the concrete was warm beneath her bottom as she sat with both feet in the gutter. She wiped her eyes, wrapped her hand in her hanky with bluebirds on it and looked for her note. It was gone, nowhere to be found.

Miss Royston didn't believe her. —Really Rita, she said, —You'll have to do better than that. You will have to stay in for detention after school. That is unlike you, Rita.

Fleur and Molly didn't believe her either, though Fleur whispered she did really, next morning in the Chevrolet by the memorial-to-the-fallen.

Fleur's golden hair swung below her shoulders, her bruised lips pouted. She danced the Valeta, she danced the Hokey Tokey, she put her right foot in she put her right foot out she put her right foot in and she shook it all about. She danced the Military Two Step. She and Audrey Wilkins, who both learnt from Miss Stringer, gave a demonstration at the Leavers' Dance at High. 'When they be*gin* the Beguine,' moaned the sobbing baritone. Fleur and Audrey swept in from behind the greenery on the left, their running steps tiny, their mauve and apricot chiffons billowing behind them, their arms extended with wide entreating fingers. 'It brings back a *night* of tropical *splen*dour,' whooped the voice. Fleur and Audrey twirled and circled, beseeching the space available. They leapt on bare feet, they flung their heads back in ecstasy, their curls fell forward, cascading over their faces as they begged in vain. 'It brings back a *memory* evergreen.'

At the end as the violins faded Audrey and Fleur sank to the ground, their faces hidden on their outstretched arms, their wrists crossed, all passion spent.

Molly and Rita stared, their mouths slightly open, their hot arms hanging. Molly was a good sort. The shy boys said so.

Molly and Fleur and Rita had been on holiday together before, when Rita was at Library School, Fleur at Dental Clinic and Molly doing her training in Hastings because the Hospital had a good name. Rita and Fleur planned every detail of their skiing trip, sitting beneath the real paintings at The Coffee Shop in the Quay drinking freshly-ground Mocha.

Molly came down on Newman's and was violently seasick all night as they crossed on the Lyttleton Ferry even though it was calm as a millpond, the stewardess said. It took for ever for the bus to get to the Hermitage and a year's savings gone phht, but worth it they all said, what a holiday.

We stayed at the Ball Hut and people were training for the New Zealand Championships and Fleur and Molly and I just landed in amongst them, well you can imagine, they were all so good. Fleur's binding was faulty. We'd hired, the skis weren't ours or anything, and men would appear all over the snow to fix it. And the air, there's nothing like it. We sang rude songs at night. No I couldn't, not now. The words are terrible but you don't care there because it's all such fun and nobody thinks about what they mean. There was one called *Roll the leg over* and everyone made up verses like—

> I wish all the girls were like Fleur Leckey,
> Who brought her own glass,
> So that there'd be plenty.
>
> Oh roll the leg over,
> Oh roll the leg over,
> Oh roll the leg over
> The *man* in the moon.

No, I can't remember mine. No, really. Something about Rita, and they thought they should beat her; and Molly's had jolly and trolley.

They used to have me at parties because I remembered the words. I'd hear Brian, he had false teeth, and he'd been in the Navy. —Where's the gash bucket? he'd say.

When he was arranging a special party in the bunkroom say, I'd hear him discussing with the other men, —And we'll have the other one who knows the words. What's her name? Rita. And we'd all sing happy as anything and not caring.

> And he stuffed her up with candy
> And he stuffed her up with cake,
> And he stuffed her up the alley,
> Coming *home* from the wake.

—*I know.*

And there was one about coming down the mountain early more a woman than a girlie.

And we sang them without a thought. That's what I *mean*.

We had to ski down at the end because the road was blocked with snow and the minibus couldn't get up. Mick the guide went first. Have I told you how some of them smelt? Not the guides only, I mean the men. There was one man, Steve, he really stank and Fleur and Molly and I didn't want to be rude, but we couldn't stand it, sitting on his knee or anything, but they were very kind, all of them, especially some.

There weren't many women. I don't know if they'd got trapped at the Hermitage or there just weren't many or what. But they were very kind to us considering, I mean we'd never skied in our lives though we did pick it up, but you know what I mean . . . They were Training.

Going down, Mick went first and we followed in his tracks, so that was easy. Just around the first bend (it was Mick, then Molly, then me, then Fleur) I heard Fleur yell, Damn, and I said, What? and she said, —My bloody binding. Well. Mick and Molly had disappeared around the next bend by this time. So I started herring-boning my way back to her because she could never fix it herself, when woosh, there was one of the really good skiers, though quite old, swooping round the corner out of nowhere like Young Lochinvar. He fell on his knees to fix it. Fleur looked so lovely, her fluffy hair sticking out beneath her skiing cap, her trousers and jacket so black against the snow, and it was snowing by now. Errol, that was his name, Errol. He said. —It's OK Rita, you go on, I'll follow and give Fleur a hand. I don't trust this duff binding. He glared at it, and I said, —But what about your training, and he said, —I'm just a hack, and laughed. —Anyway, he said, —I need a bath. I smell like a goat, though he didn't, or not like Steve.

So I turned and skied slowly down in the tracks. Mick showed me a rabbit. You wouldn't think they could live there. And a hawk he showed me, as well.

It was lovely at the Hermitage, and everyone wanted to talk to us about snow conditions because they were all waiting to go up because of the blocked road. All these experts asking us, I mean. But Fleur took it all in her stride and we had a lovely time, I'll never forget it. Errol insisted that we all had dinner with him and we had wine though we didn't usually, well not much, and he and Fleur danced afterwards, gliding and dipping, especially in the tango, with Fleur bent over backwards like Miss Stringer at the End of Year Recital. Everybody clapped at the end and Fleur sank into a chair, I mean really sank, and Errol lit her cigarette with a lighter. They weren't sitting by us. Eventually Molly said, I'm going to bed, and I said, So am I, though I wouldn't have minded dancing, it was a good band considering, and it was all so gracious, with palms and ashtrays on stands and everything.

Fleur and Molly and I were sharing a room, one of the cheap ones at the back, it didn't have a view or anything but we didn't mind. Molly and I got undressed and she dumped her clothes on the floor and I folded mine and put them on the little chair with glazed-chintz stripes, there was only one, and we cleaned our teeth and lay in bed reading *Mademoiselle* and *Man Alone* and waiting for Fleur, and we waited and we waited and we waited and then Molly went to sleep and *Mademoiselle* slipped onto the floor and Molly began snoring, she does a bit, those pale redheads often do. I just lay there with my bedside light on wondering what to do. I kept thinking, 'She came down the mountain early, more a woman than a girlie,' and I couldn't think what to do, it was awful. I couldn't go to the manager. What could I say? I couldn't ring Errol's room, what would I say? Hullo Errol, this is Rita. Hullo Rita. Then what?

Eventually, hours later, Fleur crept in, her new strappy sandals in one hand, and I sat bolt upright and I said, —Fleur! and she said —Ssssh, and put her finger to her mouth like someone saying it.

I said, —Where've you been? and she sat on my bed and said, —I've been with Errol, and I said, —Well I know *that*, and she said, —Yes, and hid her head on her knees.

Nothing happened for a while. I sort of wet my lips, they were a bit dry, and I said, —What did you do?

She lifted her head. Her eyes looked bigger than ever in the half light. —Do? she said.

—Yes.

Fleur put her head on her knees again. —We went to his room, she said.

—Fleur!

—Why shouldn't I?

I couldn't think of anything to say. Why shouldn't she.

She smiled and lay down on my bed leaning her head against the foot-board, her feet up my end.

Nobody said anything.

—Oh well, I said eventually.

Fleur sat up again, she sort of unwound herself. —He really likes the Andrews Sisters, she said. He has a daughter nearly as old as me. You wouldn't think that, would you?

—No, I said.

—And he knows all the words, she said. 'Don't fence me in,'
and everything.

—He's probably heard his daughter's, I said.

—Mmmn, she said, then silence.

—After a while . . . she said.

—Yes?

—He got pretty, you know.

—Oh Fleur! How *aw*ful.

Fleur smiled. —I kept thinking of coming down the mountain
more a woman than a girlie.

—Fleur! Whatever did you do? I felt quite hot.

Fleur didn't say anything. She just smiled and rolled over for
a moment then she got up and stretched her arms up to the ceiling
and dropped them. She cleaned her teeth and hopped into her bed.
Goodnight, she said. She was asleep in two minutes.

I turned off the light and just lay there. How *aw*ful. Poor Fleur.
We left next day.

Fleur had three husbands. The first one didn't last long. Nigel
Combes, a cousin of Molly's. They were too young. Nigel was last
heard of in Buenos Aires. The second, Trevor, canned fruit and
made a lot of money. When he died Fleur went to England for
another trip and married a retired naval captain she met at her
Cousin Bee's in Hambledon. They lived in the Close at Chichester,
where Bengy had lived with his first wife Evadne until she died. We
had ten perfect years, said Fleur. When Bengy had his coronary and
died Fleur packed the porcelain and silver herself, got Pickfords in
for the rest, and came home.

Molly married Tim who had been badly wounded in the war. She
was the staff nurse in his ward and pumped life back into his
mangled body, his dazed mind. She strode about the hospital, her
cap tipped on the back of her orange head, her belt cinched tight
about her waist, the stiff white uniform puffing out above (bust) and

below (bottom). She popped into the Dispensary. —Is my fiancé's script ready yet Mr Carfax? Tim Boulder. Oh well. I just thought I'd pop in, seeing I was passing. —Yoo hoo, Miss Broadstairs, she greeted the physio in the corridor. My fiancé's ready for physsy any time you are. Right oh. I'll tell him.

Tim won a farm in a rehab ballot and they slaved on twelve hundred acres in the King Country. Molly worked side by side with him till the children came and after, docking, dagging, drafting in the yards. He roared poetry to the hills when they were mustering. 'There was movement on the station as the word was passed around / That the colt from Old Regret had got away.' 'Strong gongs groaning as the guns boom far,' he yelled, leaning out the window of the truck. 'Don Juan of *Austria* is going to the war,' Molly screamed back at him as she held the gate wide.

Tim read to her in bed at night, only for about five minutes usually, as they couldn't keep their eyes open. —This is us, Moll. Listen. 'High are the hills and the valleys steep. The cliffs are sombre and the defiles mysterious!' Spot on eh?

The house was a wreck. Molly went through the floor of the kitchen when she was pregnant with Shaun. The woolshed was rotten. They survived, their four red-headed sons flourished. Wedding photos of Shaun, Derek, Jamie and Blair and their brides, Tina, Lisa, Lorraine and Jo, show Molly and Tim weathered as ancient totems. Molly could make two of Tim, that faded wisp of a survivor.

—Jesus Moll, he said one evening, as he pulled his boots off at the back door. —I won't make old bones.

—You've been saying that for thirty-five years, said Molly, snatching another hank of Romney-cross from the wicker basket at her feet and slamming it against the board with her carder. She had used an old shearing comb as a carding tool for years, but Shaun's wife Tina had given her a new carder for Mothers Day and she felt she'd better use it despite the clatter.

He smiled. —Moll, he said, putting his working jersey arm tight around her plump shoulders. She leant against him, her finger

on his unravelled cuff. —Look at that, she said, —Give it to me.
Now.

He had a stroke on his sixty-fourth birthday. He sat up in bed
when she came into his room at the hospital and put out his striped
pyjama arms to her. He died with his head against her breast, her
hand stroking his fine soft hair.

After Rita finished her BA in English she went to Library School,
which she found fascinating. She travelled overseas which she
adored, especially Devon and Cornwall and the Hardy country.
She met Spencer Vaughan at Wool when they were both exploring
Wessex. He was a surveyor from Warwickshire. They married and
went to New Zealand but it didn't work. They accepted his
qualifications at Lands and Survey but he couldn't settle, and he
missed the Nuneaton pubs.

Rita kept in touch with her friends. She stayed a few days each
holidays with Molly and Tim and the boys. She welcomed Fleur
home when she arrived and dashed up to help unpack the weekend
her container arrived. The holiday had been Rita's idea. She had
worked out the itinerary, made the bookings, written frequent
letters filled with queries and counter queries. —I liaised, she told
Una Benchley. —I was the entrepreneur.

—You've sat on my glasses, cried Fleur in the front seat of the
Newmans, snatching the mangled things from beneath Rita's
behind.

—Oh Fleur, gasped Rita, hobbling to her feet.

The driver ran up the steps. —What's the problem dear? he
asked, tucking a biro behind his ear.

—She sat on my dark glasses, said Fleur. —I've had them for
ten years.

—They don't owe you anything then do they, laughed the
driver, slipping behind the wheel. He picked up the microphone.
—Good morning ladies and gentlemen. Today's scenic wonders
include a windshield tour of Nelson followed by a scenic drive to

Motueka followed by . . .

—I can't go without dark glasses, said Fleur, her voice high and clear. You'll have to stop somewhere, driver . . .

—Fleur, said Molly from the seat behind.

Fleur's hand rested against her forehead. —It's the glare.

The driver turned around. —Do you think you could hang out till morning tea? he asked politely. —There's a chemist there, dear.

—Don't call me dear. Fleur was on her feet, rootling in her bright Liberty carrier bag.

—Sorry Madam. The driver slammed the bus into gear. Fleur rocked backwards and subsided against Rita.

—Insolence, she gasped. Rita didn't think she'd ever heard the word spoken before. Not by a New Zealander.

—Have mine, she said holding out her blue-rimmed Sola-voids.

—Don't be a fool Reet, said Molly.

They shared a bottle of wine with their meal each night. Bengy and Fleur had spent several holidays in the Bordeaux region which should have been more help than it was. —I'll taste for you, said Fleur. —Thank you so much, said Molly.

Rita smiled. —That'd be lovely, Fleur.

Fleur dipped her head at the waiter in the Cosmopolitan Hotel in Westport. He poured a little wine into her glass. She lifted the glass, rolled the wine about thoughtfully, sniffed it, then sipped. After a pause she lowered her smooth pale head once more. The waiter filled each glass. —Not *right* up, murmured Fleur. —Pardon? His face was young, his large hand anxious. Fleur smiled at him. —The wine must breathe, she said. —Is that right? You learn something every day. He placed the bottle on the table beside Fleur and departed at speed, dodging behind the screen to the kitchen, the napkin swinging from his shoulder.

They were in Molly's room at the Hermitage for their gin before dinner.

—Do you realise it's nearly forty years since we were here last, said Rita, interrupting Fleur by mistake.

—Yes, said Molly.

—It's like a feast in the dorm, continued Rita.

—A what? Fleur was having trouble with her naval crown. The catch seemed to be slipping.

—Feast. You know. In the dorm. Like *Trixie at St Mungos*.

Fleur's head was down as she checked the safety chain. Quite firm. She touched the brooch briefly with one hand. —I feel naked without it, she said, —that's the trouble.

—I remember that one, cried Molly. —It was yours!

Rita nodded. —Yes!

—It had an orange cover and they all had plaits. All three of them.

—No. One had curls. The one with the lacrosse stick. Binky. The one in the middle.

—They had plaits, said Molly, slapping and folding the *Press* across her knee.

—What does it *matter*, Fleur asked the pelmet.

Rita's mouth shut.

—As I was saying previously, said Fleur, after the pause, —I have every sympathy for the New Zealand farmer . . .

—That's nice, said Molly, now on her feet, battling with the ice tray at the handbasin.

—But you can't expect the European Economic Community . . .

—EEC, said Rita.

—EC, actually, said Fleur. —As I was saying . . . the French peasant farmers, for example. Why should you expect them to have any concern?

—I don't, said Molly, crunching ice between her teeth. She dropped two pieces into the oily liquid in the bottom of each glass and topped them with water from the tap. —Gin, she said happily, handing a glass to Rita and one to Fleur. She plonked her behind onto the stool in front of the dressing table unit, stuck her legs out straight in front of her and lifted her glass. —Cheers, dears.

—Cheers, said Rita as she sipped.

Fleur drank in silence.

—It's the Brits who hack me off, said Molly.

—You know nothing about it, said Fleur, lifting a hand to the tortoiseshell comb Bengy had bought her in Granada. She and Rita sat side by side on the pink bedcover, leaning outwards from each other.

—I know Tim left half his insides in Crete, said Molly.

—That's so simplistic, said Fleur, slipping her feet out of their neat little patents.

—Is that what you'd call it? asked Molly.

—Politics is the art of the possible, said Rita.

Molly and Fleur turned to her, their glasses in midair.

—I mean, well I mean. Mrs Thatcher say. Prime Ministers must be concerned for their economies, I see that, but what worries me you see is the underclass . . .

They were still staring. —I read a thing in the *New Statesman*, said Rita. —In the Library. Not ours. Down at the Central. We don't get it, not at school. There's no call. It said that Mrs Thatcher's policies have resulted in an underclass.

Molly took a long sip. —What underclass? she said.

—People who are unemployed, who will always be unemployed, who don't vote, who have no future . . .

—If they don't vote that's their problem, said Molly.

—Quite, said Fleur. Her back was straight, her head tumbril high.

—No but it isn't you see, it isn't, said Rita. The slack of her neck moved slightly as her mouth grimaced.

—Why not? demanded Molly, brushing the front of her mauve wool jersey with quick dismissive movements of both hands.

Rita wondered if she was pink. —If you take away people's jobs you see, their hopes, their hopes for their children . . .

—Nobody's taken away their jobs, said Molly.

—They have, they have.

—If Tim and I had sat around waiting for someone to give us a job . . . Molly turned away quickly, the feel of Tim's sparse hair beneath her fingers. Nobody knew, nobody.

—But don't you *see*, begged Rita. —Once you get an under-class . . . I think we're getting one here. That's what worries me. A young man with dreadlocks asked me for fifty cents the other day, in Courtenay Place . . . For chips.

Fleur looked up from the study of her glass. —What did you do?

—I gave it to him of course. He said he was hungry. Rita paused. —An underclass! *Here.* Her hands were clasped tight, her mouth hung open, the inside of her lips rosy and damp.

Fleur slipped Mother's silver bracelets up her arm and back. —When did you embrace Communism, Rita?

Molly heaved herself off the stool. Her glass was empty.

—About the same time you turned into a phoney Pom, she said.

Rita's hand leapt her mouth.

Fleur was upright on her high arches, her pale tights. She swung to confront Molly whose faded marmalade-cat hair sprang upwards from her freckled face.

Fleur was breathing oddly. —How dare you!

—How dare I what? Molly looked like a small bull, honestly a bull, something planted on four legs not two. Totally immovable. Her head stuck forward, moving very slowly from side to side.

—Molly! cried Rita.

Molly scarcely glanced at the shocked face below her. —You keep out of this.

Keep out of it. How could she possibly keep out of it.

—How dare you speak to me like that! gasped Fleur. —I didn't want to come on this pathetic little . . . junket! I didn't want to spend my time in . . . *coaches*! She choked, her voice shaking.

—Don't give me that, said Molly. —Catch you doing anything you didn't want to. You ruined Nigel's life. Ruined it! Her head was moving more quickly now.

—We are *friends*, cried Rita, in despair.

Molly swung around. —And why've you put up with it all your life!

Put up with what? What did she . . . ? Rita's hands were clasped tight.

Fleur's face was chalky white except for two round flaming spots on her cheeks.

—I've never liked you. Either of you. Uneducated peasants!

—Peasants! You'd know, Madam la Doochy. Never done a day's work in your life! Molly's scorn exploded. She was spitting, you could see it. —You've done nothing but whinge and patronise Reet and me ever since we set off. *And* you're mean as cat shit!

Fleur's proud eyes widened in shock. —I'm going.

Molly pointed a jeering arthritic finger at Fleur's wrist. —Mummy's bracelets! she yelped.

Fleur fired her last shot. —Thank God Bengy never met you.

—*Bengy*! God in heaven.

Rita leapt to her feet between them. —Stop it! Stop it. She turned from crimson face to alabaster, beseeching harmony, heavenly harmony, comfort and joy for all friends.

Tears rolled in runnels down her soft cheeks. Do something. Anything. Anything.

She heard her voice echoing inside her skull.

—We are friends, she gasped. She dragged a hand across her blind streaming face. —We have always been friends.

Molly turned to the handbasin and poured herself another gin, her hands moving with slow attentive care. She lifted her glass and stared through it as the door clunked shut.

—When are you going out next, Toony? asked Carmen, leaning against the Staff Lockers.

—Sunday. Mrs Toon smiled brightly. —I go every Sunday.

—I'll come with you, said Carmen. She paused. —No. Not this Sunday. I'd like to but . . .

—No, no of course. Mrs Toon concentrated on the collection of electric plugs on the wall in front of her. They were of different colours; unaligned, haphazard as a huddle of mailboxes on a back country road. —You've got your own life, she said.

Everybody had. Mrs Toon turned and struggled with a window, bonging a closed fist against the stuck frame. —There's never any *air* in this place.

Carmen leant across and shoved hard. The window flew open, its long handle banging. —I haven't been out to see her for ages, she said.

—Oh well.

—Sunday week then. That's for definite, as Cissie used to say. Carmen's blush surged upwards. —I'll ride the bike out to your place, Toony, she said quickly.

Mrs Toon's face moved slightly, a grimace, a clamping of the lips. —No you will not. I'll pick you up.

Carmen's mouth opened then shut. —Fine. Thanks a lot. She dragged her locker key up from the front of her T-shirt. —How is she?

—Just the same. Mrs Toon turned from the window and slapped both hands against the seat of her tartan skirt. —Just the same.

—Stephen always, you know, asks.

—Hang on, Tina! screamed an enraged voice below. Mrs

Toon stood very still. Her arms hung helpless. —Does he, she said.

—Yes, always. He doesn't write much but . . . Carmen stared at her locker key with interest. —And the boys?

—Oh, they're well. Busy. You know. It's a busy time for both of them at this stage in their careers. Mrs Toon's head nodded to emphasise the extent of her married sons' commitments, the full active involvements of their lives.

—Busy's not how you are, said Carmen, her head in her locker. —It's what you do.

Mrs Toon rubbed her fingers together in silence. Carmen had never liked Gary and Bryan.

—Sister Agnes used to say we had all the time there is, she continued, emerging with a referee's whistle in her hand. —It's what you do with it. She shrugged. —I can't talk. Sunday week then?

She gave Mrs Toon a quick hug and ran from the Staff Room, springing from her toes to make up for lost time.

—Are those fish sad? asked Cissie, pointing at the anchovies in their shiny emerald and gold tin.

Mrs Toon's fingers were busy with the inadequate opening device. Made of shit metal, her husband Scotty said. Shit metal, that's your problem. She glanced down at her youngest's upturned face and smiled. Cissie's imagination was a bonus after two pragmatic boys.

Carmen stood on her other side, her head slightly higher above the bench. She was eight, two years older and knew everything. —Flat's not sad, Cissie, she said. Carmen's head tossed with certainty. Her fingers clung to the bench with conviction. —Flat's lying down. Anyway, my Mum buys those pies. Carmen often collected them from Woolworths, her stomach balanced on the open deep-freeze cabinet, her feet waving above the vinyl as she leant across the rock-hard chickens to grab the pizzas by their heavy duty plastic. Their fronts had bright pictures of leaning towers. One sort had a bull fight.

Mrs Toon arranged anchovies on one half of the pizza for herself and Scotty and her elder son Bryan who liked an anchovy. She rinsed her hands and laid salami slices on the other half for Cissie and Gary, and it looked as though Carmen was staying too.

Carmen minded Cissie. —Don't worry Toony. I'll mind Cissie. —Spit, she said, holding out a handkerchief to Cissie then scrubbing her ice-lolly stained mouth. Raspberry was the worst. She held Cissie's hand and guided her through the hole in the hedge, positioning each foot to avoid the nettles. —Hold my hand, Cissie. Don't worry about the boys.

Cissie had rather, when she was little. They were so large and there were so many of them. Rory and Terry and Tim and Joe and Stephen who was quieter and played the guitar. The others roared about slamming in and out of the large muddled house, shouting at each other as they ran down the hill for the bus late as always, leaping over the heads of the small girls if they were sitting in the way, swearing at each other about pinched books, nicked bags, swiped shoes. Mrs Doyle glanced up occasionally, smiled, curled a long piece of grey hair around her finger and went back to Barbara Pym. She was a quick reader and had almost worked her way through the Mobile Library. —Look at them, said Mr Doyle smiling with pride as Terry jumped the gate, one hand on the top and over. —Devils to go eh, devils to go. Tearaways the lot of them. Scotty and Mrs Toon agreed. Mrs Doyle smiled.

The Doyles' house was on a ten-acre plot surrounded by poplars on three sides. A scramble of hawthorn, old man's beard and taupata separated it from the quarter-acre section of the Toons. Cissie climbed through the hedge into a wider world.

A sluggish stream covered in duckweed meandered past the house, willows trimmed to standard length by two damp-eyed Jerseys lined its sides. The Doyle milker-for-the-week boy hooshed them up across the paddock twice a day, slamming both hands against his shorts and blowing air sharply between his teeth, Hssh, Hssh, Hssh. The cows ambled towards the shed rocking from side to side. Sometimes a full udder dripped milk. Spit streamed in threads from warm rolling mouths. If it was Terry or Stephen they gave Cissie a stick and told her to stand still if a cow turned on her, but Cissie moved behind Carmen.

—They won't hurt you, Cissie, said Carmen.

—They swing their heads.

—They're cows. Carmen danced her weight from one leg to the other. —Cows are meant to, she said. Her head swept down then upwards. Her eyes rolled. She was a swinging-head cow.

—The garbos are out again, said Joe, slamming the paper on Tim's pale stomach as he lay spread-eagled on the verandah. Cissie stared, her eyes wide as they often were at Doyles as she groped for meanings, searched for clues. What was going to happen next. Half the time she couldn't guess. The words, the food, even the washing up happened differently. Everyone read at mealtimes, Mr and Mrs Doyle one at each end, Theresa, Carmen and the five boys silent for once as they sat round the long table, their books propped against Vegemite or jam pots. Arms snatched, books fell to the table as someone grabbed a better leaner and it was snatched back. Mrs Doyle lifted her eyes briefly. —Boys, she said. Anything could happen. Once a hen laid an egg before Cissie's very eyes, squawking outraged and flapping to its feet when they were playing Hide and Seek and Carmen was He and Cissie hurtled breathless into the shadowy gloom of the fowl house.

Tim lifted the paper to his eyes. —Good on the garbologists, he said. —How'd you like humping people's crappy rubbish all day. He dropped his head and lay flat. Cissie could see his ribs moving; up and down, up and down for ever. If they stopped he would die.

Terry nudged his brother with muddy toes. —But remember last time. We had to bury the stuff for weeks.

—Don't worry about it, murmured Tim, —I'll think of something. Hey you lot, come here, he shouted. Rory and Stephen were wrestling on the lawn, entwined and indistinguishable as lion cubs on telly. They sat up looking surprised, crawled to their feet and ran over, brushing bright grass clippings from their legs.

Tim directed the operation. Terry, Stephen and Joe squatted on the concrete beside the wash house wrapping the overflowing rubbish bags in crisp brown paper given to Tim by Grant at Central Meats. Tim tied reef knots with green string. —Give us a finger, Cissie. Tighter. Cissie pressed the half knot hard, the end of her finger bright pink. —Good girl.

The boys took turns to leave the neat parcels by the side of the road each evening. They were always gone by the morning.

—Bright lads! cried Mr Doyle. —Lovely stuff.

—I'm going to Denmark, announced Cissie as she guided her stick ship across the duckweed with a bamboo pole donated by Stephen from a clear-out of the back shed. She inched her stomach further along the rough bark of the overhanging willow. —Denmark. She stretched far below to poke her ship onwards. There was a good harbour ahead, a small dented hollow in the bank made by the hoof of a slipping cow. —In Denmark, she told Carmen who lay flattened on the next branch, —the cowsheds are so clean you could eat your breakfast off the floor.

—Why would you want to? said Carmen. She gave a quick forward shunt with her legs and propelled her ship onwards to Vladivostok which she liked the sound of.

Cissie's face turned to her, her cheek flat against the bark. —Miss Glanville said.

—That doesn't mean you have to. Or it's true even.

Cissie's head lifted in surprise. She rocked, clutched, then plunged head first through the duckweed into the shallow creek. Carmen dropped instant as a cat and dragged her to the bank. Water, mud and duckweed streamed from them. Cissie's streaked face crumpled. —Don't cry, ordered Carmen. —This is good fun see. This is secret. No one knows but us. Come on. Like this. Carmen in front, they crawled to the wash house leaving a flattened trail through the tall grass.

Cissie's hiccoughs returned as she stared at the structured

groups of white cells in the corners of the unlined walls. —Mason bees, she gulped.

—Mason bees don't hurt, said Carmen firmly. —Take off your frock and pants, she ordered. She squeezed the rubber plug in and turned both taps hard. The water gushed foaming into the old wooden tub. Carmen kicked an empty apple-box onto its side. —Get in, she said, both hands levering beneath Cissie's naked behind. —Gee, you've got a monty bottom, Cissie. They sat smiling and secret in the warm water, small duckweed leaves floating around them.

—Next we wash our frocks see, then we get dry and no one will ever know except us. Carmen's eyes glistened with excitement. The thing was impossible, Cissie could see that. She poked a duckweed leaf and stared at the speck of squashed green against her shiny pink leg.

—Mum will know, she said, her head down. Carmen clenched both fists and banged them together in front of her. —Not if you don't say! There was not much room in the tub and the sides were slimy. The wash house was dark and quiet. Cissie's thumb moved towards her mouth. —I don't tell Mum anything, continued Carmen standing up, the water streaming outwards from her stomach. —You've got Theresa, said Cissie rubbing her finger at a furry bit of damp wood near the tap. —And anyway your mother doesn't mind.

It was not that she wanted to tell Toony. She wanted not to tell. When her mother came to put out the light, Cissie's eyes were shut tight. —What is it Cissie? asked Mrs Toon, her hand on the black-stalked button of the light switch. —Nothing, said Cissie clenching her eyelids tighter to make her go away, her heart squeezing smaller with the effort of not telling her mother who *did* mind.

Gary and Bryan climbed through the hole to Doyles but not as often. Sometimes there were huts, beautiful wooden things with towers and old bits of carpet and ropes suspended above the duckweed, their knotted ends almost touching the creek. The Toons wanted Boys only but Carmen kicked Gary behind the knee and Bryan in front. —You're not the boss of me! she told them. The Doyle boys didn't care. —Come on Cissie, said Terry, lifting her so high her pants showed. —What a fatso, gasped Rory, pretending to stumble as he handed her across the water to Joe's waiting arms.

—Ouch, said Cissie proudly, as Rory and Tim pulled pale hairs from her head and held them to the light to see which ones were best for fishing. Her hair was better for fishing than Carmen's because it was whiter and more invisible. —My hair is invisible, she told Gary that night. —Bull, he said, leaning forward to switch to the other channel.

When the boys had fights the Doyles were all on one side against the Toons. Cissie hid behind the unused copper in the wash house if she was near enough because she wanted to be on the Doyles' side and how could she. All the Doyles were different sizes and shapes with different faces, their hair all dark and curly except Carmen's, which was yellow, and Tim's which was straight. There was more of everything at the Doyles' place. More ways to do, to be, to look even. Gary and Bryan were alike as two flattened fish though Bryan was a year older; the same height, the same still pale faces. When the sun shone behind them at breakfast four sticking-out ears glowed rosy red. Cissie thought of her own house next door on its flat section with her nice mother and her nice father and her new kitten. And her nice brothers her mother said, but often they weren't, pinching her tight bottom and muttering Sneak when she told.

—Lawns look nice, dear, said Mrs Toon to Scotty as he wheeled the mower back to the walnut tree for its rub down after mowing. —Very nice. She rested her hand on the dolphin knocker Scotty had picked up in Malta after the war and smiled at the striped grass beside the parking apron, the new Protea grandiceps which was coming away well, the small stones trapped face upwards in the exposed aggregate sweep of the concrete drive. Cissie appeared beside her clutching Caesar, the kitten. One finger pointed at the knocker. —Why is that fish standing on its head? she asked. Mrs Toon stared down at the flushed cheeks, the clear eyes. Perhaps she had a thing about fish. They said they couldn't feel pain but how could you know. She held her handkerchief down to Cissie's nose. —Blow, she said. Cissie blew, Caesar wriggled. —Lawns look nice, don't they dear? said her mother.

—The Doyles take off the dog pooh first, said Cissie. —Dad just mows it. She still hadn't told about the creek. Mrs Toon gave the dolphin a rub with the end of her apron, standing on her toes so that it would reach. —Mum, said Cissie. —Yes? The bored kitten scrambled from Cissie's arms and ran, leaping from its hind paws to dance. —Nothing, said Cissie.

—You pinch a packet from your old man and we'll pinch one from ours, said Gary to the Doyles who were draped around their verandah.

—If we want fags we can buy them, said Tim, rolling over onto his belly.

—Why buy them? They'll never miss a pack. Not from a carton they wouldn't, the way they go through them. Gary's arms were leaping sideways and upwards, demonstrating mountains of cartons, reefs of fags.

—Cissie's never even had a puff, said Gary.

Cissie blinked at the unexpected interest. —No, she said. Did she want to?

—See? said Bryan.

Carmen was playing dentists. She squatted flat-footed on the verandah, her brown knees level with her ears as she bent forward. She pressed dirt into a nail-hole molar on the verandah, spat, stirred the mud with a twig then tamped and levelled the surface with care. She held out a phantom glass. —Rinse, she said.

—Shit, it's hot, said Pat. He was fatter than the others and glistened.

Carmen brushed her hands in abrupt dismissal of the professional world. —Manny and Theresa might take us to the beach, she said. —For a picnic.

—A smoking picnic, said Gary. His pale eyebrows moved slightly as he blinked.

—Yeah, said Bryan.

Rory who was the tallest though Tim was older, inspected the sole of his foot then replaced it on the bleached wood. —What the hell for?

—You're scared shitless of your old man, said Gary.

—Yeah, said Bryan. Rory didn't bother to answer. He leant back against the post and closed his eyes.

—Theresa wouldn't take us if you've pinched anything. Carmen was definite. She hooked a strand of hair behind her ear and squinted into the sun. Her nose moved like the Standard Three rabbit the Doyles minded for the convent each holidays.

Gary minced about on skinny legs wriggling his behind. —Theresa wouldn't *take* us, he squeaked.

Carmen flicked the spare dental amalgam at him with finger and thumb. It landed on his nose and dribbled. He leapt at her. Rory, his eyes still shut, lifted a foot and tripped him. Rory sat up. —God, I wish I had my licence. The surf's good now. You ask Theresa, Carmen.

They went next Saturday, six Doyles and three Toons piled in the back of Manny's ute; a scrambled and straggled collection of legs, arms, and faces singing *Beautiful beautiful brown eyes* because Tim insisted though Stephen said he'd kill him. —You'd better come in front, said Theresa before they set off, holding out her arms to lift Cissie down from the tray. —You were sick last time, remember, on the last horseshoe by the bridge.

Cissie clamped her lips tight. —Not this time I won't be.

—OK. Theresa never fussed. —Bang on the window if she wants to toss, Tim. Tim's lip curled in exaggerated disgust as he drew his feet away. Cissie laughed, hiding her head in delight. Theresa leapt into the front seat and nipped Manny's ear. —Don't do that *now*, he groaned. —Love you, she shouted above the slamming gears. Manny smiled.

—OK, hon? asked Theresa when they arrived. Cissie nodded,

her lips pressed tighter than ever.

Theresa lifted her down. —You'll feel better after a swim. She gave Cissie's bottom a quick pat. —Hang on you lot, she shouted at the boys who were flinging togs about and flicking towels at each others' legs. —Wait for Cissie and Carmen.

The sea rolled; endless, dazzling, the best sea in the world for breakers, for sailing over the top of unbroken waves. —Watch for dumpers, cried Theresa. —Watch the rip. Mind the holes. Shark bait, yelled the Doyles as Manny's arms ploughed straight through the water out to beyond the breakers, his head disappearing at each foaming wave to surface and shake and disappear again. He lay on his back not even kicking, his face peeling to the sun. —Watch Cissie and Carmen boys, cried Theresa, her legs braced against the current, her hands retying the halter of her bikini. —Not me, shouted Carmen coming up for air. —Not me for goodness sake. She seized Cissie's hand. —Jump Cissie. Duck for the big one. Duck!

Too late. Rolled and tossed, flattened and flung in the shallows, abandoned by small returning waves, Cissie floundered to her feet laughing.

Theresa smiled and lifted her beer can, her arm stretching upwards to Manny. Her hair was stuck to her head, her stomach folded in flat brown pleats above the V of her bikini. —Here's to you, she said. —If I hadn't've met you I couldn't've let you, but I met you, and I let you, and if I met you again I'd let you again. So here's *to* you! Manny's mouth hung slightly open. You could see the dry salt on his forehead. —Theresa, he said, his knees sinking onto the tarpaulin. —Theresa. —Who's got the bloody snarlers, said Terry.

They were in the sandhills behind the beach. —There's a beetle thing that makes traps like that. Stephen poked a piece of marram grass at the funnel-shaped hole Cissie had dug. —He makes a hole that shape, then he hides here. Stephen's piece of grass touched the base of the hole. —Then small minding-their-own-business beetle things fall over the edge and roll down and he leaps out and eats them up, munch munch munch.

Cissie watched his moving jaws, his white teeth. You never knew with Stephen. —No, she said. —Yes. His hand flapped up and down and across his bare chest. —Cross m'heart.

They sat in the blazing sun smoking, the two packets and matches half covered by sand. Everyone puffed and sucked hard except the older Doyles. The younger ones' cheeks flattened with the effort of holding the smoke then blowing it out without coughing. Cissie's face was red, her eyes streamed. —You've all got to inhale, said Gary.

—D'y'reckon? said Rory, holding out two fingers for the thin hand-rolled one from Tim.

—There's a funny smell, said Cissie. Tim laughed. Rory flapped his hand at Tim.

—Come on, you berk.

Carmen's cigarette lay unlit on the sand. She was on her knees plaiting marram grass. —Did you pinch them? she said.

—Yes, said Gary.

—What a stink thing to do. Carmen let the strands of grass go. They rolled back, unweaving gradually, stretching themselves high into the air again.

—Don't you tell, said Bryan, holding his hand around the butt for a quick furtive suck.

Carmen looked at him in disgust. —I don't *tell*.

—Not even Theresa, said Gary.

Carmen picked up her cigarette, brushed the sand from it and lit up. Cissie watched her sadly. Her eyes followed the curving line of the brown hills (poor hills, poor parched hills, said Toony). There were no clouds except a small streak above the island. A gull flew straight into the sun, dropped the tuatua from its beak and plummeted down to pounce, its beak tugging at the broken shell. Was tuatua a fish? Fishes don't hurt. Cissie wanted to be home, to hide in her mother's Brasso-scented lap, to have no secrets. She stood up. —I'm going to the toilet, she said. —I'll come, said

Carmen. —I'm minding you. —No! Cissie ran up the sandhill, her feet disappearing in the falling sand. Her eyes felt hot. She looked back at them all smoking and pinching and not telling. She turned and ran on, her legs pumping through the sand, her arms stiff by her sides. She didn't want the toilet. She crossed a shallow creek, her feet splashing across the ribbed patterns of the sand beneath the water and headed up the last sandhill to find Theresa. I want to go home Theresa. I want to go home and no secrets. Cissy, cissy. Sook, sook, shrieked the high rolling gulls. Tears splashed the top of her sunfrock which was shaped like a red and white striped heart and had a frill.

She scrambled up the hill panting, her arms bent to help her legs wade through the scurrying sand. In the hollow below Theresa lay on top of Manny. Her bottom covered the top of his legs. They had nothing on, nothing. Theresa was arched backwards, her arms stiff and straight, their spread fingers digging at the sand. —More, she panted, —More! Manny's whole body shoved beneath her, his eyes were shut, his face red. Theresa sank onto him groaning and they lay still.

Bryan yanked her head back while Gary spat. The gob oozed down her cheek. —Sneak, he said. —Shitty little sneak.

Carmen wouldn't let her through the fence. —It's the boys see, she said, kicking her piece of hopscotch-wood into the number three square chalked beneath the Toons' whirligig clothes-line. —They'd scrag you. They said. She paused on one foot, ready to hop. —Dad belted them all. Tim even. *And* Rory.

—I can't believe you didn't tell me Cissie, said her mother.

—I *did* tell you. Cissie's head moved. Her eyes were shut, the kitten clutched to her chest.

—But not before. How could you not tell your own mother about stealing? Mrs Toon pushed back her daughter's fringe. —I thought we were friends.

Cissie buried her head in the soft fur of the kitten's belly. —That's why, she whispered. —That's why I told.

*

Sunday was cloudy and warm. Carmen and Cissie and Mrs Toon sat side by side gazing at the traffic that swept along the motorway on the other side of the fence.

—Three, four, five, six, said Cissie, ticking them off on her fingers.

The curved iron legs of the wooden seat were embedded in a slab of concrete. 'In grateful memory', said a small brass plaque nailed to its back. 'Dr J.C.R. Pearsall. Superintendent. 1931–1950.'

—I like your haircut, Cissie, said Carmen. The moon face turned to her. —Three, four, five, said Cissie.

—It's just the same, isn't it, said Carmen. —Her hair.

—Well, it's an easy style isn't it. A fringe. Mrs Toon touched the pale hair. —She can wash it herself under the shower, can't you darling?

—Yes, said Cissie.

—And you keep your eyes shut don't you, like Toony showed you when you were little. Mrs Toon laughed. —She hated having her head washed when she was tiny. Ampoo, Ampoo, back, back, she used to say, holding up her little arms.

Carmen moved her buttocks on the slatted seat. Merciful Jesu. There was a strong smell of urine.

—They shouldn't call them Kanga Pants, said Mrs Toon suddenly, her eyes still fixed on the traffic. —The things they have to wear. They shouldn't give them a jokey name like that.

—Maybe, said Carmen, maybe they thought it might be . . . What? Nice. Cheerful. Kind. She was silent.

—How would they like it, asked Mrs Toon. Her voice shook. —That's why she's here really. Scotty couldn't . . . She lifted the solid white hand from the seat beside her and kissed it.

—That's my girl, she said. —And Carmen's brought you some Smarties, haven't you.

—Yes, said Carmen.

Thea Sinclair thinks about Aerial Survey in 1978

Thea Sinclair sits on the opposite side of the table from Miss Franklin. She is at Miss Tamp's left hand to take shorthand notes of the first Staff Meeting of the year. She faces two large windows, from one of which the fire-escape is visible. She smiles as she remembers the unexpectedly long drop to the asphalt as she, Miss Tamp and Una Benchley exited during Fire Drill last year, the day Carmen was attacked.

Carmen's summer tan is golden unlike Thea's which is a muddy brown but you can admire Carmen without envy because she is as good as she looks. Beauty, they say, lives with kindness, but not always. In fact seldom, which is why it is difficult to be unaffected by Carmen.

Thea's eyes focus on the large aerial photograph of Girls High and its environs which hangs between the windows, taken by Aerial Survey about ten years ago—when Thea lived next door in fact, though she is unaware of this.

—Look, cried her husband Ray, one hand stiff in explanation, the other ticking off the points. —I've got to get a job, get established, get a flat, get a car. What's the point of you all coming at this stage?

—Because I'm your wife, said Thea. —Look at Mrs Raffles in Singapore. The pioneer women!

She stared at him; sandy haired, amiable, his Adam's Apple rising and descending like a bubble lift. At dinner parties he usually agreed with the last male speaker, jerking his chair forward with quick affirmative movements. Dissension troubled him. He didn't know what to do with it, other than to wish it would go away. Sometimes he went away, sliding silent from his chair when Bryan Hamble lost his temper over Closer Economic Relations or Stuart

Bickerson was caught in a direct lie. He would move to a window, open a curtain slightly to stare at the Hambles' dark plantain-spotted lawn, the Bickersons' half-painted fence. A photograph in the boys' room showed him dappled in shadow beneath a lacebark, a chameleon caught in mid-change.

Thea tried again. —I know engineers are having a rough time. His lips brushed her forehead. —True, he said.

They leant against the wall in the bedroom of their recently sold house surrounded by piles of clothes, mugs of Nescafé on the floor between them. The wardrobe door hung open revealing wire hangers twisted and jumbled on the rail or discarded on the floor, half buried beneath pinkish-grey fluff.

—But . . . She tugged her hair back with hands blackened by packing newsprint.

—They're mad about you in the office. I heard.

His hands were behind his head, his mouth now blowing kisses for the informer.

—Well then?

—Well what.

—Why-are-you-go-ing-by-your-self? she said, snipping the words into bite-sized pieces.

He leapt up, seized Freddy's ball and bounced it. Hand, forearm, biceps. Biceps back to hand. —Because Australia is a land of opportunity and cuts and thrusts and all that crap. It's the only thing to do.

She tugged both knees against her chest. —I'm coming. We're all coming.

He stopped in mid bounce and swung to her. —No. The red ball rolled slowly down the hall to the front door. —Funny. You didn't notice the slope when the carpet was down.

—We're coming! yelled Thea, on her feet, leaping to snatch the thing.

He put his arms round her, his head resting on her head as he stared up the hall to the stained glass panels on either side of the door. —God, I love you, he said.

*

He sat yarning for days to his mother, Bella, before he left for Australia, lying at her feet on the front verandah as she swung on an ancient couch beneath a faded green canopy. Bella was a large woman who moved with a continuous rolling motion. Everything about her flopped, uncorseted and generous to a fault. Her hair hung in grey tendrils which escaped from a bun as loose and uncontrolled as all her parts. Her face was serene, her skin unlined and creamy about her brown eyes, her large mouth. Her hands were also beautiful. Long bony fingers extended from wrists braceleted and solid as a baby's.

—I don't know about these Prayer Breakfasts, she said.

He smiled, one hand reaching for the paper.

—Look at this lot. 'Capital City Prayer breakfast held in Wellington Town Hall, organised by the Christian Business Men's Association,' she read. 'Minister of Commerce and Industry, Mr Adams-Schneider, reads from the New Testament.' They're all there, the whole boiling. Mayor Mr Fowler, Governor General Holyoake. She snorted.

—A touch phoney?

—Ask yourself.

He lent his head against her knee and sighed.

Vandalism, she said later, her hands clasped among the gathers of her sleeveless tub frock, was a symptom of something deeper and he agreed. She heaved herself from the collapsing couch and waddled towards the kitchen.

'It must be jelly / 'Cos jam don't shake like that!' Ray slapped her behind and swung her around the cluttered formica table which was submerged beneath the end products of Thursday's big shop. Half-frozen chops leaked pink beneath their plastic. —That should see me out, Bella had said as she dumped mounds of toilet paper on top of potatoes, bananas and one green pepper. Six chocolate fish in a little white bag waited for deep-freeze stowage beside a dew-covered carton of Tip Top Cassata. Freddy and Ben leapt about on stick legs yelping with excitement. A bottle of homogenised milk crashed to the floor. Ben shoved it between the toaster and a carton of number seven eggs smothered in Golden Kiwi tickets. —Your horizontal surfaces are a disgrace, white trash. Ain't you got no shame? cried Ray. —Not a drop, gasped Bella. She collapsed on an inadequate stool, her arms reaching to enfold the pink-faced boys. —Benny, Freddy. Freddy, Ben. Which is which of you lot? —Gran! they squealed, burying anxious laughing heads in her lap.

When Ray left, Thea rented a flat which was overlooked by Aerial Survey Ltd. A man with red hair waved to her as she and Aunt trailed in with cartons, hampered by two small boys who skipped from side to side in front of them.

—They were chained to the wall with cobwebs, exclaimed Aunt. She tugged one of the beds away from the wall to demonstrate, her hand indicating invisible ropes, layers of sticky greyness now hidden in the belly of the brown Hitachi at her feet. —The place was a pig-sty. It was filthy, to me it was filthy. She searched Thea's face for acknowlegement of her efforts, her victory.

—Oh dear, said Thea. She heard her voice limping on, crawling through the hoops of a familiar obstacle course. —I'm very grateful.

—Somebody had to do it, sighed Aunt, coiling the Hitachi cord over her arm before slipping it through the handle.

Aunt was a small woman, slim as a pin in her blue and white sun frock. She scuttled everywhere, her head well in advance of her bent waist, her busy legs. Her life was husbandry. Layers of housework, archaic rituals of cleansings and washings alternated with bottling, baking, producing three meals a day and keeping my men happy. —It's no forty hour week, she told Edith her neighbour who was an unmarried corsetiere.

Aunt was now upright. —And Bella didn't put in an appearance, she said.

Bella has demonstrated once again that she is lazy and mullecky-gullecky and as useless as a piece of fixed furniture. Aunt regards her as an irritant, a protagonist in a war-game in which the victor's prize is the major share of affection from Thea and Ray's two sons, Freddy and Ben. Bella refuses to play.

To be hugged by Bella is to know that all is not lost and that worse things have happened at sea and you can stuff the lot of them and rise again.

Thea applied for a job at Aerial Survey the week after Ray left. She climbed the cool stairs lined with photographs of local stations, the roofs of the homesteads and woolsheds tinted red or green, the names of the paddocks (Longreach, Lambing, Top Flat, Swamp) neatly inscribed in small print. The hair-like roads leading to Otahome, Blairlogie, Rongomai, were white.

She listed her secretarial skills to the receptionist. —I live there, she said pointing below to the faded grey roof, the concrete backyard, the circular clothesline whirling at speed with its frill of little boys' shorts, little boys' T-shirts, her pink-spotted pants. —So I thought I'd just see . . . The receptionist had red hair. Perhaps they all had.

—I doubt it, she said.

Thea smiled. —Yes, it's just . . . That pale papery skin must be hell in the heat.

—Oh well. The receptionist glanced at her watch. —I suppose I can ask. She rose, pushed herself up from the laminated formica and clanked away on Scholl sandals. Thea stared down at the flat. A black and white cat dragged its belly across the concrete then lay still.

—There's nothing, said the receptionist. —Not a thing. Sorry.

A BMW stopped at the Superette (Dick and Relda) below. A long-legged woman leapt out pursued by a wobbling toddler with outstretched arms. The woman scooped the squalling child under one arm like King Kong requisitioning Miss Darrow. They disappeared inside. —You see everything here, don't you? said Thea.

—What?

—Nothing.

The red-haired man was not visible.

Aunt found her a job at Beechaven Retirement Home. The matron
Mrs. Burnside belonged to Church Fellowship and she and Aunt
did the brass together, Aunt putting on the Brasso and Mrs Burnside
following, rubbing and buffing with worn nappies discarded from
Children's Ward at Public. Aunt brought her silver-brush from
home to get right into the eagle's beak on the lectern. —I can't
stand a build-up, she said.

Beechaven was set in park-like grounds surrounded by a secure
fence. The shady verandahs were lined with old ladies glaring into
the sunshine. There were few men. —This is Mrs Sinclair, said Mrs
Burnside. —She is our new secretary, aren't you? Thea shook the
hands which were offered and smiled at those who slept or stared.
An emaciated woman in a wheelchair burst into bellowing sobs as
she clung to Thea's hand, her nails digging the skin as she wailed,
—Inez. Inez.

—You mustn't mind, said Mrs Burnside. —People always
think they're unhappy when they cry. They're not. It's just their
emotions are very near the surface. She's thrilled to see you aren't
you, Miss Jerome. Mrs Burnside extracted Thea's hands and
mopped the streaming face with a Kleenex from the box on the
windowsill.

—And this is Mr Barrymore.

—They're all gaga here, said the old man, his eyes staring at the
fence, his trembling hands stroking the carved knob of his stick.

—What a beautiful stick, said Thea.

—They all say that.

—Where did it come from?

—Malacca.

—I thought that was cane.

He straightened and looked at her for the first time. —This is
wood. Carved. Teak. Look. Holding it in both hands to lessen the

tremor, he thrust it at her. The carving was very fine. Intricate fenestrations defined the heads and bodies of grotesque birds and beasts which swirled around the knob of heavy polished wood.

—Beautiful, said Thea handing it back.

—And this is Mrs Alfson. The tiny body was curled among faded cushions, the face hidden, strands of white hair were sparse above the pink scalp. Mrs *Alfson*. Good heavens . . .

Thea and Ray had camped on their honeymoon, moving up the Coromandel, their bodies salty and aching with love; sand in their hair, their sleeping bag, their stale bread and smelly chops. Ray made her a chair from driftwood so that she could lie back to watch the sun collapse into the sea at Tairua. He tied the pieces together with the tow-rope his father had insisted they take. Aunt got permission for them to camp beside the bach on Mrs Alfson's farm.

—It wasn't easy. You know what she's like. But I just kept talking. I said you're only young once and they're very careful, but you know what she's like.

As they lurched down the road to the sea the weather broke. Rain bucketed down, hissing on the overheated bonnet of the old Prefect. The windscreen wipers were hysterical and inadequate. Water poured in rivulets, streaming over the parched land.

—I'm not camping in this lot, said Ray. —There must be a key. He splashed through the vertical rain to check the outdoor safe, the door lintels. He ran bent double from pile to pile, his hands groping. He found it on the third from the door and squelched back to the car. His hair was plastered to his skull, his eyes bright as he held up the key with its plastic tag labelled Bach.

—Home and hosed, he yelled.

The temperature had plummeted. He lit a fire and hung their clothes from the mantelpiece, securing them with an ancient iron from the kitchen, two heavy doorstops and a large rock from the verandah. They made love on the rug in front of the fire, their giant shadows leaping above them. Ray rolled from her sighing, one hand flopped across her stomach. Carlights raked the wooden beams, flashing around the walls as a car jolted down the track.

—Christ! Ray was on his feet struggling into his wet jeans, kicking his Jockeys beneath the uncut-moquette sofa. —Quick, he shouted. She was flattened, ground into the rug. Why hide. What did it matter. He flung her sodden jeans at her. She shook her head smiling.

—For Christ's sake. He snatched the Indian cloth from the table and wrapped it around her, twisting her, swinging her back to him to tuck it above her breasts. It had black peacocks on a red ground. Granny Smiths from a dislodged basket rolled bouncing to the floor as she laughed. —Sit down, he hissed as the thundering knock sounded.

Mrs Alfson's son stood hesitant and dripping in the doorway, a large bald man in an oilskin. Khaki shorts hung low about his hips, rain trickled down solid legs to his boots.

—I'm Hamish Alfson, he said. —Come in, come in, cried Ray leaping around the sofa to pump his hand. —Ray Sinclair. My wife Thea.

—Mum said, said Hamish in slow embarrassment, —that as it's hosing down you might like to use the bach. —Great, cried Ray, striking his hands together then flinging them wide. —Great. Very kind. Have a beer. Bit warm I'm afraid.

Thea stared at the peacocks.

—But I'm cooking a loin, said Aunt. —I put it on specially in this heat. Pork. The boys love crackling.

—I told you Aunt. Bella asked us . . .

Aunt's stare was unblinking. —And what do you imagine I'm meant to do do with the loin?

—She asked us a week ago.

—Well that's that then, isn't it? Aunt turned away, her head high. Hoity. Also toity. She called me that when I was a child. Hoity toity.

Bella had forgotten all about it. She came out to meet them in her down-at-heel pink mules leaking threads of osprey, her arms wide in welcome.

—There's not a skerrick of food in the house, she said cheerfully.

—Kentucky fried! squeaked Ben, his voice muffled behind a Groucho mask.

—Yey, yey, shouted Freddy, jumping up and down and hitting him.

—Thea flapped one hand, yo-yoing the air above their heads.

—There's that Cassata in the deepy for after, said Bella. That's something.

—Yeah, Yeah!

—She'd see me, said Thea. —With my luck. I bet.

The jumping and hitting stopped. Faces lifted. —Who?

—She'd never go within a bull's roar. Bella's shoulders heaved. —Put on a false beard, she said.

Ben dragged off the exuberant eyebrows, the bulbous celluloid nose and shoved it at her. —Here.

Thea put it on. —Thanks, she said, liberated by Groucho.

—There's still your feet, said Freddy.

—What's the news? asked Bella later, pouring a stream of Brazilian Fiesta into a pot of boiling water. She made the best coffee in the world.

Thea dragged Ray's aerogramme from her pocket. He says Woolford and Kneebone are useless. —Not a thing he says. He's in a cruddy little bed and breakfast in the Cross. I'll give you the address. Bella nodded. —Surrounded by pros continued Thea, that's what he says. —What sort of a word is that, snapped Bella. —And it's hot, continued Thea. Thirty-eight. She paused. —The prawns are great. They do barbecue them.

Bella glared at her, a cross, inflated globe-fish.

—How does he know?

—And he sends you his love.

—What the hell's he think he's playing at? Bella puffed back to the table with two Snoopy mugs and made her slow descent onto the gingham cushioning her chair. She glanced at Freddy and Ben who stood silent, watching from the doorway. —It must be something educational, she said, picking up the TV programme. —*The World around us. What's wrong with the sun?* Bad as that, huh?

—She's splendid, Bella said to Aunt. Splendid. I don't know.
    —Well if you don't know . . . replied Aunt, dusting the telephone with her hand, slipping around the cradle with care.
    Bella put the receiver down.

Relda in the Dairy was also concerned. She was lean and rangy, dark eyes snapping beneath thick eyebrows. Her sinewy hands gripped the counter. —It's a long time to be on your own with two though, isn't it? How long is it now?
    The Superette was so handy. There were lights at the crossing so the boys could run over. It was open every day from eight till eight. And they had Golden Kiwis. Dick had sold a winning ticket once. —Didn't you get anything? asked Thea. —Not enough, the miserable bastards, said Dick, his hands moving with speed as he slammed the Reizensteins into their steel cages.

The boys were all right. They liked their new teacher Mr Cridland who played 'Michael row the boat ashore' on his guitar. They liked the new dunnies in A Block, the Beasley twins next door and taha Maori, which was new. Thea was home from Beechaven each day before they scrambled in to dump their bright school bags and hurtle off. She threw out the half-eaten banana sandwiches and brown cores. She waved to the red-headed man. He winked and lifted one hand.
    Mr Barrymore sought her out at Beechaven. He stood at the office door muttering at her beneath his untrimmed white moustache, his hands clasped on top of his stick. —You're a pretty woman, he said. Shit and hell. —Tell me about your stick, Mr Barrymore. He edged gingerly into the small office space walled off

from one end of the verandah and lowered himself onto the upright chair from which Thea snatched a tray of correspondence. —I lived all my working life on Carey Island, he panted. —Island off the coast near KL. Been there? She shook her head. —Ran a palm oil plantation. Soil acidity's the problem. Know anything about the water table? She began typing as she shook her head once more. He was now onto the aboriginal people of the Malaysian archipelago. The Orang Asli. —Small. One hand lifted to wave within her range of vision at about four feet. —Friendly, know what I mean? Dying out.

—And they gave you the stick? Her eyes flicked to the grotesque thing. She saw the endangered tribe assembled, dark feet shuffling in the dust of the jungle clearing, wide-eyed babies at foot or breast, the shy smile on the face of the diminutive head-man as he made the presentation.

—God no. Malacca. Got it in Malacca. Told you.

—Yes I know, but I thought . . . Mr Barrymore leant forward and placed a trembling hand on her knee. —Always liked fair girls, he said.

—If I were you, said Aunt, tugging her end of the sheet they were folding with such vigour it flew from Thea's hands, —I'd just pack up and go.

—Can't be long now, said Bella leaning back on the flat's overstuffed sofa, the *Listener* balanced on her stomach open at *Life in New Zealand*. —'Mount Victoria. Two bedrooms. Renovated. Won't last long.' Her body shook as tides of mirth rolled over her. —Where do they get them!

—People send them in Gran, explained Ben, draped across what was left of the arm of the sofa. —See. It says.

—Yes, but where'd they get them? Bella heaved a handkerchief from the leg of her doublet-like bloomers and blew hard. —Any day now he'll ring, she said to Thea who was slapping Vegemite onto Ryvita. —You'll see.

The flies settled and lifted beside Thea on the formica. One tipped backwards to scrape obsequious front legs, then swung into a handstand to rake its rear extremities. Thea brushed a hoverer from above the sugar bowl. —You need one of those wee net things with beads, said Bella, replacing the handkerchief with effort. —Covers. I haven't seen one since Ida died. She mopped her face with a nearby tea towel. —But then I can't crochet.

> I am the man from Sodom
> And I want to fuck your bottom

announced the pink-chalked graffiti on the asphalt outside the Superette.

Thea nodded as Dick lurched in with a milk crate, his white veined-marble legs hairless below maroon shorts, his mouth lop-sided with effort. —Shit, he gasped, dumping the crate at Thea's feet to wipe milky hands down the front of his T-shirt. —Pardon my French.

—If Dick didn't come home every night I'd die, said Relda, flattening a five dollar bill on the counter before slipping it beneath its steel restraint in the till. —Well he's home anyway but you know what I mean.

—Yes, said Thea.

—Where does the time go? gasped Pam Bickerson, one hand attempting to restrain her youngest, Tommo, as he flung his head between the uprights of the bike-rack outside the Superette.

—I don't know said Thea, her hands tight about the newly-acquired Chux recommended by Aunt.

—I feel so guilty about you though. I mean we haven't had you round or anything.

Thea pointed to a trail of granular yellow baby-shit seeping down Tommo's leg. Tommo rocked on his feet, peering down at it with interest and an exploratory finger. —Oh No! Pam's hands flew to her hair. —He's had it for weeks. Thanks, she said, grabbing the proffered Chux. —Stand still!

*

Thea took the boys to the river after school, humping the basket over the round stones to make a detour past the prostrate couple on the grass who lifted glazed eyes to the procession then re-entwined. The river flowed slowly, shallow and smelling of mud. It was cool beneath the willows. I must leave Beechaven. Enough's enough. She sat hunched, her skirt wrapped tight against the sandflies, watching Freddy and Ben splashing and damming below. They were very busy. Each knob of each backbone was visible as they heaved and tugged, their fingers scrabbling at huge stones.

—Use the smaller ones, she called.

Ben's head lifted, his face frowning. —What?

She tucked her skirt into her pants (God your legs are beautiful) and demonstrated.

—We need Dad, she said.

—Why? said Freddy, still tugging at an impossible boulder.

—He's an engineer. Quick. There's a cockabully.

They trapped it in a mini pool and offered it bread, squatting on damp haunches, their voices gentle as the crumbs sank around the fluttering transparent dorsal fins, the speckled body.

—No, you can't take it home, she said. —It'd miss the other cockabullies. Momma bully, Poppa bully, all the little bullies.

—Where are they? said Freddy, his legs braced against the current as he stared upstream.

—This is a rogue one.

—What's rogue?

—One that got away. A different sort of cockabully, she said, bending to kiss the hot stubble of his hair.

—Different how?

—What do you think that's sheep's name is?

—Which one? asked Ben.

—The one staring.

—They're all staring.

—Betty! called Freddy, his feet slipping on the smooth stones. —Here Betty. One of the sheep moved to the fence, pricking its way on trim black feet.

Freddy swung to her, his eyes round. —That was the *one*.
The cockabully had disappeared.

—He's just lonely, said Mrs Burnside. Surely you can see that.
　　—Oh sure. Thea gazed at the nursing medal on the bosom in
front of her. Her mother had had her Medal.
　　—Well then.
　　—He can be lonely at someone else.
　　—That's not very kind.
　　—I'm not very kind.
　　Mrs Burnside's lips tightened. —There's no one here for him
to talk to. He's intelligent, well-educated. It's very sad. He doesn't
mean anything.
　　—It gives me the creeps. Every time I look up I see that stick.
The contorted primitive shapes flicked into her mind, writhing
bird's head melding with snake. —I dream about it, she said, lying
for the second time in the conversation.
　　Mrs Burnside sighed. The medal lifted and returned. —I'll see
what I can do. Her plump pigeon hands rested on the desk. Blue
and pink roses tumbled on curtains and two small covered chairs in
the over-heated room. Photographs of My girls and the littlies,
previous employees and their littlies covered the walls and tables.
A brass vase of flame-coloured gladioli stood on the mantelpiece
above the unused fireplace. There was a mixed bowl on the desk.
There were always flowers, a source of pride. And comfort.
—Matron does them herself, said the exonerated relatives. —It's
those little touches.

Thea dumped the washing powder on the counter and smiled at
Relda, the exact change in her hand.
　　A bus driver crossed the buzzing threshold, his blue uniform
shirt and shorts straining to provide coverage. —Who owns the
blue Morris? he asked.
　　—Me, said Thea.
　　—Sorry lady, he said smiling. —We've backed into it.

—What! She leapt across the doorstep. —It's uninsured, she gasped, staring at the crushed radiator, the drunken hanging headlamp.

The driver shook his head. —Uninsured. That's not so good. He took off his cap, wiped the inside band with a handkerchief and replaced it on the back of his head. —That's a bummer.

—It wouldn't have been a bummer if you hadn't bloody backed into it! She stepped into the gutter to peer at it, to touch the mangled thing.

—Wasn't me, he said. —Him. Under training. The driver indicated a stolid youth a few feet away.

—I don't care who it was! She heard her voice rising. Like a woman's.

—Can I help? She straightened to find herself level with the red-headed man's shirt pocket. It had a biro in it.

—She's not insured, said the driver.

The sandy eyebrows rose slightly. —That's a pity . . . he said.

—Oh don't you start, said Thea, storming back to her Persil. He followed her. —They're still responsible, he said.

She turned on him, her fists tight. —Of course they are. I know that! I'll deal with the creep in a moment. Thank you, she said to his departing back.

—You've got enough on your plate haven't you, said Relda after a pause, —without buses backing into you. She stared at Thea, her mouth moving. —And I hear someone's nicked your pants, she said.

Thea snatched the Persil to her breast. —Who told you?

Relda's two front teeth closed over her lower lip. Her hands rearranged the cellophane-wrapped carrot cakes in front of her. —Someone, she shrugged. —I don't know.

The cop was an elderly Scot with a crew cut. He sat on an upright chair beneath the vase of toi toi provided by Aunt, his legs wide apart, a small pad balanced on one knee.

—You left the washing out overnight then did you, Mrs er, Sinclair? he asked.

—Yes. It saves time in the morning.

He shook his head. —Not a good idea. I imagine it's a man—a wee bit perverted man, you see, he said gently. —You wouldn't want them back, would you? The knickers?

Thea shook her head, her eyes on the drooping toi toi heads. Some people dye them.

The cop made a note and glanced up. —Are you insured Mrs Sinclair?

—No.

'I have always been honest with you' writes Thea on airmail paper. She rips out the page, screws it up then stares at the crumpled thing on the floor. She writes the words again on the next sheet and continues, 'so I'm writing to say I don't know what's going on and if you want to leave me and your sons . . .' She crosses out 'your sons' and writes 'the boys'. She screws it up and starts once more. 'Why don't you say so?' she writes.

If I'm so honest why haven't I said . . . Quite a lot. Everything. Everything what.

One elbow feels sticky. She lifts it, wipes it quickly then drops the cloth and does nothing at all. The bracket clock in the centre of the mantelpiece gives a preliminary wheeze then strikes three instead of five.

Thea has written to the bus company. Yesterday she handed in her notice to Beechaven, received with displeasure by Matron among the chintz and mixed bowls. She has promised to visit Mr Barrymore who is a lonely old man. She has applied for a job as secretary to the Head of Girls High. She has withdrawn her custom from the Superette.

She jumps from the kitchen table and turns on the cold tap. She runs it until it is really cold, testing it with quick flapping movements of her hand, then bends to drink. She straightens, wipes a hand across her mouth and runs into the backyard.

The red-headed man is looking out the window. He sees her

and turns back to his work. Plastic pegs smack the concrete as Thea grabs a towel and the line whirls. He looks up. The late afternoon sun casts shadows from the tall building right across the yard: almost as far as the whirligig and the woman in bare feet who snatches washing from the line as though her life depended on it.

She waves. —Come on down, she yells. He opens the window. He still can't hear her but he understands the message of her waving arms. He smiles, then disappears from sight.

Carmen and Margot do not know if Jared was planned which is odd as they discuss everything with Sooze, or almost everything. There are one or two things Sooze does not discuss: Bryce for example; and whether or not Jared's arrival was intentional.

If Bryce is on the night shift at Southalls he minds Jared during the day. Sooze makes up the formula before she leaves for school although Bryce would be happy to make the stuff, and as he says, he's got the time. But Sooze insists. It's the least she can do, she says, slamming the powder into the clear plastic jug and holding it at eye-level as she measures the water. If Bryce is on day shift Sooze leaves Jared with his formula and his extra clothes and his small bear in the red jacket at the crêche on her way to work.

Jared is very happy at Day Care with Cuddles. Sooze and Bryce tell each other this and Jared lies on his back and smiles, his hands moving without volition as they do at his age. Sooze demonstrates Jared's dimples to Bryce who has seen them before; on his cheeks, the base of each finger, each elbow. She kisses each finger and changes his Treasures which are another thing Sooze refuses to feel guilty about as she is teaching full-time and doesn't want to anyhow. Jared has no hair, only fluff. His head is smooth and warm, blood heat beneath his father's cheek as he holds him in his arms.

Bryce was in Futures before the crash. He left to catch the unit each morning in his dark suit and white shirt with his briefcase and sometimes his good fawn raincoat. Occasionally he carried a rolled black umbrella though even the expensive ones blow inside out on The Terrace. Brownstone and Cutler were an old established firm and he enjoyed the work; rolling the money, adrenalin pulsing as you watch the millions go go go, the telephones screaming, the other sharp guys.

The firm held an annual sports day and everyone trained for months, pounding along the wide footpath at Oriental Bay, crashing into the surf, manoeuvring past the occasional piece of orange peel to swim out and around the Fountain in the lunch hour. Bryce won the triathlon. It nearly killed him. Mrs Cutler, upholstered in blue, looked worried as she presented the cup. —Are you sure you're all right, Bryce? she asked, shoving the thing at him as though it was a dead fish.

It was a long day but he unwound in the train going home to Paraparaumu, deliberately not reading, watching the slumped women passengers, the rough paddocks, the idle cows flick by.

—You realise our jobs are in jeopardy? said Nev Skinner, resting one buttock on Bryce's desk the day after the crash.

—Jeopardy, huh? said Bryce. —D'y'reckon. He wished he had something to do with his hands, a pencil sharpener, anything. He straightened a ruler he never used and stared out the window. Brownstone and Cutler's office was on the tenth floor. Far below two lipstick-red tugs were nudging a great white whale of a cruise-ship into its berth. Soon, disconsolate male and female American tourists in permanent-pleats and good quality reversible wind-jackets would be wandering around Courtenay Place wondering where the good bit was, and how to get there.

A flock of gulls wheeled in front of the window and swept up and away, screeching across the harbour.

—You don't often see that, said Bryce.

—What? said Nev. —I wish to hell I still smoked.

—Gulls flying like that.

—Like what?

—All together like that.

Nev stood and adjusted the turn-up of his bird's-eye check trousers. —Is that right, he said, moving back to his desk.

*

Sooze was convinced it would be all right. Bryce couldn't understand it. She had always been the worrier, the insecure one, clinging to him each night as she poured out the latest crisis at bloody Girls High.

—Balls, she said. —Why should they sack you?

—Make me redundant, corrected Bryce from the floor. —Get it right. Chuck us that thing. One hand reached out to Sooze for the disposable nappy, the other was held above Jared's penis. He was sick of getting it in the eye.

Sooze swung her feet under her and sat up straight, her hands smoothing the checked cover of the sofa. —OK. 'Make you redundant.' Look at your CV.

Jared rolled obligingly from side to side as Bryce changed him, chewing and dribbling on a pink plastic duck. Bryce rolled up the wet Treasure and held it in his hand as he lifted his son and held him against his chest. —Look at everyone's CV. There's no one there who isn't good.

—You're extra good, she said, leaning forward to insist.

—There's been a stockmarket crash for God's sake! He pointed to an empty New World bag on the sofa beside her. —Ditch that. Plastic bags can kill kids.

—I know that. She screwed the thing between her hands. —It's for my knitting.

He stood up with Jared in his arms and walked to the ill-fitting French doors of the bach. They opened onto a small terrace of concrete slabs which were sinking unevenly into the sand. Beyond lay the marram-covered sandhills and the sea. Kapiti was purple.

—Ditch it, he said.

—I need a big one for my Kaffe Fassett.

Bryce swung round to face her, Jared's head hidden against his chest. —Ditch it!

She put the plastic bag to her lips and blew. —Don't take it out on me, she said.

*

The rumours at Brownstone and Cutler were hard to handle. Bryce thought of the tensions of the triathlon. They were as far away, as hazy and irrelevant as the dreams and hopes of childhood Christmases.

Selwyn Cutler called the whole staff into his office three months after the crash. The soft leather chairs sighed as the seniors sank into them. The mahogany desk was uncluttered by any photograph of Selwyn's dependants. The plants, including a six-foot Moreton Bay fig in a brass bound tub, were crisp and green, maintained each week by Plants without Pain. There was a large painting behind the desk of smooth rounded stones. The bar was hidden.

Decisions would be made that weekend, Selwyn said. He was afraid to have to tell them (and he looked it) that some redundancies were inevitable.

—If only I'd got out before, Bryce said for the five-hundreth time.

Sooze sat beside him on the sofa and kissed his ear. Bryce stopped wearing his earring years ago and the hole was almost invisible.

—Why don't you wear your earring again? she said.

She was pale. Good legs. He'd think so if he saw them on the train. Long long legs.

—What's that got to do with it? He fingered his large and convoluted ear, shiny as the giant plastic model in the Audiology department where he had once taken his grandfather for testing. —It's gone, he said, meaning the earring or the hole or both.

—We'll have Margot and Cam up tomorrow night, Sooze said. And Carmen. People round here. Have a party. To hell with them.

— No. Bryce dragged his hand across his mouth and sighed. Her eyes blinked.

—Why don't you want them?

—Because Carmen makes me feel guilty and I don't want to sit around talking to that thicko Cam about four-by-twos all night.

I didn't rape her.

—She wasn't raped. And Cam doesn't talk about four-by-twos.

—And he never takes his eyes off your boobs.

She was on her feet, tugging at the hem of her miniskirt. —What's the *matter* with you?

—What does he talk about then? Go on. Tell me.

She was getting angry. His eyes watched the pinched nostrils, the pale mouth.

—There's not much point is there? If they're not coming. She moved to the sink, snatched lettuce leaves from the water and held them dripping in front of her. —I have never heard Cam talk about four-by-twos or six-by-eights or . . .

He was getting there, edging gently. —He never talks about anything else.

—He does! She shook the lettuce with conviction. Beads of water splattered the faded red vinyl. —*Why* don't you want them?

—Because I fucking well don't, he shouted.

—Then don't fucking *have them*, she screamed.

His shoulders sagged. Sooze mopped the floor with the dishcloth.

—If I do that you give me arseholes, he said.

Sooze stood very still staring at the nineteen-thirties Kitchen Memo Minder which hung on a nail above the sink. The little red tin flag pointed at Condiments. Why didn't it say Salt, Pepper, Mustard, like a sensible Memo Minder. She smiled.

—What's the joke?

—Why don't you go for a run? she said.

—I don't want a run. He heaved his shoulders from the doorway and moved to the french doors.

Sooze filled the kettle for the potatoes, put it in its safety cage and pressed the switch. He was staring at the sea.

—What *do* you want?

—A good fuck.

—We can't fuck all weekend.

He didn't turn. —Why not?

Her eyes pricked with rage. After a moment she shook her hair back in the sweeping parabola of a shampoo advertisement and walked the few steps across the room. She put her arms around him and buried her head against his chest like Jared. —Tomorrow's Saturday, she said.

He didn't return her hug. —So?

—Have you read *Tristram Shandy*?

He stared outside. —No.

—They fucked every Saturday. Tristram's parents. After he'd wound the clock.

He pulled away. —I'm going for a run, he said.

Selwyn Cutler and his hatchet man, Clive, had had a hell of a weekend. They told the assembled staff so on Monday morning. How difficult, impossible almost, it had been for them to come to redundancy decisions when all the staff were of such high calibre. They spoke, their faces twisted with pain, of their discussions, their concern, their traumas. Bryce, Nev and two trainees were declared redundant. As from next week.

—I'm not going to sit around and mope, said Bryce, sitting at the table that night demolishing lamb chops and Pasta Fresca. —And I'm buggered if I'm going on the dole.

He seemed to be on some sort of a high. —No, said Sooze. The meat was pink, undercooked. The pasta slid from her fork.

He took a swig of carton red. —I'll get some shitty job so that I can be available for interviews, see.

She gave up and cut the green slippery stuff with the side of her fork. —Yeah, good thinking.

—Commercial cleaning, say. Any fool can do that.

Sooze's head lifted in silence. Her mouth was full.

There were no interviews. No jobs in the money market.

He preferred the night shift at the cleaning job. It was better for Jared-minding, he explained. And he didn't have to see the smart-arses who overflowed their wastepaper baskets, spilt their coffee, fouled up his toilets.

—Even when I put the rubbish bin bang in the middle of the toilet door they still charge in during the day, he told Sooze. —Girls and all.

—Why wouldn't they? If they want to go?

—Wouldn't you realise that some poor sodding cleaner had *put* it there? To show the bog's being cleaned. It's a huge thing. He demonstrated the four-foot used paper towel receptacle with its flip flop roof.

—No. Her eyes were worried —Perhaps you could get a sign.

He flung down his fork. —'This unit is being sanitised for your convenience'?

—Well, why not? It doesn't have to be idiotic. Nobody's going to know what a bin in the door means.

—Can you see old Thunderguts giving me a sign!

—Make your own sign! Don't be so unenterprising.

He stared at her, chewing slowly.

—I'm only trying to help, she said, bending to pick her crushed paper napkin from the floor.

—That's just about the crappiest statement anyone can make. Ever. His thumb pressed hard against the button of the wine carton. He took a swig from the overflowing glass. —Y'know that?

Sooze's face was a foot from his, both hands clutched the table as she shouted at him. —It is not my bloody fault!

Bryce quit cleaning for Southalls in the New Year the day Nev told him about the job in the morgue. There were still no interviews and he knew he'd go mad minding Jared for ever. Nev had come in to see his bank manager and they'd met in the Calypso Coffee Bar. Nev was shooting through, he'd had it. —But the morgue's OK, nothing wrong with the job. He touched his blond moustache. A crumb of ginger crunch fell onto a plate decorated with palm trees.

—They don't advertise. It's word of mouth. I'll put in a quick snivel for you with Charlie, but you better be quick.

Bryce ate the tomato slice which had slid from his filled roll. A pip was stuck beneath his partial-plate. —You mean guys are queueing up?

—There's a lot of interest.

—Job satisfaction? That sort of thing?

Nev scrubbed his moustache with the inadequate bit of paper. —OK smartarse.

—This guy Charlie, asked Bryce. —When's he knock off?

—Four-thirty.

If he skipped the bottom floor, skidded through the cloakrooms. Anything'd be better than Southalls. —I'll be there, said Bryce. —Sometimes, he added, scratching his top lip, —you wonder why y'don't go on the fucking dole. Why had he said that. When you say something it's out. In the air. Said.

Nev was silent.

—I mean when you think. Some people, guys we were at school with even, people like that. Some of them're dead now. Bryan Coulter. Remember him? Skinny little guy with red ears. Hemi Ryan?

Nev nodded.

—So what are we worried about.

—I'm not worried. Nev pushed the ginger crunch crumbs to one side of his plate with his forefinger then licked it.

—Me neither. Let's have a beer.

Nev stood up. —No, I've got to go to the bank, then get back to suck up to Charlie. So don't you, he'll smell it.

—No.

—See yer.

—See you before you go!

They nearly shook hands on the Quay but changed at the last moment to a half wave. Nev disappeared, leaping between the line of slow cars outside Whitcoulls. At the other side he turned, lifted an arm and ran on.

Any fool can clean and any fool can leave it half done and who bloody knows. Bryce finished an hour early, wondering why he'd ever been such a berk as to do it properly.

He hadn't been on a bus for years. You see a lot on a bus and the thing was almost empty. Most hospital visitors'd be coming the other way at this time. He sniffed his hands. Pine. That shouldn't worry Charlie.

An Indian youth, slight, insubstantial as a shadow, master-minded a radio-controlled model car on the pavement below. It flung itself against a wooden fence, trying to mount it, its wheels buzzing, frustrated as a sex-starved kakapo attempting union with a log.

—See that? said Bryce to the man in the seat in front of him. The man's face was pale and damp beneath his synthetic fibre hat. The band was dark with sweat.

—What?

—That car.

—Which car?

Bryce wanted to hit him. He leant back. The man shrugged. At the next stop he climbed out, clutching a small green suitcase to his chest with pudgy hands as he negotiated the steps.

Charlie was a sad-eyed sick-looking man, not tall, not short. His arms seemed over-long as they swung from his sloping shoulders. He was very professional, he knew what he wanted.

—We can't have weirdos here, know what I mean. And you're a friend of Nev's. Nev was OK. Sorry to lose Nev. Charlie explained the job in some detail. —Don't worry, he said, —we'll give you on-the-job training, if you get it. I'll let you know. Tomorrow. Next day. They shook hands. The place seemed empty as Bryce left, his footsteps clanging down the brightly lit corridors.

Bryce was so late home he missed Jared. —Couldn't you've kept him up? You know I like saying goodnight. He could feel the warm head nestling against his shoulder.

—He was half asleep, said Sooze. —God knows what they do with them at that place. She wanted to tell him about Carmen. She was worried about her, well not worried exactly but . . .

—What's wrong with the place?

—Nothing's wrong with it.

—You said God knows what they do with them . . .

—It was a joke. I want to talk to you about Carmen.

—What about her?

—I'm a bit worried. She doesn't seem to be coping too well. Not with work I don't mean. I mean . . .

Bryce stretched his arms high then flopped them back onto his knees.

—Women who're born beautiful are a pain in the aspidistra. They think the world owes then a living. Look. OK. She's had a traumatic experience. Life is a traumatic experience! I've had a traumatic experience, for Chrissake.

—Not sexual violence.

—Any moment now you'll be telling me she needs counselling.

—Nothing wrong with counselling.

—It's done to bloody death. Look at them all standing round like vultures waiting to counsel the survivors when the door flew off that aircraft. Counselling! You've got to get on with life.

—Carmen is.

—Then what're you on about?

—This guy Cliff . . .

—Yeah?

—He's a nice guy and he obviously likes her but she . . .

—Of course he likes her. He sees the Rolls Royce chassis, doesn't see the Skoda motor.

Her hands flew to her face. —You are a *shit*. A pathetic sexist shit. Comparing women with cars was dead in Uncle Morrie's day.

—Joke, he said. —Uncle Bryce's joke.

He pulled off his jersey which also smelt of pine.

—Look, he said, sitting down beside her, —I'll never forget the day it happened. The three of you all at the flat in town when I came home. There was a chicken defrosting and you were all sitting round the table and Carmen was crying and I came in and you all looked up, all three of you looked at me as though I had *Rapist* carved on my forehead. As though I'd raped every woman on the block. OK. She's had a nasty experience. OK. I'm sorry. One guy! Don't blame the rest of us. He paused. —I've applied for a job in the morgue.

—You've what! She had really round eyes, the blue exactly in the centre.

—I've quit Southalls. I had an interview at the morgue.

—The *morgue.*

—Stop looking like that!

—You can't work at the morgue. Her voice was shrill.

—Better than shitty cleaning.

—But. But. She seemed to be having problems with her hands.

—It's temporary, for God's sake.

—But you'll be . . . It'll be dead people. You'll be touching them.

—You bet your sweet life it'll be dead people. Her mouth was hanging open, not far, the bottom teeth were hidden. —What's wrong with dead people?

—I know. I'm sorry but . . .

—Dead people are live people who've died, for Chrissake.

—Yes but . . . she leant back. —Anyway you haven't got it yet.

—Oh great, he said. —Thanks a lot.

He did get it. —I quit, he told Thunderguts's stomach. The satisfaction of the B-movie phrase was fleeting. Thunderguts unwrapped a new Spearmint pack and flung a piece in beneath the drooping moustache. He screwed up the wrapper and dropped it in the giant yellow bag hanging from the cleaning trolley. He looked Bryce slowly up and down and nodded his polished head. —I always knew you were a quitter, he said.

Bryce found the job interesting and he liked Charlie and the other orderly and the pathologist. It was just Sooze.

She seemed to have gone somewhere else, and be hating it. She was bright, too bright, too quick, when he came home.

—It's, it's . . . she said when he pressed her, insisting on reasons . . . it's just that I'm scared of death. Of being dead. Of not existing I mean. I know it's mad . . .

She was tense under his hands as they made love, her face turned from his. —It's your hands, she muttered.

—What about them?

—They . . . It's the dead people. He could see a streak of tears on her cheek.

—Bugger it! he shouted. —Sure! I weigh dead people. I cut up dead people. I scrub up after dead people. He flung himself to his side of the bed as Jared gave a sudden squeal in his sleep. Bryce could hear the dull roar of the sea. —Death is part of life! he yelled.

—Yes, Yes I know. I'm . . .

—And stop being sorry!

—I'm not.

Bryce snatched at the duvet. —You're scared of life, not death. That's your trouble, y'know that? What do you want? Do y' want me on the fucken dole. Is that what you want?

He could see the moist gleam of her eyes as they stared at the ceiling. —Shut up, she said. —You'll wake him.

He tried to jolly her out of it.

—Morgue, he said briskly next day as he picked up the receiver in Charlie's office, his eyes on the saccharine calendar supplied by the Hospital Store. Two soulful kittens peered from a basket decked with blue satin ribbons. It wasn't the kittens' fault. Nothing wrong with them.

There was a pause. —Bryce?

—Good morning Madam, he said. —Did you want to make a booking?

—Yes, she said.

The pathologist, Dr Vern, trusted him, and Bryce began

assisting at post mortems. Dr Vern was a born teacher like Sooze, but in a one-to-one situation. Bryce was quick, he had a quickness, and he admired Dr Vern: his dignity, his reverence, his swift movements, one finger resting along the handle of the scalpel as he guided the blade with precision.

—It's always interesting to watch an expert, Bryce told Sooze later. —A real expert.

—Yes, she said, her face against Jared's bullet head as she stared at him. —Anybody who's good at anything. Carmen shooting goals. Cam hammering nails.

—Into four-by-twos?

She dropped a kiss on Jared's upturned palm and smiled.

—You should come in and see the place, he said next morning.

—I could. Yeah, she yelled from the shower.

—Sort of homeopathic cure.

—Mmn.

—Then do it. Margot'll drop you off. The water stopped. He turned from the mirror, the razor in his hand as he handed her a towel.

—Thanks. She stood dripping on the mat. She always dried in the same order, breasts, arms, under arms, buttocks, back, then legs and finally between. Her bush was darker than her other hair, but that's usual.

—Except there's no point. She was drying carefully now, between her toes, her breasts hanging. He watched from the mirror, one hand holding the skin taut for the razor.

—Why not? If you've got such a thing about it.

—I've told you. It's not the death of a body I'm fussed about. It's the spirit. I've told you that.

—Right, so why're you fussed about where I work?

She scrubbed the towel against her face. —I don't know, she muttered.

*

Bryce hadn't looked at the worksheet before he entered the p.m. room next morning. The first thing he noticed was the expanse of stainless steel. The size of the body was a shock. The baby's eyes were closed, cherub genitals lay between chubby legs.

Dr Vern looked at Bryce. —These are the worst ones, he said, placing his cufflinks on top of the instrument cupboard.

—How old? asked Bryce.

—Age? Dr Vern glanced at the form. —Five months.

Bryce cleaned up afterwards and left. He got off the bus at the Caledonian, went into the downstairs bar and ordered three jugs. He drank them one after the other, pouring the stuff down his throat as he stared out the window at the fence of the Basin Reserve, the thundering red buses, the mad people. Jesus. A cot death. Bryce was breathing hard. He stumbled to his feet and blundered out, knocking against the tables of the docile afternoon drinkers. He'd get a taxi. But he kept walking, head down, weaving a little at first, then gradually straightening as his legs sliced through the miles to the station.

He hid in a corner of the carriage with his face to the window, tears sliding down his face. He'd like to go and see them. The parents. I understand how you feel, he'd say. Would you like to talk about it. I know how you feel.

By the time he got home his head was roaring with pain, one eye seemed to have gone wrong, its image was blurred. He tested it, holding a hand against each eye in turn. It was the left eye.

Jared was staying in town overnight with Sooze's mother. They were meant to be going to something. He couldn't remember what. Something. Bryce pulled the curtains in the musty box-like bedroom, dragged off his shoes and fell on the bed. They must get him back. Tonight.

He woke to see Sooze sitting on the edge of the bed beside him. He heaved himself up against the pillows and put a hand to his head. Christ.

—What's wrong?

—My head.

—What is it? She put out one finger and tracked the line of dried tears down the side of his nose to his mouth.

—I'm going to toss. He lurched to the door and into the bathroom. He didn't make it to the lavatory. He ran the water hard and sloshed the stinking mess down the hand basin, then bent for the Vim and rag from the floor. A mistake. Sooze was at the door.

—Go and lie down.

—Clean m' teeth.

She stayed propped against the doorway, then followed him back as he crawled onto the bed.

—What happened?

His eyes were closed. —We must get Jared back.

—Why on earth?

—We're not going anywhere. Not now. He remembered not to shake his head. —Not tonight.

—Mum's all set. She's borrowed a cot and everything. I said he didn't need it but she borrowed it anyway. We can't just . . . She stopped.

He lay very still, his eyes closed.

—What happened? she said.

—I drank too much.

—Why?

—I just felt like it.

—Bugger that. Why?

His head felt a bit better. He opened his eyes and sat up carefully.

—I just felt like it, he said.

She was wearing her green dress with the white collar. Her school dress she called it. A car backfired, farting its way down the street. Sooze sat down and pulled her knees up on the bed. Long, long legs.

—The new guy at school, she said. —Cliff.

—Yeah?

—He wants to paint me. He asked me tonight.

He stroked her leg. —Why not?

The corners of her mouth curved upwards. —You know. Nude.

—Stuff that!

—Why not? If I say so.

—Because . . . He shut his eyes. The *length* of stainless steel, the vacant expanse beyond the body. He blinked, stared at her. She was too thin. Too tense.

—I love you, he said.

She shook her head. —That's nothing to do with it.

—No. You're right. One hand circled her right ankle. —Good old Rock babe. Why not? Why shouldn't he have a go.

She sat up straight and wrapped both arms round her knees.

—Listen, she said. —Don't worry about things.

—I'm not worried. She was too pale as well. Far too pale.

—This is just a bad bit see. It won't last. Not for long. Soon we'll have our own place with a daphne in the front and a lemon out the back and a whirligig clothesline and a drive-on garage and Jared'll be running around and you'll have a beard . . .

He moved his head very slightly. —Why a beard?

—Why not?

—Not many beards in the money market.

—You could start a . . . There was a sharp cry outside. Sooze's head lifted. She laughed. —Sounded like Jared.

—We must get him back.

—Not tonight.

—Yes.

—You're nuts.

He put out his hand. Sooze picked it up and kissed it, gently at first, finger by finger, then quickly, snatching it, covering the back and palm with quick nipping bites. Bryce lay received by pillows, staring at the lopsided hair falling across her face. His eye was all right now.

—Watch it, he said, his hand moving beneath her mouth. —You'll draw blood.

I like Route 1 out of Wellington, cruising up the coast, the sea different every time though hidden by that concrete wall at the best part near Paekakariki. The tape deck is shot. I think about Carmen. I fantasise about Carmen with her legs in the air. I stop quickly. I think about getting off my butt and taking my stuff round the dealers which is the worst job in the world, but that's why I came to Wellington isn't it. There is only one thing worse, which is An Opening and I've only had two of those. Yes. Well. I think about *Sooze in the Carpark*. Monet painted his wife on her deathbed after she'd died. He was appalled at himself but he couldn't resist trying to get the skin colour—yellow, blue, grey.

Raeburn painted his dead infant son. While he was doing so, he said, 'I almost forgot he was dead.' That doesn't surprise me. I asked Sooze to sit when she was explaining about Carmen. Who is in my every dream. The car swerves and I concentrate on the road. Fuck everything.

The bach is a dump really. Fibrolite flung together in the thirties I would think, before baches became holiday homes and motor mowers ripped the air to shreds. Right on the beach though, a good place to live. Sooze comes out the back door wiping her hands briskly on short pink shorts. Her legs are just as good further up. —Hi, she says.

—Hi. I start dragging my stuff out of the car. I hold out a bottle screwed tightly in brown paper. —Oh, she says as though she's never seen a wrapped wine bottle before in her life. —Thanks very much. She is shy so I make it worse. —Why did Bryce change his mind?

—He didn't. It's my decision. Her cropped hair hangs unevenly, slanting across her eyes.

—You said he wouldn't like it.

She is not going to tell me. She shoves a hand through her hair as though punishing the stuff.

—I don't know, she says. —Something happened. She has a shy smile, Sooze. Not like Princess Diana leering sideways, but you can see Sooze doesn't swan through life. —I'm a liberated woman, she says.

I'm shy now. Liberated women don't say that. Not now they don't. —Hell yes, I say.

Bryce comes round the corner in old rugby shorts carrying a baby in the crook of his arm. Whacking thighs, sinews, muscles all over the place, he holds the baby with care. His other hand comes out like a clamp. —Hi, he says. This is Jared.

—Hi Jared. What would *you* say.

Jared's dimple appears then he hides his face against his father's hyper-expanded chest.

—I hear you're going to paint Sooze starkers, says Bryce.

—Yes.

—Good on you. He puts an arm around Sooze who is standing looking miserable and kisses the top of her head. A territorial gesture. —We're going down to the beach, he says. —Get out of your hair. I'll take his sleeping thing, all the gears. Sooze stares after them chewing her bottom lip. Bryce turns at the corner of the bach. —That was Carmen on the phone, he says. —She's coming out.

It's going well. It's good. It's very good. I've done a few quick sketches, mainly angles, lines, nothing really, because I can't wait to get on to it, to start getting the paint on, to start laying the colour on the canvas. Miss Bickerstaff's rickety old easel is set up where the kitchen becomes the lounge. Sooze is staring straight ahead. She is in front of the kitchen table, her bum just propped against it. I can put the mudguard in later. It might even be an indoor car park; more threatening, but I want the flattened capitulation of the paper: the uprights, the fence. And the crosses of the cyclone netting. It's just the pose I'm trying to get now. She can't have her feet dorsi-

flexed all the time either. That will come later. Her thin arms support her either side, she leans forward slightly. Her breasts are small, very round, one hangs fractionally lower than the other. There is a false nipple below the left one. She is so vulnerable it would break your heart not mine. She doesn't say a word and neither do I. I am too happy for one thing. Eventually she moves.
—Look, can I have a rest? she says.

I am full of apologies. Tt, Tt, God in heaven, What am I thinking of, all that. She pulls on an old towelling dressing gown and plugs in the kettle which has one of those safety cages, I suppose for Jared later. I have been painting for half an hour. She hands me a mug with a blue cow on it and moves to the easel. I spring in front.
—No, not yet. She smiles and takes her mug to the open French doors and squats on the doorstep looking out to the beach which is hidden by sandhills while I fuddle about in front of the easel thinking about the black mostly.
—OK? I ask, meaning get back you silly bitch, not that she is a bitch, I'm grateful don't think I'm not. So on we go. There is no sound, no time.

Carmen walks in the French doors behind me. —Hi, she says.

Sooze leaps for her dressing gown as though it's a cop raid. I swing round guarding the easel.
—Don't look! I tell Carmen.

She pretends I mean Sooze. —Déjà vu, she says. —I've seen it a thousand times. She walks over to hug Sooze. She is hauling things out of a faded blue and brown bag, one of those round African ones; long loaf, pâté, cheeses, green peppers. My hands twitch as Sooze thanks her. Get out of that thing, Susan.
—That's it for now, Cliff, I guess, says Sooze.

I can't believe it. —What!
—Well. Sooze shrugs. —Anyway it's time for Jared's juice. She moves to the fridge. —He'll be dry as a crisp by now.

I am nearly sobbing but I bite it back, I can feel my jaw locking.
—I'll get them, I yell and charge out the door, leaping and swearing

over the sandhills, spraying sand, my throat tight with rage.

I calm down of course, but when Bryce and Jared and I come in the French doors the two women are standing in front of the easel in silence. I heave in front of it like a bloody stag at bay. —I told you not to look at it!

Bryce and Jared stare at it, both also silent. —You needn't worry Soozie, Bryce says. —El Tampo isn't going to recognise that. He holds his son high above his head with outstretched arms. —Spot of your old painterly abstraction there, Jared, he says. —Your rock 'em, sock 'em school of modern art. Jared chortles, you'll have to believe it. Fairies are being born all over the grotty bach.

After the juice ritual we go down to the beach. Carmen's shorts are yellow, not pink. Her breasts are bigger than Sooze's I know, but I'm not looking at her because she hates me and I hate her.

Bryce and Sooze have stopped on the way up the beach to see the wreck of an old coaster they tell me lies buried in the sand. They wish to demonstrate the delights of seaweed popping to Jared who travels on Bryce's back in a sort of roofless sedan chair. They squat around on their haunches popping the bladders of flapjack. Minute hoppy things leap in the air disturbed by the unprovoked attack on their habitat. Jared is only mildly interested but points one finger at a high flying gull.

—Seagull, says Bryce.

Carmen and I keep walking along the hard sand which is the colour of gunmetal; blueish pewter where it's wet. —I'm sorry about last Saturday, I say.

Carmen turns to me. Her eyes are huge. After staring at Sooze for so long they seem out of proportion. —You shouldn't have locked it. The door.

—No.

—How's the hand?

I show her. —Flesh wound.

—Your fault.

I don't say anything. Bugger it.

—You couldn't know, she says.

I am tired after painting. Not tired. Languid's the word. Like after sex. Not too crisp, but I get it eventually. —Did you ask Sooze to tell me?

—Yes. At the Staff meeting. She drops on her bare heels to pick up a bit of driftwood. Splatters of wet sand fall from it as she heaves it into the tide. —I should've told you myself.

—Oh. Now I am breathing deeply, the air is going right down. You can see all the way round to Foxton. Now I am grinning at Carmen who could break your heart because she is so beautiful and a one-off job and not vulnerable at all. A survivor. I like survivors.

—I'm a bit, um, she says. —A bit sort of . . .

I don't say a thing. I just look at her.

Her hair is tied back but bits blow about in the wind. She smiles at me. —Have you got a sense of humour? she says.

—Asking someone if they've got a sense of humour is like asking them if they're a good driver. No one's going to say no. I'm still looking at her. —Why?

—I just wondered. She points one finger at the white shape of the mountain a hundred miles away —Look. That's Ruapehu. How about that.

—Amazing.

She stares along the beach. —Where is the wreck anyhow? she says, as though I who know nothing and have never seen the thing would know.

12

Miss Tamp thinks about the school —an audiovisual aid

Thea	I didn't realise you had a whole house. Hallo. Puss, puss, puss.
Tamp	He's Faraday. Don't be a nuisance, Faraday. What were you expecting?
Thea	A unit. A town house, I mean. Yes, Faraday, you are beautiful.
Tamp	I've been here five months now.
Thea	Five months. Just goes to show as my aunt used to say.
Tamp	It's shaming that you haven't been here before. You're just along the road as well.
Thea	Oh well. It's very nice though.
Tamp	I like it. I got fed up with the Hutt Road.
Thea	Yes. Lots of sun, I suppose.
Tamp	Yes, it floods in.
Thea	Where's north?
Tamp	Over there.
Thea	Is that right? Yes. Yes it would be.
Tamp	When I get home from school the place is like an oven.
Thea	How lovely. And you'd be sheltered from the northerly as well.
Tamp	Not entirely. Faraday's taken to you.
Thea	I love cats. Especially Burmese. They're so . . . patrician.

Tamp	Do you have sun?
Thea	No.
Tamp	Oh.
Thea	There's a bit in Ben's room, but we're the wrong side of the tip.
Tamp	Oh. Oh dear. Well do sit down.
Thea	Thanks. The ex-tip actually. It's filled in now. Come on Faraday. Oops.
Tamp	Would you like a drink.
Thea	Oh, thank you.
Tamp	What can I get you?
Thea	Oh. Um.
Tamp	I'm having a gin and tonic. And a slice of lemon.
Thea	Lemon. Do you have any sherry?
Tamp	Flor fino?
Thea	Thanks. Why the camera on the tripod? Tape recorder, all this stuff?
Tamp	They're Jenni Murphy's audiovisual equipment from school. The video camera's new. She's very proud of her vidcam. She's practising on the cat. Literally. 'A day in the life of Faraday.' She leaves the camera running. Sort of *cinema verité* type thing I gather. Andy Warhol made a film like that apparently. Not cats though.
Thea	Why's it all here?
Tamp	She's staying with me at the moment.
Thea	Oh. Why?
Tamp	She's very direct, Jenni, isn't she.

Thea	She certainly is. A tough bunny inside that pixie.
Tamp	She said, —Miss Tamp, my relationship has just split and I have to get out of the flat. Can I stay with you till I find another one?
Thea	Relationship?
Tamp	Flat, I gathered.
Thea	That's Jenni all over. Why didn't she ask one of the young ones?
Tamp	She explained that. She said that most of them are in relationships and that Carmen is too beautiful.
Thea	What a damn cheek.
Tamp	(*Laughs.*)
Thea	Why on earth did you let her come?
Tamp	She requires a cosy vacuum. Time off, I gather from the *sturm und drang* of her rich emotional life. She regards me as amiable but chemically inert. She virtually told me so.
Thea	Patronising little creep. God the young . . .
Tamp	Well, it's all in the mind as they say. I find it rather flattering. Her wanting to come. Is Faraday being a nuisance?
Thea	No. His purr's a real racket isn't it. Kids, I don't know.
Tamp	No one patronises cats.
Thea	I didn't mean . . . But you're the Headmistress! And what about the vegan bit?
Tamp	Oh, she does her own meals. I find her good company. Delightful, in fact. Not of this world in some ways . . . She's gone to some Dance thing with Carmen.
Thea	She's chaotic! Sometimes I think she's slightly mad. I

mean mad. Completely irresponsible. Gets everything wrong. Day. Week. Place. Not an ounce of time sense. Always the last to have anything in. Reports. Registers. Whatever. I'm sorry, you can say what you like but she drives me insane. Look at this lot. Just dumped. I get so fed up with people who swan through life leaving a mess for boring old Marthas to clean up. Oh, I'm sorry. I'm so sorry, I didn't mean . . . I meant me. Ben and Fred do it all the time.

Tamp   In some ways she's very efficient. A good teacher. Technology at her fingertips. Audiovisual aids. Anything of that nature. She's set up a video team of seventh formers entirely on her own initiative. They're going to record school events, sports, Leavers' Play that sort of thing. Hours of work for Jenni.

Thea   I read a woman in the paper the other day. She said that violent TVs and videos are having an effect on children's concentration.

Tamp   It is a worry. A terrible worry.

Thea   She said that it was harder to switch kids on. That teachers have to be as upmarket and impacting as a video.

Tamp   And they say teachers are overpaid. Perhaps that's why Jenni succeeds. Not upmarket but certainly impacting.

Thea   'Those whom the world call mad, are really fey . . . and can believe in fairies.'

Tamp   Pardon?

Thea   It was a children's play. I was about nine.

Tamp   What happened?

Thea   Not a great deal. I had the main part. In a golden wig. Those were the last lines.

Tamp   Oh.

Thea   Why did you want to see me tonight? If you don't mind my asking.

Tamp   I wanted to talk to someone I could trust.

Thea   Oh. I thought there might be some of the others, but nobody seemed to . . . I mean I asked one or two on Friday . . . Una Benchley, people like that.

Tamp   I've always known about the loneliness of command, of course. My father was in the merchant navy. A captain. That's why I like ships.

Thea   But they're sailing ships aren't they? On your curtains. Tall ships?

Tamp   Yes. And the footstool. I brought them with me from the Hutt. I can't discuss it with the Board of Trustees at this stage. I shouldn't discuss it with anyone. I should just . . . accept . . .

Thea   Oh, I know what you mean! Any moment soon I'll have to charge out to Makara and scream to the hills —'My shitty kids are driving me in*sane!*' Sorry.

Tamp   How old are they now?

Thea   Ben's fifteen and Fred's sixteen.

Tamp   I've never taught boys. Are they worse?

Thea   Different. They were such loving little boys. I used to tell them they smelled of Mr Cridland's room when they rushed in after school for a hug. Hot wool and chalk.

Tamp   Does their father keep in touch?

Thea   No. I can smell it now. We could go to Makara together.

Tamp   And scream to our separate hills. Yes.

Thea	Yes, and you Faraday. Don't you love the way they pat your cheek for attention.
Tamp	He is a character, aren't you?
Thea	I'd stop stroking him you see. All right. All right. Look at the shine on that coat. I don't trust anyone now. Not really.
Tamp	It is a luxury. One shouldn't need it. Why do we expect it.
Thea	Have you ever noticed there are people you like but don't trust, and people you don't like but trust.
Tamp	Yes.
Thea	Odd though, isn't it?
Tamp	Not very.
Thea	There aren't many you like and trust, are there?
Tamp	No. You know what I wanted to talk to you about.
Thea	Miss Franklin?
Tamp	And the school. Yes.
Thea	Have you noticed Cliff Marden and Carmen lately?
Tamp	I imagine they're in love. Or something.
Thea	They're lit up. They glow from within. They drag each other's names into every sentence. They sit cheek by cheek. They hold hands. They gawp. He's been besotted for months, of course. She seems to have caught it now.
Tamp	I hope she doesn't get hurt again.
Thea	Hhh.
Tamp	What do the Staff think of Miss Franklin, Thea?
Thea	They admire her control in classroom situations.

Tamp   Yes. She has control.

Thea   And she's an excellent teacher.

Tamp   She is impossible. And getting worse. Obstructive. Disloyal. Last year was bad enough. This year . . . And at a time like this with all the *Tomorrow's Schools* upheaval! How can any school plan ahead without knowing their financial grant to the last cent.

Thea   I don't know.

Tamp   It's all paperwork, endless soul-destroying paperwork. I don't *need* Miss Franklin's obfuscation at this moment in time . . . All right, Faraday. All right. I think he wants to go out. (*Door opens.*) T'mon t'mon. (*Door closes.*)

Thea   Did you know the previous Head? Miss Sargesson.

Tamp   We never met.

Thea   They were very good friends. She and Miss Franklin.

Tamp   Yes. What was she like?

Thea   Charming. She had a lot of charm.

Tamp   Yes. And she was very efficient wasn't she?

Thea   Oh yes. Very.

Tamp   Yes.

Tamp ⎫ She must have been quite young . . .

Thea ⎭ In some ways . . .

Tamp   Yes?

Thea   Sorry. You go on.

Tamp   I was going to say she died young, didn't she?

Thea   Oh yes. Only in her forties.

Tamp   Tt.

Thea   Miss Franklin nursed her almost to the end. With
        domiciliary care of course. Still.

Tamp   And ran the school as well.

Thea   Yes. Everyone was marvellous of course. Una Benchley,
        people like that.

Tamp   Yes. Yes, she would be. What were you going to say?

Thea   Oh never mind . . .

Tamp   I'm coming Faraday. (*Door opens.*) Well, why did you
        pretend you did want to then? Come on. Come in. (*Door
        closes.*)

Thea   I was going to say she was rather . . . unexpected.

Tamp   Unexpected.

Thea   You didn't always know where you were with her if you
        know what I mean. Oh you old snuggle puss. Come on
        then. Did he have any trouble settling in when you
        moved?

Tamp   No.

Thea   No butter on paws then? That was a good boy. I mean . . .

Tamp   Yes?

Thea   I shouldn't be talking like this.

Tamp   I asked you.

Thea   I admire loyalty very much don't you?

Tamp   Yes. I do.

Thea   Yes. I saw a thing just the other day. About the Captain
        of the Graf Spee shooting himself after he scuttled his ship
        after the Battle of the River Plate. It was a review. I
        haven't read the book.

Tamp   I'd describe that more as honour.

Thea	Nobody would do it now though would they? Not in the West.

Tamp	I don't know. I just don't know.

Thea	Look at Nixon, say. Not that I agree with it necessarily. Shooting himself, I mean. As I was saying, I remember years ago at Prize Giving. Mr Smythe, the Chairman of the Board of Governors as he was called then, he was making his speech and he was going on rather you know how he does, and I happened to glance at Miss Sargesson and she was sitting there all in her gown and everything twiddling her thumbs under the table.

Tamp	How very odd.

Thea	He couldn't see or anything but I just thought it was, you know . . .

Tamp	Unexpected.

Thea	Exactly. And she was very conservative for someone so young. About hats, that sort of thing. She wasn't what you'd call innovative in any way. It was funny I thought. Her being so young.

Tamp	Miss Franklin means to destroy me.

Thea	Oh, surely.

Tamp	I know it's not the sort of thing one says but every girl in the school is precious to me.

Thea	Yes.

Tamp	I still believe, I still believe that education is the only answer. The one essential. It's only if people are taught to think, that melioristic evolution has a chance.

Thea	What evolution?

Tamp	That things can get better, will get better. That the world's problems can be solved.

Thea	What about the profit motive? There's some graffiti in the women's lavatory at the Central Library. It said McDonald's are politically unsound. It said that they're cutting down rain forest for cheap grazing for their cheap cattle.
Tamp	That's a case in point! No one educated, taught to think, would do such a thing.
Thea	But I don't see . . .
Tamp	I'm about to take the matter of Miss Franklin to the Board of Trustees. But I have to clarify things first. Talk it through. That's why I asked you over.
Thea	But I'm not a teacher even. All right, Faraday. Way you go.
Tamp	I've no intention of being destroyed.
Thea	No. No, of course not.
Tamp	I've assembled this dossier.
Thea	Heavens.
Tamp	I'd like you to read it.
Thea	I'd rather not thanks. I mean I don't see . . . (*Door opens.*) Oh . . .
Tamp	Oh. Hullo Jenni. I thought you were going to that thing with Carmen.
Jenni	So did I. (*Door closes.*) But hunk of the month appeared.
Thea	Hullo Jenni. That's not like you.
Jenni	Hi. To peel off? No. Carmen said to stay. She wasn't expecting him or anything and I could see she was getting all steamed up and was going to insist on him shooting through and she went all pink, you know how she does, and he was getting all sort of . . .
Thea	I am surprised. That you left.

Jenni	Mmn. So'm I. Anyhow when I got outside I thought I couldn't be bothered slogging over to Boys High by bus, I mean it would have been different on Carmen's bike, so I went to the Western Park Tavern but the band was lousy so I caught the unit and came home. C'mon Faraday. Ptt, ptt, ptt. There's a good man. Don't you love the way he stretches? Arms up, legs right back. Like a nude Marilyn Monroe. T'mon Faraday. T'mon then, Smoocherama. He seems to like you.
Thea	Yes. What are you doing with that thing?
Jenni	Just adjusting the angle to get you all in.
Thea	What!
Jenni	It's trained on the floor for Faraday. It'll be all legs and laps. I left the vidcam running for 'The day in the life of'.
Tamp	But those things record sound as well, don't they!
Jenni	Yes.
Thea	Heavens above!
Tamp	Give me that tape or whatever it's called. You've recorded a private conversation!
Jenni	No sweat. I'll just tape over it. I don't want to waste one. Rubbedy scrubbedy. Be clean as a whistle.

13

Miss Hobbs thinks about the peonies at the Kamikaze Pilots' Memorial at Etajima

Marcia Hobbs stares across the kauri table at the new Art man's hair and swallows. It is the wrong colour, not the blue-black sheen of Senri's but it has the same springing strength: each hair seems to leap from the scalp. The parting is definite, a white track on the left-hand side. Mr Marden turns his head and Marcia sees that it begins from a similar whorl of hair on the back of the head. At the base of the man's stomach where the hair begins, Marcia knows, individual hairs tough as wire will lie against the curve of his white belly.

Before she went to Japan Marcia had always been conscious that she had not done enough with her life. She thought of it flowing back over thirty years to dolls' tea parties beneath the flowering currant, her finger anchoring the lid of the teapot in imitation of Granny's. Her flowered teaset had a red Japan stamped on the underside of each piece. There had not been a lot of action in Marcia's life since those days. Not a lot of endeavour, thrust you might say. It had all just as it were happened, as though she had fallen into a stream and drifted along like Ophelia with weeds in her hair and a faint smile on her lips. She had not taken her life by the scruff of its neck, moulded and hacked it, knocked it into a shape she could visualise—of which she could think, Marcia Hobbs: This is Your Life.

She was astonished at the vigour with which the younger members of the staff, Margot, Carmen, Susan, to say nothing of Jenni, attacked life, flinging two or more lives into each day as they dashed about after school kicking life into motor bikes, snatching up babies, attending seminars to keep up to date. And still taught well, cared, had relationships.

And not only the young. Look at Miss Franklin for goodness sake.

Perhaps it was because she had never learnt to rush. There had never been any need. There had always been plenty of time. No man or woman ran yelling out the door each morning scrambling for a bus, a slice of bitten toast clutched in one hand. Granny went to her room to change, to prepare a face to face the world an hour before she left the house, which was seldom. Her hair alone took half an hour to coil and sweep into a French roll, to anchor and stab with pins.

Marcia's father, a top dressing pilot, had been killed in an air crash in the Rimutakas when Marcia was two. The Cessna just fell out of the sky according to a farmer who happened to be watching. The wreckage lay hidden in deep bush (rugged terrain the papers called it) for months before it was found. Her mother sold up in Tawa and went back to her widowed mother and Aunty Pat over the harbour at Eastbourne. Aunty Pat worked for a local accountant; she just had to pop round the corner. Granny worked in the garden. Marcia's mother knitted. The sun shone.

And you certainly couldn't rush with music and Marcia was musical from infancy, hanging on her mother's every hum, lisping the names of the great composers familiar as household words. All the family were musical. Very musical. Good music surged through the house. Bad music was rigorously excluded. They all played. Marcia began piano at five. They listened to good music on the Concert Programme and their stereo, which was the most precious thing in the house. —If there's a fire, said Granny, settling herself on the sofa for a Brandenburg, —remember. The stereo first. Aunty Pat drove them in to all the concerts, sweeping around the harbour in her Escort in plenty of time for a good park.

Marcia had an excellent start and all the encouragement possible, except that her mother wouldn't let her play in the Comps though Miss Engelbretsen thought it would be good for her. Mrs Hobbs tied back Marcia's pale fluffy hair. —There's too much pressure, dear. Pushy mothers and pert little girls and that sort of thing. You wouldn't like it.

It became obvious that Marcia was not concert platform material. —She plays beautifully, said Miss Engelbresten rubbing her knobbled fingers together. —But . . . There was some thought of private pupils. —But then with private pupils there'd be all the financial side. I mean think of it. Bills and everything. You know how hopeless you are at Maths. And dealing with ambitious parents. Just think.

Marcia decided on a private school in Mount Eden. It did mean moving to Auckland which was probably one of the few non-drifting decisions she had ever made. It worked out all right though and she loved Mount Eden, she liked the girls, she enjoyed teaching even, except for the ones with talent who wouldn't try, wouldn't practise, wouldn't damn well *care* about their precious gift.

In her second teaching term Marcia attended a course in Asian ceramics at the Museum. It was very good. Excellent in fact. After the first lecture the class moved *en bloc* to the Asian Hall to look at examples. Marcia stared at the thick creamy surface of the early Imari bowls. The cobalt underglaze grasses were a few vivid brushstrokes. Her eyes swam with tears of pleasure.

—I'd like two like that, said a woman behind her. —One for cream and one for icing sugar. Marcia turned, her eyes blinking. The pleasant face smiled.

The unlabelled saucer in the next case had been been mended with clamps. A line of gold divided its surface. The larger side was translucent white except for a small spray of plum blossom; charcoal flower, terracotta buds, leaves of turquoise and greenish gold. On the smaller side exuberant patterns of fine black lines covered the turquoise glaze which was splashed with deep violet peonies. That is the most satisfying man-made object I have ever seen, thought Marcia. I shall go to Japan.

She sat on the steps of the museum and stared across the harbour to North Head, then walked around the monolith of the Cenotaph. It was inscribed 'Our Glorious Dead'. 1914-1918 was carved on two sides; 1939-1945 on the others. 'This is consecrated ground' said the bronze notice.

I'll go quite soon. It appeals to me.

But then Granny died in her sleep and Aunty Pat said she couldn't stand it another minute and went to Nelson. Marcia came home to Eastbourne because Mother was nervous on her own quite naturally. She was lucky to get a job at Girls High in the middle of the year. The previous music teacher had left, just like that. Una Benchley said she would be happy to come to some arrangement about lifts from Eastbourne but Marcia had to learn to drive because of the concerts and taking Mother. She hadn't enjoyed the driving lessons. Especially stopping and starting on hills with her heart in her mouth and the ABC instructor smoking his head off. But it was lovely walking out to the carpark after the last lesson to find her Mini waiting instead of being dependent and fitting in. Marcia felt like stroking it.

She took over the garden at Eastbourne. —It's growing on me, she told her mother, once she had mastered the need for mulch in sandy soil and the role of compost in the production of deep rich friable loam. She spent hours on her knees among the peppery-scented leaves of the geraniums attending to the paths of broken shells which were such a thing to weed, Mahler tapes blasting from her cassette recorder.

Life flowed on until suddenly Mother died. Her head dropped forward during Beethoven's Fifth and she was gone.

—She went just as she would have wanted, sobbed Marcia to Aunty Pat who had come over for the funeral. Aunty Pat picked a piece of apple peel from between her two front teeth. She stared at the yachts lilting and tossing on the harbour and ate the scrap. — Mnn, she said. —I'd better cook a tongue. And a chicken.

—Go for God's sake. Go! Get out, cried Aunty Pat at the airport tightening the strap around her old green suitcase and giving it a quick kick before handing it over to the young woman behind the Check-In counter. The airport was packed. It had been closed by fog for two days. Slack-faced men in track suits and dirty running shoes milled around shouting at each other. A child submerged beneath an orange anorak howled, banging its head against a distraught young woman's thighs. The woman dropped onto her three inch heels. —Shut up or I'll belt you, she screamed at the streaming face.

Aunty Pat gave the suitcase its final heave and turned to Marcia, her face pink with effort, her forehead puckered. —Look, she said. You've always wanted to go, God knows why. When I think of what they did to our boys . . . Look! If you don't go now you never will. She paused, her tongue flicked her top lip. —The money's there. And go on your own!

—But *Japan*, pleaded Marcia. —It's so . . . She couldn't say foreign.

—You know a bit of the language don't you?

—A bit. Years and years of University extension courses, for this very moment.

—Perhaps a tour, said Marcia, her top teeth resting on her lower lip.

—Go on your own, shouted Aunty Pat as her flight number crackled above their heads, almost indecipherable in the uproar. —It's the only way to go. She hugged Marcia, her eyes on the man at the desk behind the doors leading to the departure gate. She nodded at him slightly as though to indicate she was just coming, she wouldn't be a moment.

—Travel, she cried as she charged forward, —is an intellectual Outward Bound. She turned at the doors and waved. —A challenge! she yelled.

The aircraft was full but she did have a window seat. The man beside Marcia was large and informative. He leant forward in his distressed-leather jacket, his stomach expansive above the safety belt. —It's my mother. She's far from well. Terminal.

—Oh dear, said Marcia, her eyes on the flickering figure of the well-groomed man demonstrating emergency procedures on the TV screen. He adjusted a yellow oxygen mask and smoothed his hair back. He was followed by a black man and a white woman who crossed their arms and leapt onto an escape chute. They hurtled down stiff-legged, their smiles bright. Into some ocean presumably.

She dragged her eyes from the screen. —I'm sorry. The pores of his nose were huge.

—In Japan? she murmured.

—Good God no. The nose retreated. —In Manchester.

Her scalp tightened. —But we're going to Japan!

—Sure. Sure. I'm doing some business on the way. I'm in Plexiglass.

—Oh. Gratitude to this beautiful blue-jowled man flowed through her. —The announcing thing quacks so doesn't it. Though of course they wouldn't let me on if I'd got on the wrong one would they. Her voice trailed away.

He understood perfectly. A hand patted her knee.

—Tell me about Plexiglass, said Marcia.

He told her. Eventually he clutched the back of the seat in front of him, heaved himself up and backed into the aisle. —Toilet, he said.

Marcia dipped her head in consent and leaned back. Someone was kicking the back of her seat. Chestnut curls appeared above the seat in front of her. The small face beneath had the dark eyelashes and hooded eyes of the born vamp. The little girl removed her thumb from her mouth and pouted. Marcia sat very still. Smile and you've got them for the duration. —Hullo, said the child. Marcia stuck out the tip of her tongue, rolling it like her childhood friend Bernice whom Mrs Hobbs had declared *persona non grata* after the problem with the rhubarb. The head disappeared.

Her fellow traveller reappeared and eased himself into his seat. —If you'll excuse me, he said, —I think I'll get a bit of shut-eye. It's a long way to Manchester. The plane bucked briefly. —Clear air turbulence, he said, closing his eyes. —No problem.

Marcia shared a taxi with him from the airport. —Thank you, she told the departing back, but he was gone, leaping sideways onto an island swept by streams of hooting traffic.

Miss Franklin had told her to print the name of her hotel on some cards. —It's the only way, she said. —There are no street signs or numbers or anything as I suppose you know.

—Yes, said Marcia, her pile of School Certificate theory books flattened against her chest.

—They smile and nod and you think they understand but believe me they're only smiling and nodding and anyway nodding means No in Japanese. Or so I understand, continued Miss Franklin. —You can always get back somehow to the hotel if you have a card, even if it's not in Japanese. Or that was Jean's and my experience. She banged a wet strength tissue against her nose and sniffed. —For what it's worth. And when you get to the hotel take one of their matchbooks with you whenever you go out. That's even better.

Marcia had drawn the name of the hotel in Japanese characters as well. The driver nodded and smiled and they continued on their way to her hotel. Each step was a minor adventure. Checking in, the money, tipping the bowing taxi driver, all were simplicity itself. They could understand her halting phrases, or appeared to. Marcia could scarcely believe it. I can do it all. I can do anything. I am a traveller in Japan which is the land where I wish to be. I am completely at home. Escorted by a diminutive porter who with smiling insistence shouldered her hand luggage as well, she marched across the gilded foyer with her room key. The child porter pressed the arrow pointing upwards.

The lift door opened and Marcia was face to face with a man in ceremonial dress. He wore a wide pleated and divided skirt of black and white striped silk tied at the waist, a short black coat with two circular white crests covered what Marcia knew to be a black and white under kimono. He stood very still, his head high, his face unsmiling. He was magnificent, Marcia could see that.

The man's head moved fractionally.

—Are you coming up? he said.

Marcia shook her head. —No.

I am a traveller in an antique land.

The doors shut.

The porter stared up at her, puzzled. —Madam up next time?

She inspected the cluster of unsolicited mini-gifts in the bathroom, a shower cap, a shampoo, a sachet For Removal of the Stain. A blue and white *yucata* in a plastic bag hung on the door. The lavatory flush water had a most disconcerting swirl. Marcia bathed, changed, and went downstairs in search of food.

Near the reception desk stood a cavern of glass and light labelled *Sushi Bar*. A large sign on one wall displayed coloured photographs of delights within; boiled shrimp *sushi*, cooked egg *sushi*, raw fish *sushi*. A good idea. A solution. Better than waiters and a formal dining room, and anyway *sushi* was real Japan. Marcia hoisted herself onto a high stool at the bar and watched the slim young chefs dance before her, their knives flashing as they chopped vegetables, seaweed and raw fish with life-threatening speed. She ordered, pointing and smiling, made confident by attentive courtesy. The young man smiled back and whipped a small celadon-green bowl in front of her. It was filled with steaming liquid on which floated one dark unrecognisable leaf.

Soup? A finger bowl? Her stomach clenched, she blushed with shame at not knowing, at shame at caring about not knowing.

—It's a finger bowl, said the man on the stool beside her. —*Sushi* can be eaten with the fingers.

—You've changed, she said. Banal beyond banal.

He smiled. —So have you.

—Your . . . your clothes, were so beautiful.

—Uniform. He smiled. —I was returning from my niece's wedding.

—Oh.

—Do you know about Japanese weddings?

—No.

—I will tell you.

—Thank you. She shifted slightly on her stool.

—The main thing about Japanese weddings is the expense. He looked at her, his face concerned. —The money. You know?

She nodded.

—The kimono my niece wore cost two hundred and ninety-six thousand yen to hire. That would be . . . His fingers moved, a quick strumming of air as he worked it out. —Something like a thousand American dollars. Marcia shook her head. —Ttt, she said.

—The bride and groom must give presents to all the guests which should be equal in value to those they receive. It is not easy you know. It is extremely expensive. Nowadays many couples are married outside Japan. His hand gestured. —Your food.

—Thank you, said Marcia gazing at the plate of edible art as though he had given it to her.

—We Japanese eat with our eyes.

—Yes. She turned to eat. There were mirrors everywhere: the dancing chefs, the food, glass, the shimmering steel, all were reflected endlessly. Amongst it all, incongruous as an uncooked bun in a fish factory, a small pale face looked back at her. She could stare at the man more easily though.

—Some of them come to New Zealand, she said with the quick stabbing pride of the native abroad. —To be married, I mean.

—New Zealand? Ah! Sheep. He glanced again at her plate. —You pick each piece up you see. He indicated a small saucer of dark sauce. —Then dip one side in that then . . . His hand gestured towards his mouth.

The For Removal of the Stain might be necessary. —Chopsticks would be easier, said Marcia.

Chopsticks appeared.

The pale bun face smiled. —Thank you.

He tried again.

—Many sheep.

She had managed chopsticks for years but the *sushi* parcels were not easy.

—That's right. Millions of sheep.

—It is a very beautiful country.

—Yes, she said, chasing an egg *sushi* around the curve. Any moment soon he'll mention the Milford Track. But what a face, what pared down beauty of line and form. —Especially the South Island, said Marcia.

—There is a walk, a very beautiful walk through mountains.

—Yes. 'The finest walk in the world.' The Milford Track.

—*Track*, he said, one palm slapping the mahogany formica counter.

—People come from all over the world to walk it.

—So I have heard. His *sushi* plate and round bowl were placed in front of him.

His hand was beside hers. The fingers were long, tapered, almost transparent when seen against the light. —Why have you come to Japan?

—I have always wanted to. It's such an interesting culture, she babbled. —So many beautiful things.

—And pollution. His right hand moved with speed, seeking, dipping, despatching. He rinsed the fingers in the finger bowl. Traces of soya sauce swirled in the warm water. —I am free at the moment, he said, picking up a rice-paper napkin. —I could show you things.

—Thank you, said Marcia to her startled face, the dancing lights, the acrobatic young men leaping behind the *sushi* bar.

As Marcia notes the exact way Cliff Marden's hair springs from his scalp she remembers surprise, amazement, but no regrets. For it is better, is it not, to have loved and lost than never to have known at all. And anyway she didn't lose, not in that sense. She was not ditched like Carmen, who told the Staff Room so last year in as many words. —I've been ditched, she said. She has no shame, Carmen, she wears her heart on her sleeve for all to see which Marcia knows is a sad mistake and never did, nor does. Not of course that there was anyone there to watch Marcia's sleeve for squealing tell-tale hearts. That was part of it, probably, her complete anonymity. Otherwise how could she possibly have had the sense, the wit to accept the Outward Bound challenge of Senri. She kept nothing from him. Her passion, her astonishing abandonment, her willingness to try anything once and usually again and again and again. Is it better? Is it better? Marcia's slightly bandy legs are crossed beneath the staff room table. They move slightly, the top one presses down. Carmen smiles at her. Carmen smiles too much. Cliff Marden can't take his eyes off her. Anyone can see that. Marcia rocks back and forward a couple of times. Senri's body was also compact and beautiful beyond words.

He was home on leave from the Japanese Embassy in Washington he told her next day. —I am a minor functionary, he said, pleased with the phrase. —We can travel together. I can show you things.

—All right, said Marcia.

The bullet train's speed was 180 kilometres per hour according to a speedometer attached to the wall of the carriage. They stared out the window, searching through the mist for the perfect cone of Mount Fujiyama. —There it is, said Senri. Marcia turned to laugh at him in an attempt to hide her disappointment at the unconvincing glimpse. Behind his head an arrogant young Japanese with a crewcut and a lasso glared at her from an advertisment for Marlboro cigarettes.

—Why do so many Japanese men smoke?

—They think it's macho. He paused, his eyes on the advertisment. —I gave it up when my wife died. In Washington.

—I'm sorry.

He bowed, then picked up her hand and kissed the palm. —Don't talk, he said. He looked out the window at the clouded landscape spinning by.

—Did he tell you about *wabi* at your classes? Your teacher? Did he tell you? He turned again to the window.

—Melancholy restraint?

He nodded. —That view has *wabi*.

He kissed her palm again and lay back, silent and still.

It is good to know nothing. To wish to know nothing. *Wabi* discarded, she leant back, hand in hand with the surprise of her life.

—I'd like to stay in a Japanese inn, she said in bed that night.

He opened his eyes slowly. The solemn beauty of his face, the angle of his cheekbones moved her almost to tears.

—A *ryokan*? I don't think you'd like it, he said.

—But why?

He leapt up from the crumpled bed and strode around the room. His body was hard, smooth as pale jade.

—You would feel like a cow in a china shop, he said.

She snorted with laughter.

He stood on his toes, his arms above his head. —I am tall for a Japanese. *Ryokans* are designed for small ladies and gentlemen. He patted the air three feet from the ground. —Everything is the size for dolls. And your room lady comes in always, to unroll the futon, to roll the futon, to serve the food, to help with your kimono. It is a bowl for goldfish. There is no privacy.

—Oh, said Marcia.

He cupped one of her breasts in each hand, weighing them. —Exactly. They rolled back on the bed.

—I like teets, he said later.

She leant on one elbow, startled. Did he mean tits?

Marcia had not heard either word since the educational whirl of Eastbourne Primary.

His hand reached up to stroke the nape of her neck. —Japanese men like this area also. That's why Utamaro's courtesans all have low necklines at the back. Their kimonos. His hand sketched a sweeping curve. —Very seductive.

—A reverse décolletage? But she had to explain it. Every difference pleased them, they rejoiced in each discovery, each small gem of language or custom mined and ferried from a foreign land.

—Your legs are bandy and you walk pigeon-toed. He demonstrated, fingers closed, as he flapped the strong hands one in front of the other. —That's very beautiful. But you can't walk like a

Japanese woman, you see, because your teets are too big. He glanced at her face. —I am telling you this, so that you will understand.

—I don't want to walk like a Japanese woman. I am not, said Marcia, dismissing thousands of scuttling females from her mind, —a Japanese woman.

He was on his knees, the sheet dragged tight around his thighs.

—You are wonderful. More wonderful than any. My golden lady.

Please choice carefully, said the sign above the mini-bar.

—Anyhow, he said thoughtfully. —I have never stayed in a *ryokan* with an English lady.

—And I am not an English lady.

His hand stroked her stomach.

I am here. I will stay here. I will leave Girls High. I will go to Washington but first we must go to Eastbourne to settle things. Walk along the beach. She saw his footprints beside hers, their line very straight, the toes turned out.

His parents are dead, which is a good thing.

—Haydn, he said one night lying flat on his back in Nagoya. —Haydn is for happiness. For when life is good. We should have Haydn. The Kaiser Quartet.

She took his hand.

He was a perfect guide. He knew everything, he understood everything, he never told her too much. Marcia walked pigeon-toed beside him, incandescent with happiness as he explained the ritual of the tea ceremony, the structure of an Edo screen. They climbed hand in hand to a small temple. It was empty except for two young women who danced the foxtrot in silence, their bodies moving in unison, a Walkman clamped to each impassive head. Senri smiled. —Technology, he said.

They followed Marcia's travel plan; from Tokyo to Nagoya to Kyoto. He insisted on paying for meals. Her room was pre-booked and every bed was vast, his supply of condoms inexhaustible. It was all very simple. It could not have been better planned.

They were surrounded, mobbed almost in the gardens of Mijojo castle by schoolboys in black uniforms and peaked caps. —English, they cried. —English rady. Please to speak English. Where you from, rady? Senri barked one word and they fell back, their arms hanging, their faces blank beside the scarlet maples.

—What did you say? asked Marcia.

—I asked them to stop, said Senri. He took her hand. —Come. I'll show you the nightingale floor.

The sprung wooden floor squeaked at every step, singing to warn a sixteenth century shogun against surprise attack. Nearby were panels and painted screens on which butterflies hovered above shimmering silver grasses; high-stepping roosters, their tails plumes of gold and red, strutted beneath branches of plum blossom.

An identical rooster skittered in front of them later in the afternoon as it chased a recalcitrant hen back to the fold behind a Heian shrine. Senri bowed low before the altar, clapped his hands together once and bowed again. He signed the book. She watched him as he drew the strokes of his signature, enchanted with every move he made, each aspect of his different being.

She heard her mother's voice answering an unheard comment from Granny on the sunporch. —Marcia is simply not interested in men, mother. I've told you that before.

—The Shinto religion is a very agreeable one, said Senri later, opening his lunch box with careful fingers. —It has no sin. He picked up a small red crab from its compartment with the chopsticks provided and put it in his mouth, gazing across the grey lake beside the bench on which they sat. —We've just missed the cherry blossom. It is always more sad when you have just missed something.

—I like the way it doesn't last long. —Ephemeral, said Marcia, eyeing her red crab with doubtful eyes.

He stared at her. —Would you do something for me?

She smiled. After all, she didn't have to eat it. —Of course.

—Would you come with me to Etajima? His mouth puckered.

—It is not an idle request.

She smiled at his pride in the idiom. —I'd like to very much.

—Yes. The Inland Sea is not too far away. The pollution is very sad. But there is a memorial to the Kamikaze pilots.

The lake was very still. —Oh, said Marcia.

—There were over two thousand of them. They chose forty to represent all the others. For photographs, displays. One from each province. There were too many you see, otherwise.

—Yes, I see.

—My mother's brother was one of them.

—Oh, she said again.

—My parents were very proud, my family. Especially as he is one of the forty as it were. One of the ones chosen.

—Yes. They would be. (Of course they would be. They would have to be, wouldn't they.) Did they . . . ? I mean . . .

—But I have never seen it. The memorial. I must do that.

—Yes, of course. A sharp breeze swarmed across the lake, scurrying the surface into miniature waves.

He bowed. —Thank you.

The main thing was their youth. Large photographs showed boys in pilot's uniforms, some serious, some smiling into the eye of the camera. One or two were laughing.

—They were so young, said Senri. —Expert pilots who volunteered as of course many did, were rejected. They were needed, you see, as teachers and escort pilots.

Marcia said nothing.

—My uncle was twenty. He indicated a proud face above a white scarf tucked into the neck of a uniform. The eyes stared straight through her.

—He looks like you.

—I look like him. His name was Senri.

Forty large display cases contained articles of uniform, a sword, books. Some attempt had been made to indicate an individual life. A group of laughing young men lounged against a training aircraft.

They sang around a piano. They swam naked. A smiling Kamikaze tied his comrade's white headband as he sat in his cockpit. It was all beautifully done.

—His *hachimaki,* said Senri pointing. —They were worn by samurai warriors. A symbol of coolness and courage. They all wore them on their last missions.

There were poems. Extracts of letters. 'May our death be as sudden and clean as the shattering of crystal.'

'I shall fall like a blossom from a radiant cherry tree.'

A giant photograph of the final ceremony before take-off covered an end wall. A young man in an old-fashioned flying helmet, his face calm, drank his final toast to the Emperor. Both hands were raised to lift a small pale saucer to his lips. The man beside him waited his turn.

She felt ill, sick with rage. Rage for all victims of war, willing and unwilling, rose in her throat.

—The last toast, said Senri, —is always drunk in water.

Marcia put out her hand to the cool marble wall. The heels of her sandals clattered on the tiled floor. —I'm going outside. She turned to grope her way to the door.

His face was contrite. —I have upset you.

She looked at him in astonishment. —*Upset* me? She lurched across the high entrance hall in her silly clacking sandals and went outside. Clouds of smog covered the beautiful harbour, misty islands rose from the shadowed sea. Unheeded boundless destruction. Waste waste and more waste. Marcia's hands were clutched tight against her chest, she was panting with rage.

A line of small children lead by a slim young teacher trailed across the courtyard chattering and calling to each other, bright parakeet schoolbags on their backs. They swept around the corner and disappeared. She could still hear them, but only faintly.

Senri was at her side. —It was a long time ago, he said. —Come. Look at these.

The tree peonies stretched down one side of the memorial. Hundreds of varieties, few of which Marcia had seen before, had burst from their tight buds into a blowsy profusion of pinks and white; white with strong gold stamens, maiden's blush to fat-lady rose, deep crimson to dark wine, the flowers swayed above or hung their heads from exuberant grey-green bushes.

Several of the blooms had small paper umbrellas above them. Marcia stared at one, speechless.

Senri smiled, his hand on her arm. —For protection, he said. —You can understand that. They are very fragile, you see.

Jenni Murphy, who thought about her sexuality during the first Staff Meeting of the year, is still thinking about it in June when Mrs Hopere brings up the subject of 4F. Her sexuality is something she thinks about quite a lot. Her blank gaze is fixed on the wall opposite but she is having an interesting if confusing time inside her head. Periodically she glances at Cliff Marden whose left hand is busy making convoluted, rather sinister patterns on the cover of a small sketch pad which lies on the table. His legs are crossed, the top one hangs parallel with the other. Sometimes he wraps one leg right around the other. Jenni tries this but finds it impossible as her legs are too short. Cliff flings both legs straight in front of him. His thick red-brown hair flops over his forehead, his fingers are exceptionally long. Artist's fingers thinks Jenni, who sometimes but by no means always likes to get things classified. Which is why she is working on her sexuality. It is about time she made up her mind. Exploring your sexuality is all very well but it can go on too long, especially nowadays. It must cease. Jenni realises this.

When Jenni was at secondary school she decided she was a lesbian and acted accordingly. She had happy and unhappy relationships which was exactly what happened later when she decided she was heterosexual. Some men treated her badly, some women. Some women were loving and generous, some men. Jenni decided she was bisexual; but Bryony, her lesbian lover, was no more pleased with this decision than her friend Anthony who made the most extraordinary fuss and flung a rather nice Pet Rock (a gift from Bryony) against the mirror wall of the bedroom in their flat, and broken glass as well as the rock fell down on Jenni and Bryony who were in bed together at the time.

Jenni, who looks like Miss Bun the Baker's daughter gone wild, is sexually amoral. Not immoral, she has standards as regards cheating, lying, and ditching, though she is ambivalent about two-timing because what does it matter. If she likes (read loves) someone she sees no reason why she should not welcome them with the same warm friendliness bestowed upon Captain Cook's sailors by the women of Tahiti. As Sooze says, —If she likes them she loves them. Carmen agrees. Margot thinks it's a bit much. —I mean, honestly.

But now the threat of Aids has changed things for the promiscuous and the friendly givers. Jenni must decide, must settle for one kind and preferably one of that, which is why when she is not staring at the pleasing angles made by Cliff's folded legs, the authority and speed of his moving hand, the particular way his hair falls and the line of his jaw, she is concentrating on Carmen. They are both good physical specimens, worthy examples, as it were, of their species. But Jenni's amorous propensities are moved as much by the swell of Carmen's breasts against her T-shirt, the dip at the base of her throat and the small blue vein in the inside of her elbow as they are by Cliff's harder edge. Angles excite her as much as curves. Classical or Baroque, Georgian or Art Nouveau. Jenni sees no reason why you should have to pick one style, let alone one lifestyle, when there is such God-given abundance. Except that now she does see, and must do so.

Jenni Murphy is regarded with affection by most of the staff although they cannot place her. She is unslottable. She is friendly and hard-working, a conscientious teacher of Social Studies and expert in the use of audio-visual equipment, but she never seems to know what's going on. She doesn't seem to notice, let alone care. Her clothes are from a child's dressing-up box, not even Op Shop as a rule. She favours bright Christmas tree colours, red and white, green, wreathes of gold or silver stuffs with sparkle. She is so cute you could die. The girls like her too. They regard her with bemused tolerance and a touch of wistful envy. Why doesn't she care that she looks like a used cracker, a battered kewpie doll from the topmost branch of yuletide who has come down late as usual to spring across the quad in pink gym shoes, to attempt the jump of playground puddles too wide for leaping.

Jenni comes to and pays fleeting attention to the staff meeting. She suggests they should have an amnesty for the return of the Clothing Room scissors, like the supermarket trolleys in Dunedin. Had anyone seen it? They had seventy-eight returned no questions asked. She makes a further comment on the supermarket round the corner and goes back to her contemplation of Carmen's neckline.

The Staff Meeting finishes at last. Jenni jumps to her feet and adjusts her white leg warmers. She smiles at Cliff, picks up her gear and hurtles round the end of the table to her locker. Carmen leaps to one side in an attempt to avoid collision but it is too late. Her papers are knocked from her hands and she and Jenni drop onto their heels to scrabble for them beneath the table. Carmen's breasts are presented as on a plate when she leans six inches in front of Jenni's nose. —Have you ever had a lesbian relationship? asks Jenni under the table which used to belong to the Chairman of the Board of Trustees and his wife Grace.

Carmen sits back on her Adidas. —What?

—A lesbian relationship.

Carmen laughs. —Jenni, she says.

—Have you ever had one?

—No I haven't. I'm hopelessly heterosexual. It is fairly dark under the table. There are cobwebs between the members of the frame. —Why ask me now? Why wait for an under-the-table situation?

—I just thought of it, says Jenni.

—So you said it?

—Yes.

Carmen shakes her head, still smiling. —Come on, she says. They crawl out clutching papers. There is no one left in the staff room. —Oh good, says Carmen holding up a photograph which has fallen from the pages of a tennis coaching book. —Great. I wondered where that'd got to. She holds out the photograph to Jenni.

The photo shows four large young men and Carmen farewelling another woman in what looks like an airport lounge. The other woman is going somewhere, a large suitcase is at her feet, Carmen's arms are around her, her head is half-buried in the traveller's shoulder. Arms are around waists, shoulders, two men are waving at the camera, everyone except Carmen and the other woman are laughing.

—Thank God, says Carmen, taking it back. —I thought I'd lost it. —That's my sister Theresa going off to be a nun in Australia. I must get a frame for it.

—Where's your mother? asks Jenni.

Carmen gives her a quick glance. —She doesn't like airports. Dad took the photo. Carmen props her behind against the table and stares at the photograph.

—I thought you had five brothers, says Jenni.

—Yes. Steve's been overseas for seven years. He'll never come back.

—Why not?

Carmen is still staring at the photo.

—You know Mrs Toon's daughter?

—The brain-damaged one?

—Yes. Carmen rubs one hand down the leg of her green tracksuit. Her fingers are spread wide. —She fell off the back of Steve's motor bike. When she was nineteen. That's how it happened.

—Shit.

—Yes. Carmen lifts her eyes. —They were, her hand moves, a quick sideways flick, —you know, sleeping together.

The corners of Jenni's mouth pull down in a grimace of horror.

Carmen puts the photo back in the book. —Mmn, she says. —Terrible.

—Why a nun? asks Jenni after a pause, peering over Carmen's shoulder at the photograph.

—You're a Mick aren't you? I always imagined dozens of Murphys lying about all over the place.

Jenni shakes her head. —My mother died when I was two days old.

—Oh, Lord. I'm sorry.

—Not your fault.

—No.

—I had a lovely Gran, says Jenni.

Gran who spoilt her rotten so they said. Who let her have meals in her own room when she wanted to finish the book and couldn't stop. Who gave her bed-baths when she was sick, carefully exposing each limb one at a time to wash and dry it, then re-covering it with warm towels as she had been trained to do fifty years before. Gran who simply filled a grey cardboard suitcase with Jenni's clothes and took her back to her house and the bantams when she was three and her father married again. —You're much better here darling, she said. —Snug as a bug in a rug, eh cuddle-bun, she said that night, tucking both sides of the bed so tight that Jenni lay in a deep hollowed trough of comfort and love.

Best of all, Jenni now realises, Gran who, when Jenni discovered at an early age that the meat on her plate had once pranced in the paddock with the bantams and refused any part of it, had looked up what ancient vegetarian recipes she could find and begun doggedly making nut-cutlets, imitating the rejected.

—Lucky you, says Carmen.

—Yes.

Carmen is still staring at the photo. —Are you a lesbian? she says.

—I'm not sure.

Carmen can't stop smiling. —I wish I'd known your Gran.

—She was lovely.

—One of my brothers is gay, says Carmen, pointing to a large man in a white T-shirt who has one arm around Theresa. —Terry. He says in lots of places, Morocco say, they don't have this division thing. Some guys'll be homosexual one day, heterosexual the next, what the hell. Women too.

—Mmmn. There's Aids though, says Jenni.

—Yes. Carmen puts the photograph back in the book.

—It would be a waste to be a nun, says Jenni who knows nothing of the contemplative life.

—You didn't know Theresa. When she left we had a code. 'My suitcase got scratched' meant the Mother Superior is not my favourite lady.

—I bet she never wrote it.

—No. Just a jokette. Carmen sniffs. —I think she was trying to pretend to me that she hadn't gone completely.

Jenni is thinking hard. —Do you know anyone asexual?

Carmen sits on Le Nid, her feet on a chair, elbows on her knees, her face in both hands as she considers. —One, maybe, she says. —Why?

—I'm thinking I might try that next, says Jenni, pulling up her leg warmers yet again.

Carmen's eyes disappear briefly as she laughs. —Let me know how you get on, she says, one hand reaching down her front for the locker key which hangs round her neck on a length of cord.

Jenni watches her. —Have you ever been a dancer?

—No.

—You'd be good at it.

—No. I got sick of discipline when I was diving. —I love modern dance though. *Limbs* and stuff like that.

—There's a women's dance group on at Boys High on Saturday. In the Memorial Theatre. Carmen's eyes are beautifully shaped, like a sole. They have the tiniest flick upwards at the tear ducts.—Why don't we go? says Jenni.

—Are they any good? I can't stand that stuff where they lift an arm every five minutes in a meaningful sort of way. I like action. Carmen demonstrates. —'Hurry on down, Hurry on down, Hurry hurry hurry on down,' she cries. Her body is swinging, strutting to the urgency of her command. One hand knocks *Lake Annecy* off the wall. She is now the other side of the table, fingers snapping, plait leaping. —'If y'don't come soon I'll have to call Sam,' she moans. She stops short and replaces *Lake Annecy*.

—I don't know anything about them, says Jenni faintly. —I'm going to find out. Why don't you come?

—Well, says Carmen, —I'm not quite sure about Friday. She inspects the end of her plait and brushes it thoughtfully against the tip of her nose. —No, she says. No. Why not? OK OK. Sure. I'll come.

—If I come to McFarlane Street, says Jenni, we can go on your bike and get a meal at the Cantina afterwards.

—OK says Carmen.

Jenni arrives early not that it matters. Carmen comes to the door zipping her miniskirt, a towel over one shoulder. She wears a red and white striped T-shirt with long sleeves, a black miniskirt, very fine black pantyhose and her favourite black shoes which her father calls beetlecrushers. Her waist and hips are slim, her breasts full. Her hair is not quite dry. The dry bits fluff up from the wet and curl about her face. The wet hangs down her back and over her face when she bends.

—Hi, she says. —Come in.

Jenni admires the view. —It's like the south of France, she says, looking beyond the yachts moored tidily in the marina to Tinakori Hill, —not that I've ever been there. She sits cross-legged on the sofa in the half lotus position and leans forward. It is all quite interesting.

Carmen is very fond of her flat. She found it after Barry dumped her. At first it was just a roof and a double bed and who the hell cared but now she has taken a running jump at the place. She has spent a lot of time up a ladder scrubbing and painting with the stereo roaring and the light flooding in through the tall windows. She is not going to have curtains in the living room because she likes the moulded frames of the sash windows which she has stripped down to the original wood and polyurethaned. She is proud of the old window catches which she found in a demolition yard and was able to buy from the owner even though he said, tipping his chair and

closing with reluctance the lurid covers of his Dairy-porn paper-
back to deal with her, that if he had any sense he'd flog them to an
antique dealer for real dough. They are brass with bulbous white
porcelain tops above the catch part.

Carmen says that anyone who is keen enough to make the
effort to peer through a telescope from Wadestown is welcome,
though she does have curtains in the bedroom. The walls of the
living room are Aztec Red. Carmen wondered if it would be a bit
much but the only way to find out was to paint the whole thing and
then decide, and in fact it looks great. Her two posters of the Te
Maori exhibition, those of the greenstone adze and the Pukeroa Pa
gateway, hang side by side. When Carmen can afford it she is going
to buy a kilim rug and fling it over the sofa which is losing its stuffing
in one corner. She got the idea from a postcard Steve sent her of
Freud's couch in Hampstead. She is going to have cushions too, all
over the place.

—Wine? she shouts from the kitchen.

—Have you got any fruit juice? Jenni can't sit still. She picks
up an oval box which is pale gold in colour and sits on a small table
beside the sofa. —What's this?

—Carmen appears around the door with a glass in each hand.
—It's cherrywood. Handmade by the Shakers. Steve sent it to me
from the States. She hands Jenni her drink and sits very straight on
a large waisted cushion which Mrs Doyle called a humpty. When
she was little Terry or Steve or any of them used to tie a rope around
its waist, put the other end round their shoulders and give her
chariot rides on the verandah, thundering up and down at speed.
Mrs Doyle murmured occasionally that she didn't think it was
doing the humpty much good. Carmen puts down her glass of wine
and picks up the oval box to stroke it. —It's beautifully made, she
says, putting it down carefully.

—Whose fault was it, the accident? asks Jenni.

—What?

—When Mrs Toon's daughter was, you know. Was it your
brother's?

—Not if you mean whose traffic offence was it. No. There is an edge in Carmen's voice. —A car shot out from a side road. Steve swerved to avoid it and they went into a skid. It was raining.

—Well why can't he come back?

—He can come back. What on earth do you mean? Carmen sits even straighter. Steve lifts a hand to her. Turns in a doorway laughing.

—You said he'd never come back.

—Really Jenni you're a bit much. Carmen slaps one hand over the other. She leans forward on the humpty. —He feels it's his fault. He loved her for God's sake.

—She needn't have gone if she didn't want to. For the ride on his bike.

—That's not the point.

—Yes it is. It wasn't his fault.

—Of course it wasn't his fault. But he feels guilty, he feels . . .

—Why?

—Don't you ever feel guilty?

—Not if it's not my fault.

—In his mind it is. In his conscience. Your mind, inside your head, isn't a hollow pumpkin with a candle! Carmen's hands are moving as she searches for words, snatches them from the air. —It's another place, another world with it's own transport, geography, storerooms. If you think a thing, it is. And anyway he loved her. Ask yourself!

—If he feels like that he'd be better to be here and go and see her. Look after her even.

Carmen tugs at the frayed cord of the humpty. Her face is flushed. —Would you?

—No.

—Then don't tell me what he should do. You know nothing about . . . nothing about anything! What gives you the right to . . .

Jenni's round face is startled. Orange strands swing from her head as she leans forward. —I just thought it was interesting, she says. She puts one small hand on Carmen's knee and smiles. An enchanting smile, eager and friendly as a child's. —Sorry, she says.

Carmen laughs. —Feeling guilty?

—No, says Jenni.

The doorbell rings. Carmen's head lifts quickly. She is not pleased. She leaps to her feet and moves to the door skipping sideways and swinging her hips to avoid contact with the back of the sofa. She tugs at the door which is rather stiff.

—I told you I was going out with Jenni, she says as Cliff walks in.

—I know.

Jenni concentrates on a large yacht with a blue sail cover which rides at anchor in the marina. Shitsville. Also bugger.

Carmen usually wears her green track suit at school. Cliff takes in the stripes, the miniskirt, the legs. He is not interested in the shoes. —Hi Jenni, he says at last. —I'm not staying but I had to give a guy a lift to the airport so . . .

—Well. Carmen's eyes are on his face. —I don't know, she says and walks back to the kitchen which opens off the living room. Everything opens off the living room except the bathroom.

Cliff sits beside Jenni on the sofa, up the end with the stuffing. —Hi, he says again. He pushes a bit of stuffing back with his thumb and pats it.

—Hi.

—Great view.

—Yeah.

Carmen's face appears. It is pink. Her eyes are sparkling. —I told you at school, she says.

—What the hell . . .? Cliff is on his feet. —I was just . . .

—OK. OK. Do you want a beer or something?

She is glowing, absolutely glowing. Cliff and Jenni are sure of this. Rage, health, something is making her glow as though she has just run in from an icefield.

—Beer'd be great, mutters Cliff. —Seeing you're so keen.

Carmen comes into the living room and hands him a beer can. Conversation is desultory. Carmen strokes the faded brown cover of the humpty and watches her shoes.

—What've you been doing since school? asks Cliff.

—It's only two hours ago. Carmen lifts both feet off the ground to examine the tops of her shoes more carefully then places them together on the floor in front of her.

Cliff tries again. —Jenni?

—I took Faraday for a walk.

—Who?

—Miss Tamp's cat. He's a Burmese.

—Oh.

—He follows you for miles. Jenni scratches her head vigorously with one hand then inspects the nails. —Burmese often do.

—Is that right.

—Yes.

Cliff puts his hands behind his head and leans back. His legs are stretched in front of him. His jeans are new, dark and crisp. You don't often see jeans like that.

—I like those trees, he says, his eyes on Tinakori Hill. —Real Altdorfer trees.

—What? says Jenni.

—A German. Great guy. The first real landscape painter. He did trees like that. It's a bit far away here. You can see them better in Tinakori Road. Cliff's right hand moves straight up and down. —Dark. Strong verticals.

—Someone said you're painting Sooze, says Jenni. —With nothing on.

Cliff tugs at the stuffing. —Yeah, he mutters. —Nude.

—How's it going? says Jenni.

Cliff's head is still down, his hand busy. —It's not. Not at the moment. It's, you know, on the back burner.

—Someone said you were so keen about it, says Jenni, staring at him with round eyes. —That's what I heard.

Cliff has stopped tugging. —Yeah, well . . .

Carmen is on her feet. —Cliff, come into the bedroom. Excuse us Jenni. I'll be back in a minute.

Cliff jumps up and follows her into the bedroom. The door closes. Jenni's mouth moves. She would like to know what is going on.

After a few moments she creeps across the room and squats with her eye at the keyhole which is large and situated on the horizontal panel halfway down the kauri door. There is a large gap beneath the door as the previous tenant took his carpet with him when he left. Jenni can, with difficulty, both see and hear Carmen who is in full flight. She is standing with her hands on her hips.

—I told you! she says. —I told you this afternoon not to come. I'm going out with Jenni!

Jenni can't see Cliff even by twisting her neck but she can hear him. —I just wanted to see you for Christ's sake. All right. All right! I'm going. Go to the bloody dance thing. I'm not stopping you!

—I'm glad you came. Glad! says Carmen. Her hair looks dry now.

Cliff mutters something which sounds like Well then.

—And I'll tell you why. If you go on like this we'll be finished before we've started and I'll tell you why because I know about this see, and I'm not talking about woman space and man space and Dialling Out and all that crap. Sure I'm mad about you. Sure I'd rather stay here and (a hand waves)—but if I say I'm going out I'm going out and you don't crawl round . . .

—What d'you mean crawl round!

Jenni is still squatting. She shifts her weight from one leg to the other. Carmen pushes back her hair. —I know about this. And I'll tell you how I know! Because I killed all the love, whatever Barry had for me and it was a lot. Killed it stone dead. I wouldn't give him an inch. I wanted every ounce, every teaspoon of the poor bugger. I wanted to eat him, live him, *be* him. I wanted to fuck him till he couldn't stand. She is shouting now. —I want to fuck you till you can't stand!

Jenni moves slightly. She can see tears of rage.

—Nobody, yells Carmen, —can eat their fucking lover and have them.

—All right! All right! shouts Cliff, —I made a mistake. I'll go.
—It's not that. It's not that! sobs Carmen.

There is no sound. Carmen has disappeared. Jenni can't see a thing except the pale wall of the bedroom. She stands up rather stiffly; her eyes blink several times. She moves back to the sofa, picks up her unfinished fruit juice and sips it slowly as she stares out across the harbour. The wind is freshening. Dusk lies near Tinakori Hill, the bloody verticals of the trees darken, lights are coming on. The mown patch of grass on the northern slopes of the hill has lost the last of the sun. Jenni remembers this from when she lived in Roseneath with Bryony not so long ago. She remembers noticing it, how that bit changed more than the rest when the sun went, how its colour deepened from sharp green to olive.

Miss Tamp said Was there any further business before she discussed the end of the year Leavers' Play?

Mrs Hopere said that she would like to bring up last year's 4F.

Ms Jenni Murphy said 4F.

Miss Tamp said that as she was sure Mrs Hopere realised, they were no longer 4F, not even last year when by rights they should have been called 4C.

Mrs Hopere said that Yes she did realise that, but as everyone still thought of them as last year's 4F there did not seem much point in calling them anything else.

Ms Murphy said that she did not think of anyone last year as 4F, and which lot were they.

Ms Carmen Doyle said this year's 5C, last year.

Ms Murphy said Oh. Them.

Mrs Hopere said last year's 4C then, and that she would like to discuss them and their problems. That she had tried to bring the matter up several times at previous Staff Meetings.

Miss Tamp said that Mrs Hopere had the floor.

Mrs Vaughan said that 4F had been a real problem in the Library last year. 4C, she should say.

Miss Franklin said that she had never had any trouble with last year's 4F.

Mrs Vaughan said that they had punctured two bean bags in the library already this year and that she had caught Tess Nation at it. You know, jumping.

Miss Franklin said In mid flight?

Mrs Vaughan said Yes. That there were those white plastic chip things all over the place and that Tess Nation was a big girl and that the beanbags were not made for that sort of thing.

Ms Margot Murchison said that if Mrs Vaughan thought Tess was big she should see Annabelle.

Ms Murphy said Which was Annabelle.

Ms Murchison said The sister.

Ms Doyle said that Annabelle was lovely though.

Miss Powdrell said that she agreed.

Miss Tamp said that the beanbags had been donated to the Library as a civic gesture by Big Save, and did anyone remember Pauline.

Miss Franklin said Couldn't they get off the beanbags.

Mrs Hopere said that her point was that last year's 4F individually and collectively was under a lot of pressure.

Miss Franklin said How?

Mrs Stillburn said that if you gave a dog a bad name you might as well hang it.

Mrs Hopere said Exactly.

Mrs Toon said that if the beanbags were a problem perhaps they should be replaced by something less easy to rupture.

Mrs Vaughan said that the beanbags were not a problem. That the problem was last year's 4F. C rather.

Mrs Hopere said that that was her point. What were Miss Tamp and the Board of Trustees going to do about last year's 4F? Now 5C.

Miss Tamp said Do?

Mrs Hopere said Yes. Do.

Ms Powdrell said that last year's 4F had been the bane of her life. B. A. N. E. Capitals.

Ms Murchison said that they had to be seen to be believed in the Clothing Room. That she had had to have eyes in the back of her head. That they had managed to uplift two pairs of Cutting Out scissors even though they were chained to the tables.

Miss Franklin asked Ms Murchison if she was sure that it was this year's 5C who had been the, shall we say, uplifters.

Ms Murchison said Yes because she checked after each class because scissors that size could be lethal.

Miss Hobbs said Where were they now then? The scissors.

Ms Murchison said that they were presumably in the home of some 5C.

Ms Murphy said that they could have an amnesty like the supermarket trolleys in Dunedin. Had anyone seen it? That they had had seventy-eight returned, no questions asked.

Mrs Toon said that questions were now being asked though about no questions being asked. Was it legal?

Miss Hobbs said Was what legal?

Mrs Toon said Offering an amnesty, no questions asked.

Miss Tamp said Ladies.

Mr Marden pulled one hand down the side of his face and stared at the palm.

Miss Franklin raised her eyes to the clerestory windows.

Miss Murphy asked whether anyone had tried the new Superette.

Miss Hobbs said that she thought Ms Murphy said it was in Dunedin.

Ms Murphy said that now she meant the one round the corner.

Mrs Toon said What corner? Sorry.

Miss Tamp said Had Ms Murchison reported the loss of the scissors at the time?

Ms Murchison said that Yes she had, and that did not Miss Tamp remember. That Miss Tamp had been wearing her taupe jersey suit at the time. With her blue nylon blouse.

Miss Tamp said Had Mrs Hopere something specific in mind as regards 5C?

Mrs Hopere said that she had one or two thoughts. That she was concerned for them. For all of them.

Mrs Stillburn said Me too.

Miss Tamp said Yes indeed.

Ms Powdrell said that 5C weren't the only ones. What about Lower Fifth Commercial or whatever they're called now? And others. 4D say.

Mrs Stillburn said that she never had any problems with Fifth Form Commercial.

Miss Franklin said that in her opinion all commercial teaching should be abolished.

Mrs Stillburn said Why?

Miss Franklin said Because schools were designed to educate.

Mrs Stillburn said that typing skills, to say nothing of computer skills, were a great deal more use than French in the real world of the marketplace.

Miss Franklin asked Mrs Stillburn if she thought that that was the real world.

Mrs Stillburn said that Yes she did and that she was not afraid to say so.

Miss Tamp said Ladies. Please.

Mrs Stillburn said that there was a great deal of nonsense talked about education.

Miss Franklin said that she entirely agreed.

Miss Hobbs said that 5C were a nightmare in Community Singing in wet weather in the Hall. That they had to be seen to be believed.

Mr Marden said What did they do.

Miss Hobbs shook her head. She said it was infuriating as Tess Nation had a wonderful voice. That she could do anything with it if she tried.

Miss Tamp asked the staff if they would please allow Mrs Hopere to offer her suggestions.

Mrs Hopere said that she had never said anything about suggestions.

Miss Tamp said Thoughts then.

Mrs Hopere said that she thought that the problem was one of peer pressure.

Mrs Toon said Peer pressure.

Nobody else said anything. Mr Marden pulled a packet of cigarettes from his pocket. Miss Franklin shook her head. Ms Doyle smiled. Mr Marden offered the packet to Ms Doyle. Ms Doyle shook her head.

Miss Franklin said Peer pressure in what way. That she had never had any problem with the form in question. In either its F or C mode.

Ms Powdrell said that she admired Miss Franklin's control, but that it was tough on the kids who wanted to learn like Mavis Kanji.

Mrs Hopere said that Mavis Kanji was not the only one in 5C who wanted to learn.

Ms Powdrell said No indeed. That she had not meant to imply that in any way.

Ms Doyle said that it was not so bad in Phys Ed because the slack kids hide in the toilets.

Mrs Hopere said Peer pressure.

Miss Tamp asked Mrs Hopere if she would like to expand on that statement.

Mrs Hopere said Certainly. That at that age, the age of the girls in 5C, the most important thing in life was to be accepted by your peers. That this put pressure on the girls in 5C to conform with the other girls in 5C.

Miss Franklin said that she was sure Mrs Hopere was right but why was it that peer pressure was always used as an excuse for indiscipline never discipline.

Mr Marden said Not at Waiouru. Or West Point.

Miss Franklin said that she would like to thank Mr Marden for his helpful comments and that she was sorry but that she had a thing about doodlers. That she had never been able to take them seriously.

Ms Doyle smiled.

Mr Marden kept drawing.

Ms Powdrell said that she thought another factor was ringleaders. One or two trouble-makers like Tess Nation, though she knew it wasn't Tess's fault.

Miss Franklin said Then whose was it?

Ms Powdrell said Background.

Miss Franklin said Ah, and blew her nose.

Ms Murphy said Which was Tess Nation?

Ms Murchison said Huge. Red hair. You know. Annabelle's sister.

Ms Murphy said Oh. That one. That she could not think for a moment, but that now she was on net. Wamberdammy. Heavy duty eh.

Ms Murchison said that surely it should be possible to get rid of a few of the trouble-makers such as Tess Nation.

Miss Franklin said How?

Ms Murchison said that with any luck she would leave at the end of this year.

Nobody said anything.

Miss Tamp thanked Mrs Hopere for bringing up the subject of last year's 4F, now 5C, and said that she would look into it and discuss the matter with the Board of Trustees.

Miss Franklin smiled. She said that that solved that problem.

Miss Tamp looked at Miss Franklin and said Thank You.

Miss Franklin said nothing.

Miss Tamp picked up her ballpoint which had fallen on the floor and said that she would now like to bring up the end of year play, the Leavers' Play, for discussion.

Everyone stared at the table.

Miss Tamp said that she had brought the matter up now even though it was only June because she realised that the Leavers' Play as well as being the highlight of the School year and looked forward to not only by the School but indeed by the whole city did mean an enormous amount of work for a great many people and how lucky they were to have Mrs Benchley and had she any ideas? As to which play?

Mrs Benchley leant back. She said that she had been responsible for the end-of-year play for twenty-five years now and that she thought someone else might like a turn.

No one said anything.

Mrs Benchley said that after all she might drop dead. Or go to

Los Angeles. Anything could happen.

Miss Tamp said that she hoped not and that would anyone else like to be responsible for the play this year.

Nobody said anything.

Miss Tamp said Mrs Benchley?

Mrs Benchley said Oh all right. But that this would be positively her final production.

Miss Franklin smiled.

Mrs Benchley said that she had always wanted to have a go at Brecht. That it was odd that she hadn't done so before and what about *Mother Courage*.

Miss Tamp said Brecht.

Mrs Benchley said that she would discuss it with her ex-husband who was something of an authority on Brecht.

Miss Franklin said Could she suggest Tess Nation as the lead.

Ms Murchison laughed.

Mr Marden also laughed. He said that he knew Tess.

Mrs Hopere said that she thought it would be a very good idea and not a joke either.

Mrs Stillburn said So did she.

Ms Doyle said that self image was the thing.

Mrs Benchley said that she was open to suggestions as to casting but perhaps later. She produced a piece of paper from her bag labelled Loot. She said that she hoped everyone who had helped last year would be available again and that she could only do so much. That with Miss Tamp's permission she would read through last year's list to make sure.

Miss Tamp said Certainly. That Mrs Benchley had the floor and that everyone was very grateful.

Mrs Benchley read Mrs Stillburn? Assistant director?

Mrs Stillburn blinked and said Certainly.

Mrs Benchley said Mrs Hopere? Front of house?

Mrs Hopere said Sure.

Mrs Benchley said Mrs Toon, Tickets?

Mrs Toon said Yes.

Mrs Benchley said And you of course Miss Franklin will have overall control. You know there is always something.

Miss Franklin said that she did indeed and that she would be happy to help in any way possible.

Mrs Benchley said that she would ask Mr Gilchrist if he'd help with the lights again. That he enjoyed backstage work. That his mother had been a dresser for Anna Neagle.

Ms Murphy said Anna who. That she was only asking.

Mrs Benchley said Wardrobe. Margot?

Ms Murchison said OK but that she hoped Sooze would be able to help again.

Ms Powdrell looked worried. She said that they were out at Paraparaumu now and that there was Jared.

Miss Franklin said that to her mind if people had babies out of school hours that was their problem.

Ms Powdrell said that she didn't think that remark was up to Miss Franklin's usual standard.

Miss Franklin nodded.

Mrs Benchley said Could Carmen help again with Movement?

Ms Doyle said Sure.

Mrs Benchley said Orchestra. Marcia?

Miss Hobbs said Yes.

Mrs Benchley said Could Mr Tysler, Sorry, Sorry. Mr *Marden* take over the set such as it was—she intended to keep it minimal of course but there would be the cart and things.

Mr Marden said Sure and smiled at Ms Doyle.

Ms Murchison said that the other guys, Cam and Bryce, had helped last year. That it had been quite fun. In a weird sort of way.

Mrs Benchley said And Jenni. Can you do backstage? Props?

Ms Murphy said Okey Dokey. That she and the Video Team would be making a film of the play. That that reminded her. Had anyone seen one of her VHS tapes. That it must have dropped out of her bag. That she remembered seeing it at some stage.

Miss Franklin said Yes and that she was glad to hear who owned it. That she had picked it up last night. That it had been lying by her car.

Mrs Sinclair glanced at Miss Tamp who was writing something in her diary.

Miss Franklin said that she would give it to Jenni later.

Miss Tamp said Was there any further business before she declared the Staff Meeting closed.

Nobody said anything.

Miss Tamp said that she declared the meeting closed and that she thanked everyone very much for their offers of help with the play.

Miss Franklin asked Miss Tamp if she could have a word with her.

Miss Tamp said Certainly and sat down beside Miss Franklin in the seat vacated by Mrs Vaughan.

Miss Franklin said that she thought perhaps Miss Tamp might prefer to talk to her in Miss Tamp's study. That it was more private. That she was only thinking of Miss Tamp.

Miss Tamp said What did Miss Franklin mean, and stood up.

Miss Franklin heaved herself up from the table and said Now?

Miss Tamp said Certainly.

Miss Tamp stands behind her desk. Miss Franklin remains planted in front of it, ignoring Miss Tamp's hospitable gesture towards the chair beside her.

—Well? says Miss Franklin.

What on earth is she talking about. Miss Tamp gazes out the open window at the Old Block. Her eye follows the concrete path beneath the plane trees which leads to the Sports Pavilion where Carmen was almost raped last year. A netball game on Number Two court stops short at a Sports Prefect's whistle. The Prefect seizes the ball from the ground, both arms are bent above her head as she throws it with force. Play is resumed. Miss Tamp turns from the contemplation of her world. Perhaps Miss Franklin is deranged which would solve a lot of problems.

—Won't you sit down? she says, repeating her gesture, her invitation to sit.

Miss Franklin remains standing; her white hair quivers.

—I have never been so disgusted in my entire life.

Miss Tamp is relaxed, uncomprehending. —I've no idea what you're talking about, she says.

The intensity of Miss Franklin's stare is worthy of a strong-eyed heading dog.

—Jenni's videotape, she says at last. —I played the video of your conversation with Thea Sinclair.

Miss Tamp's knees fold beneath her, she sinks onto the imitation grey leather of her revolving chair. —Jenni told me she had erased the tape, she murmurs.

Miss Franklin's expression changes. She is near to smiling.

—Well, she hadn't.

—So I gather. Miss Tamp straightens her shoulders. Her permed head lifts, the curls move. —You had no right to watch that. A private conversation.

—I had to identify the tape.

—You could have done that within seconds. Miss Tamp's voice rises. —You should have turned it off!

—Would you?

—Of course.

—So you say. Miss Franklin moves to the other window which overlooks the carpark. She sees her waiting car, the scraps of waste paper, the road beyond. She turns. —What I found most despicable, was your asking Thea Sinclair about Jean. Jean! A woman of her calibre to be discussed by . . . discussed by . . . Miss Franklin turns again to the window. Her shoulders move. She blows her nose.

Marcia Hobbs appears below and runs along the concrete path to her Mini.

—Like you, I wanted to know. I did nothing dishonourable, says Miss Tamp. Her eyes focus on her hands. She closes them briefly. —I presume you watched the whole tape.

—I did. And very boring it was too. Brown carpet, black shoes, an occasional cat. Miss Franklin's eyes are bright. —It was the conversation that interested me.

—How despicable. Miss Tamp stands. She leans forward on the tips of her splayed fingers which press against the desk. —Despicable! she says.

Miss Franklin laughs. Her hair flicks back. —Conduct unbecoming?

—Beneath contempt.

Miss Franklin's eyebrows leap upwards. They are not white like her hair. —*You* call *me* beneath contempt.

Miss Tamp sits once more and leans against the adjustable back of her chair. She tugs at one sleeve of her taupe suit. She has heard Carmen speak of tactics, the importance of timing. She smiles, not a happy smile, but her lips move, her face creases. —I plan to show a dossier to Mr Smythe, complaints about what I might call your lack of support.

—Your dossier! Mackerel Charlie! snorts Miss Franklin. —Much good may it do you! Her nostrils widen, extend sideways, flare.

Miss Tamp's voice is quiet. —Why were you not appointed Headmistress when Miss Sargesson died?

The prefect's whistle pierces the silence. Miss Tamp waits.

—That remark is inexcusable, says Miss Franklin at last. —Beneath contempt.

Miss Tamp nods. —Yes, she says.

Miss Franklin rallies. —I have no respect for the Chairman of the Board of Trustees and the rest of them but they would never dismiss me. Never. Not with my teaching record.

Miss Tamp's voice is even quieter. —Possibly.

—Whereas if I may say so, or even if I mayn't, your record . . . Hh! Miss Franklin is now under full sail, surging ahead, armed at every port. Miss Tamp stops listening.

She feels oddly tired. She glances around the familiar room where she solves problems; gets things done. She sees the high bookcases, the Apple Macintosh, her pictures, Mother's majolica plate. She stares at the large reproduction of Piero della Francesca's *Madonna del Parto* which shocked Mr Smythe.

He had stared at the swollen abdomen beneath the unbuttoned robe indicated by the Virgin's hand. —This is a girls' school, Miss Tamp, he said. —After all.

Miss Tamp's eyes continue around the room. —I hold no brief for some of Mr Smythe's views, she says. Her voice is sad, hesitant. She despises herself.

—He was a friend of your father's wasn't he? she says.

The day Margory Stillburn stopped thinking she had loped around
the corner as usual to do her lengths. She flipped her season ticket
at the bored young custodian with his feet up, tugged on her cap,
adjusted her goggles and stepped into the shimmering blues of the
shallow end. She swam to the diving board and back twelve times
in stately high-necked breaststroke then climbed out puffing
slightly. After a quick glance at the wall clock to check her time she
squelched down the lane in her jandals wearing an old towelling
shirt of Derek's over her wet togs and worrying about Azerbaijan.
She stopped beside the wooden bridge across the open drain to
check the padlock of the cyclone-netting gate. Once a workman
had left it open. Margory had run all the way home to ring the
Council. She explained, panting down the telephone, that the lane
was used by primary school children and running water was such
a temptation, to say nothing of the watercress.

Margory turned into Titoki Avenue. The broken-winged
rusty old car belonging to the young man next door was still parked
in front of the Stillburns' house. She had asked him and asked him.
—Darren, I know it'll seem silly to you but would you mind
leaving your car in front of your section rather than ours? It's just
. . . She always finished there, flinging her hands apart in silly-me
appeal. —Sure, said Darren each time. —No mucken furries. The
thing now bore a new sticker alongside 'Plumbers do it backwards'
and 'My other car is a Merc'. The letters were red on yellow, their
message clear. 'Don't worry. Be happy.' Margory stared at it, the
early morning sun gentle on her back, chlorinated water trickling
down her legs. The words sang at her, beat in her head; staccato,
simple, sublime. She whispered them to herself and smiled. 'Don't
worry. Be happy.' Her burden, her crushing responsibility for the

whole world lifted; she felt weightless, her hands rose by her sides. Dazed by peace of mind Margory stood dripping on the asphalt at her gate.

She stared at the white mare's-tail clouds sailing through the sky above Wright's Hill.

—Thank you, she said and walked up the concrete path to the back door.

Margory had been a thinker since infancy; a troubled worrier for the sins and pain of the whole world. Photographs of her as a child show a sharp-nosed hesitant face between two large bunched ribbons tied by her mother who hadn't a care in the world. Margory's red Barnardo's box was the heaviest all through Primary School because she could see; she could see the ragged boys, urchins even, transformed into merry crop-headed lads by caring. She could see the plight of refugees eased by UNRRA; the homeless housed, the hungry fed. There was much to be done.

Margory and Derek had been married for over thirty years. They inhabited the same house. She cooked their meals, he washed up and hung the tea towel neatly above the stove to dry. They awoke side by side. Their lives were silent, rhythmical, ordered. They spent a fortnight at Thames each Christmas with their daughter Betsy, their son-in-law John, and the girls. —Will you be sad when Nana's gone? Margory asked the youngest. The candid eyes flicked briefly from *Sesame Street*. —No, said Chloe.

Derek had never shared her concern for the whole world. Margory, her hair still wet, watched his mandibular movement across the dinette. Perhaps she wronged him. Perhaps his caring took a different form.

They had their first fight, their one and only flamer really, when he had refused to collect for Corso . —Certainly not, he said, heaving on his jacket and putting a clean handkerchief in his trouser pocket. He turned to her, neat at all points, ready for anything a day at Sun Alliance Life could throw at him. —The poor buggers'd be better off dead, he said. —Keep this lot alive and what've you got? What've they got? More starving kids. Stop them, stop the poor sods breeding! I'll give you a tenner for that.

The intensity of Margory's fury shocked them both. She sprang at him, gibbering with rage. She couldn't live with him. How could she possibly live with him. She was desperate, she stormed with anguish, she wept.

Appalled at her outburst they became more cautious, more conscious of territorial limits, more silent.

Margory picked up the clipping from the *Dominion* which Derek had placed beside her muesli. 'Green Stress', announced the sub-heading. It detailed cases of International Corporate Executives who were under pressure from conservation groups to clean up industrial waste disposal systems, pollutants, to remove harmful additives from their products, and who were thus liable to develop undesirable Green Stress. —Mad, snorted Derek above the purple and green leaves of the coleus. What was mad? The article, the executives, the conservationists? Margory didn't ask. She discarded it later as she had discarded his clipped messages all their married life. Cuttings which detailed corruption in the distribution of famine relief, thefts of powdered milk, mutilation of child beggars in India by their parents, the uselessness of any organised attempt to assuage hunger and pain. —Who do you think you are? he had asked her years ago as he lay naked beside her.

—That's all I'd like to know. Just who do you think you are.

'Margs Ancient and Modern', Miss Franklin called Mrs Stillburn and Ms Murchison. Margory's walk was much imitated at Girls High. She seemed to veer slightly to the left pursued by the rest of her body. —'Five miles meandering with a mazy motion,' Miss Sargesson had commented to Miss Franklin when Mrs Stillburn joined the staff nine years ago. Her upper teeth protruded, the canines sharply pointed. Her hair was a nest of tangled grey. She looked like a small anxious rodent and the girls liked her because she worried about them whereas Sooze's equally genuine concern infuriated them. —Why doesn't she drop dead? enquired Tess Nation when Sooze explained once more to 5C their chances of attaining School Certificate.

Margory Stillburn has pared the syllabus down for survival. She has been teaching Typing and Keyboard Skills for a thousand years. Computer Skills are a new excitement. Her girls' pass rate in School C is excellent. She is also a good Counsellor, a help to aggressive girls, even to the withdrawn girls who trust her and tell her things which she can hardly believe but does. She fights for them. She liaises with Social Welfare. She cares.

Margory thinks about the joys of peace of mind at the Staff Meeting next week, her eyes on Miss Tamp's overpermed head. She is still calm, relaxed, deeply grateful to be absolved from overall responsibility for the sins of the whole world though she will continue to do what she can. Derek was quite right. Who did she think she was? Her previous temerity, her self-inflicted agonies stunned her. She couldn't claim caring battle fatigue or whatever they called it, not for the whole world. She had not spent her life doing anything to save it other than donating as much as she could and worrying her soul-case out. She felt like singing, hopping around Le Nid on one foot, hugging Derek for goodness sake. Margory sees the dark eyes, the wistful face of her World Vision adoptee, Enrile. She had always worried that perhaps it might be wrong to help him and not his siblings. Would they hate him? Margory almost laughed. Who was she. Who was she.

—Mrs Stillburn, Assistant Director? read Mrs Benchley.

Mrs Stillburn blinked and said Certainly.

Una Benchley stands four square by the coffee machine and claps her hands. —May I have a word with all those who have offered to help with the Leavers' Play? Except for Mrs Toon and Miss Franklin whom we needn't bother at this stage.

Miss Franklin lifts one hand and continues marking. —I'll be there, she says. Heads around the kauri table lift or are kept bent rather fixedly. —Thank you, says Una. —I'd like to have a preliminary meeting, just an informal get together to clear the decks as it were when Margory and I have finished auditions.

—What're we doing? asks Margory.

—Oh. Una smiles. Brecht. *Mother Courage*. I said.

—I thought you just said you'd like to have a go at Brecht.

—No. I did mention *Mother Courage*. That's why auditions are so important.

Margory tucks her white blouse into her skirt with quick shoving hands. —Yes indeed. Mother Courage is *Mother Courage*.

Una's smile is even more friendly. —Exactly.

There are problems, almost insuperable problems involved in getting six women and one man together after school. Margory stops listening. Someone will tell her and it makes no difference to her. Any day will do. —And please try and read the play first, says Una handing out blue Methuens. Cliff Marden is surprised. They all seem serious about the thing. Even Carmen.

—Now Tess, said Una Benchley, —just read Mother Courage's speech, will you, on the bottom of page four. It's a song really, but Mrs Stillburn and I would like to hear you read it.

Tess Nation sat on the empty stage in the Assembly Hall, her feet together, her knees apart, a drape of Titian hair obscuring half her face. Implacable, a dingo on the prowl, she leant forward and announced in a husky voice.

> —Business folk.
> You captains, tell the drums to slacken
> And give your infanteers a break:
> It's Mother Courage with her waggon . . .
>
> The new year's come. The watchmen shout.
> The thaw sets in. The dead remain.
> Wherever life has not died out
> It staggers to its feet again.

The voice finished. There was no sound in the dusty hall. Margory's skin crawled. Goosebumps pricked her arms. She rubbed them briskly and turned to Una who was smiling.

—She even looks like Helene Weigel, she whispered.

Una looked at the long brooding face and nodded.

—Thank you Tess, she said.

Without a glance Tess lumbered to her feet and strode off the stage. —Hang on you fucken kids, they heard her shout.

—But why *Mother Courage*? said Margory. —The morality of the play is so . . . Why not a New Zealand play? *The Caucasian Chalk Circle* even.

—She'll be incredible, muttered Una. —Endless work of course, but still. She shook her head. —Incredible.

—Certainly, but. They'll get it all wrong, said Margory, her hands clasped tight around *The Complete Guide to Personal Computing*.

—Get what all wrong? Una ran a pencil line under 'staggers to its feet again'.

—It's negative, nihilistic even. There is no love. Just greed. Virtue is not rewarded. Mother Courage never learns.

—The fact that she never learns is the whole point! That war teaches people nothing. That the poor lose. That virtue is not rewarded. We're past *The Sound of Music* for school leavers, said Una, shoving *Mother Courage* in her bag labelled Loot.

Margory riffled the pages. —'Standing around like Jesus at the Mount of Olives,' she read, —'leads his men up shit creek.' There is no love, she repeated.

Una clapped her hands together. —It'll be an enormous amount of work, she said happily. —Enormous.

—Are we all here? she asks next Monday, standing on the stage with her behind propped against a table. She turns to the bearded man beside her. —This is Brock Benchley, who has kindly offered to help us with the production.

Heads lift to inspect Una's ex. The table rocks as Brock stands. —This table's a little you know, he says. Una smiles reassuringly.

Carmen is not in her tracksuit today. She wears a sleeveless white vest beneath a sleeveless black jersey pinafore which stops at mid thigh. Her skin is still gold over brown and looks good beneath both the black and the white. Cliff Marden glances briefly from his contemplation of her kneecaps at the man in the red T-shirt with HARVARD printed on it. Camp as a row of tents. Carmen's legs are now crossed. She dips the top foot at Cliff and smiles.

Brock gives them a burst on Brecht. He himself personally does not feel that Brecht is old hat nor ever will be. That's the sort of thing people say, says Brock, but to his mind it's suspect. Brecht is a genius. No doubt about that to Brock's mind. Sure, he's challenging even if you skip the distancing bit, the alienation, the *verfremdungs-effekt* if you must, but to Brock he is all things to all men.

—And women? asks Carmen gently.

—Sure, sure, says Brock. He goes on for some time. Illusion must always be recognised as illusion he tells Marcia Hobbs who agrees. Details must be tested, he says. Improvisation is a non-event with Brecht. Brecht's message in this play is that no sacrifice is too great for the struggle against war and Brock would go along with that. Margory Stillburn nods thoughtfully. The cart must be a cross between a military vehicle and a general store. Cliff sits up, his pen upright in his left hand.

—And of course, continues Brock, —the cart must get more battered. Twelve years of the Thirty Years War go by after all. The canvas covering can be just a rag at the end. The clothes also must get worse. —How? asks Margot Murchison. Brock replies that they may find Brecht's Notes useful though of course they don't want to get locked in.

Everyone stares at the floor except Carmen. Una speaks briefly. —Don't let Brock worry you, she concludes smiling. —He's an expert and we are an amateur school production.

Brock strokes his beard and smiles. —Sometimes, he says, —there is a freshness . . .

Margot Murchison's hand waves. —Is Mother Courage, I

mean . . . Is she a good role model? Her children do have three different fathers after all . . . Carmen looks at her with interest, her head on one side. —Does Miss Tamp, you know, does she know the play? continues Margot. —It seems so . . .

—Yes. Una scratches her wool jersey behind. —It's a war play, she says. —People don't live happily ever after after war. Usually they don't live at all.

—Oh. Oh well. Margot's shoulders wriggle. She looks like a small ruffled bird. —It's just that we don't want to get all the clothes, there'll have to be two lots if they're going to get worse, and then suddenly discover it's *The Caucasian Chalk Circle*. Do we Sooze?

Sooze smiles. —No, she says.

—This cart, Cliff lifts a hand. —It's important, you say.

Brock heaves his buttocks from the table. His hands tug at his white canvas belt. —Very. He gives Cliff the information man to man, his voice solemn. —It's a metaphor, if you like, for the whole message of the play.

—Ah huh, says Cliff, and begins sketching a cross between a military vehicle and a general store.

—I saw a production of the play years ago in London, says Sooze, —and the cart changed.

Brock's behind is propped once more. —That's exactly what I said.

—Yes but I mean one minute it was a cart, Sooze's hands carve the air, —then they pulled a couple of bits off it and it was a tent and then it was a ship or something . . .

Cliff smiles at her. —Watch it sailor, he says. —Whose side are you on?

Sooze smiles back. Her head moves as she laughs at herself.

Brock's forehead is creased. —Ship? he asks.

—Don't you think, says Margot, —that it's asking for trouble attempting something which specifies a revolving stage. She flings her hands at the Assembly Hall. —Here!

Carmen's chair is tipped back, she balances on her track shoes, both hands hold her plait on the top of her head. —That's no problem, she says. —They just walk round and round in circles going the same way all the time like Boys High when they did *The Caucasian Chalk Circle*.

—Most people, says Jenni Murphy, stowing a packet of tofu in her kete, —see time as moving from left to right.

—Not the Chinese, says Cliff, —they're cyclical.

Carmen pinches his behind. His hand clamps her wrist. His mouth is wide open as he smiles at her.

—I saw it somewhere the other day, said Jenni. Carmen and Cliff watch her in silence, her head is still down, her quick searching hands visible beneath her tangled orange hair.

—Shit, she says. —I thought I'd lost another tape but I've found it. It's funny, isn't it, it's better when you find it than if you hadn't lost it in the first place.

Margory smiles. She likes Jenni who is an amoral atheist. — 'Rejoice with me,' she says, 'for that which was lost is found again.'

—Getting back to Brecht, says Brock firmly.

—I'm still worried , says Margory, —about the tone of the play.

—I'm worried role-model-wise, says Margot.

Brock's hands slam his head like cymbals. —We're talking about theatre!

—We're talking, says Margory, —about a play performed in a girls' school. We're talking about the fact that Mother Courage is incorrigible!

—Did Tess Nation audition? asks Carmen.

Una's moves her head slowly from side to side. —Superb. A natural.

—As long as she doesn't get sick of it, says Margot, brushing the front of her skirt. —She could leave you with your sarong hanging, that one.

—Like *The Loneliness of the Long Distance Runner?* says Jenni.

—She won't, says Una.

—Come on! says Brock. —Let's . . .

Marcia Hobbs sits very straight, her feet close together. —You realise, she says, —that the music, the songs are very difficult.

—Oh dear, says Una politely. Her face brightens. —But you said Tess has a wonderful voice. I remember.

—She has. But there are other songs. The Chaplain, the Cook, Eilif. Five or six really good voices will be needed.

Una smiles lovingly. —But surely in the whole school?

—The songs are very difficult. Marcia leans back, her eyes on the whorl of toffee coloured hair at the back of the head in front of her. —I'll do what I can, she says.

—It still seems odd to me, says Margot. —Role-model-wise.

Brock is bored. He watches Cliff who has given up on his cart sketch for the moment and is watching Carmen who is watching Margot. —Yes Margot? says Una.

—Tess Nation's been a pain ever since the third form right?

Assent is given. —You can say that again, says Jenni.

—And then she gets given the star role in the end-of-year play.

—Because she's the best, says Una smiling.

Margot's shoulders huff about her ears. —It just seems odd to me.

—It may be the best thing that's ever happened to her, says Sooze.

—And, says Margot, she's only a fifth former.

—But she is a Leaver, says Una.

—Yes, thank God, grunts Margot.

Una's smile broadens. —You mean it's not fair.

—If you knew what I've had to put up with . . .

—We all know.

Margot is not giving an inch. —Not as Form Mistress.

Una is now behind the table on the stage. She leans forward, her large speckled hands are flat on the table. Her face is serious. —But Margot, she says gently, —Life is not fair.

—Cam'll need all his design skills for this bloody cart, says Cliff later in the carpark.

—He's no slouch, Cam, says Carmen. She is now in her

tracksuit. Her green-covered legs stretch either side of her bike. She holds her helmet in both hands and smiles up at him.

—Where'll we go tonight? she says.

Margory Stillburn is liaising with Cliff and Cam at a *Mother Courage* Work Day several weeks later. She leans over the back of a wooden chair staring at a large working drawing of Cliff's original waggon which lies on the floor, her hands obscuring a small bronze plaque (Adele Rosenholm 1946-1950). The men squat side by side below her. Cliff's finger points, explains, insists the thing will work.

Cam sits back on his rump. One blue jandal is now flat on the floor, the other still bent. —You're going to have a problem with weight, he says, —if you use wood, hundred-by-fifties say.

Bryce who has been rocking on the back legs of a chair donated by Sally Leveson in 1967 glances across at Sooze who stares straight ahead. Bryce decides he mustn't get bitchy about Cam. Nothing wrong with the guy. Nothing a transplant wouldn't cure.

—Nnn, says Cliff, shoving the hair out of his eyes with one hand. —I hadn't thought of that.

—No problem, says Cam. —I can make her out of hardboard.

—But it's got to look like wood. Seventeenth century wood!

Margory smiles into Cliff's eyes and nods. She knows good looks are irrelevant but they are pretty to watch.

—I can tart her up, says Cam in his slow drawl. —Veneer or something.

Cliff gives him a quick grin. —Great.

Cam drags a small pad and flat pencil from the back pocket of his shorts. —Do y'want wooden wheels? he asks politely.

—I don't know. Cliff glances at his research assistant again.

—I imagine so, says Margory.

Cam nods, his face impassive. He stands, his boxer shorts are like a bright pelmet above yards of dark window frames. —Let me know, he says. —Tell Margot.

Miss Franklin touches his arm en route to the stage. —I knew a man who walked the Milford Track in those things, Campbell, she says, pointing at his size eleven jandals.

Cam smiles at her, a gradual illumination. The white creases beside his eyes disappear. —No kidding? he says.

Miss Franklin nods and continues briskly, her clipboard clutched in one hand.

Bryce watches Carmen who is moving slowly around the stage in a circular direction. —You want to try and make each movement, she says, —well not each movement, but you know what I mean, make each movement circular. Her arms demonstrate.

—We're pulling the ruddy cart, says Mother Courage.

—Yeah, say Kattrin, Eilif, and Swiss Cheese.

—Only Eilif and Swiss Cheese at the beginning, says Carmen, —and anyway that's not the point. Movement is always important in drama, but especially in this one, see. You can tell how things are by the way they move. And always think circular. Otherwise it doesn't make sense. It's time as well, isn't it Mrs Benchley?

—Yes, absolutely, says Una, who is checking her prompt copy while Carmen takes Movement.

—Look, says Carmen. She demonstrates optimism, pragmatism, despair moving in circles. Her body exults, strides, struggles. The kids begin to catch on. Bryce glances briefly across the hall at Cliff whose face is blank as he also watches Carmen.

Cam is watching Sooze who sits at the back of the hall with a Quick Unpick ripping apart old fawn stage curtains which might do for Mother Courage. Beside her on the floor Jared rocks in his Bouncette, talking to himself. Cam sits on the floor beside him and rocks it harder. Jared roars with laughter, pale strands of baby hair lift from his head. Cam watches him with interest. —He's neat, isn't he, he says looking up at Sooze. Her eyes blur with tears. —God, you're a nice man, she says.

Cam stares at her. He notes the wide apart eyes, the swing of her short cropped hair, the quick ripping movements of her hands. Cam likes Sooze. He likes her so much he would like to go to bed with her. He has thought of this before, but only briefly. It will require further thought. Her breasts are smaller than Margot's. And

Margot loves him. And he loves Margot.

—Aw shit, he says.

Sooze laughs. The underside of her chin is white.

Cam rearranges the fullness of his shorts. He must get out of here. —Shall I take him for a walk in that thing, he says, nudging the wheel of Jared's stroller with one foot. —Give him some fresh air.

—That'd be great, says Sooze. —Thanks. She turns to Jared who is still bouncing. —You'd like that, wouldn't you, hon? She jumps up, tucks Jared in his yellow and grey stroller and belts him in. —Walk? she asks as though giving him the option. —Big walk with Cambo?

Cam smiles. You could fall into her eyes. —Cam, he says.

She laughs. —Sorry. Cam.

It is all too much for Jared. He blows consonants. —Bb, bb, bb.

—Stick to the paths, says Sooze, who is bossy like all teachers. —The hockey field's a bog after that rain. Cam lifts one hand to salute his new found love.

Bryce has appeared. He puts one hand on the stroller. —Where 're you going? he says.

—We're going for a walk, says Cam. Prick face.

—I'll take him, says Bryce, now with two hands on the stroller.

—Look, cries Carmen from the stage. —I'll show you once more. All watching?

Bryce lets go. —OK, he says.

—Gee thanks, says Cam and wheels the stroller out the Main Door of the Assembly Hall.

—Cam, calls Sooze. —Hang on.

Cam turns on the concrete path by the Sports Pavilion. His smile embraces her. Jared lifts a courtly hand and smiles also. Sooze brushes past them and tries the door. —It's open, she says. The space is quiet, empty, shadowless in the cloudy light. —Cam, says Sooze. She clutches him, holds him tight. Tears pour down her cheeks, she wipes a hand across her face. —I'm sorry, I'm sorry, she gasps, and returns to his arms which have abandoned the stroller.

—It's just, it's just, she gulps against his checked shirt. His arms are around her. She is taller than Margot. The top of her head is level with his nose. —Sssh, he says. —Sssh. His lips move down one side of her face, find her mouth as she lifts her head to tell him.

—I'm so sick of it, she says later, more breathless than ever. —Being always , being always . . . I do try, Cam. Her words are falling out, tumbling, hiccoughing, but he knows what she's on about.

—It's not your fault he lost his shitty job, he says, one hand stroking her hair.

—And they were shitty too. I couldn't stand them. The money people. It's not my fault is it? Is it, Cam?

Cam shakes his head. His hands move. —No, he says.

—Women are meant to be so strong, aren't they? she begs. He nods.

—I do try. Being supportive and stuff. I do try. But now he's left the morgue and I hated that and I hated the money market, what's the poor sod to do? Her voice is muffled against his chest.

Cam is breathing deeply. His hands are on her breasts. He drops one hand to swing the stroller around so it faces the other way. Jared is fascinated by the movement of the naked plane tree branches above the skylight. He lies chatting and waving at the winter sky.

—Sssh, says Cam, his hands now making circular movements beneath Sooze's T-shirt. —Sssh, it's all right. Sssh, my love. They subside onto the slatted bench by the lockers. Her breasts are small, perfect. Cam bends his head. He falls on his knees and pulls her onto the duckboard beside the bench. They lie smiling, panting slightly, staring at each other.

—Cam, says Sooze. —Darling Cam. Her hand strokes his face. —You're so . . . You're like a bloody rock. It's not that I don't love him. Oh God, I'm a feeble bitch. She heaves herself onto all fours and comes face to face with the back of the stroller. Her laugh is a gasp, a yelp. —Come on. Let's get out of here.

Cam's voice is gentle. —No, he says.

*

—Where's Sooze? asks Margot, who has just arrived from the Clothing Room with a pile of costume patterns she has been drafting.

Cam pushes Jared and his stroller with one foot. —She's gone out for some air, he says. —It's bloody stuffy in here.

—Yes. Margot nods. She bends to kiss his forehead, a quick connubial peck.

—Look Sooze, cries Margot waving the patterns at Sooze who has just walked in the Main Door. —It's a start, anyway.

Sooze is pale. —Clever old you, she says. —Let's have a look.

Cam looks away. He stamps his jandals and sits staring at the floor.

—Why's your hair wet round the edges? asks Margot.

—I had a shower, says Sooze.

Margot is puzzled. —Why on earth?

—It was so stuffy. I couldn't stand it.

Margot looks at her, the patterns move in her hand. —Where?

—In the Sports Pavilion. There's a dead towel there.

Margot shakes her head. Her shiny black hair moves as she laughs. —I must remember that, she says.

—Jenni, calls Carmen from the stage, —could you bear to run over to the Sports Pavilion for me and collect some hoops?

Jenni is on her knees. She looks up from the collection of general store artifacts she is sorting, a battered saucepan in one hand. —Hoops? she says.

Bryce is on his feet. —I'll go, he says.

Carmen smiles. —Thanks, Bryce. It's not locked. There are some hoops in the corner. Bring about six. She waves one arm. —Thanks a lot.

Brock is now man to man with Cliff and Bryce. He leans back in his chair, his gut solid beneath the Harvard sign as he continues his in-depth dissertation on Brecht. He explains Brecht's ambivalence in some respects. —I'll put it this way, he says. —He was a survivor. He had an ability to survive.

—I like survivors, says Cliff. He wears green cotton trousers and a black T-shirt. His hair is clean. He looks very together.

Brock sits up straight. He is very serious. —So do I, man, so do I.

—I've nothing against gays, says Bryce later in the Men's lavatory which does not boast a urinal because the Chairman of the Board did not consider it a viable option when the Administration Block was built.

—Some of your best friends are, are they? Cliff bends his head for a drink from the cold tap.

Bryce's hand shoots out and clamps Cliff's head rigid beneath the running water. Cliff is helpless, spluttering, his blind hands tearing the air as he searches for Bryce's.

Brock walks in. His step is bouncing. He springs from the balls of his feet.

—Hi, he says happily. —Boys being boys, is it?

Bryce leaves quickly as Cliff staggers to the paper towel dispenser.

Brock sees his face. —You all right? he asks.

Cliff nods, his eyes are glazed, focused on the distant scene when he will kill Bryce even though he is a pacifist.

Brock moves nearer, his face anxious. —You're sure?

Cliff leans against the wall breathing carefully. —Yes thanks, he says. —I'm sure.

—Nothing I can do?

Cliff shakes his head.

Brock nods and moves to the cubicle unzipping.

Cliff walks out into the arms of Margory Stillburn who is lurching past the Men's in her search for Marcia Hobbs who doesn't seem to have turned up. She looks up at him and stops.

—Are you all right? she asks.

Cliff nods.

—Why's your hair wet? She touches it gently.

Cliff has a mad desire to tell her. To sink down to her height, to explain to her loving little potoroo face, to tell her everything.

To be absolved from rage though he doesn't want that. He smiles and shakes his uncombed head yet again. Water sprinkles the back of her hand.

She watches the drop which lies in the V of two dark raised veins. She glances up. —You're sure?

—Sure.

He can't tell Carmen either.

—Oh well. Margory smiles again and moves away licking the drop.

Miss Tamp has slipped into school on her way home from the Saturday Market. It is not as good in the winter. It is really the herbs and the exuberance of summer vegetables which she enjoys; the seductive shine of yellow green and red peppers, the purple glaze of eggplant, the gleaming tomatoes, fresh ridged zucchinis. However she has got into the habit of shopping there and she enjoys the crowd. It makes a change. Miss Tamp smiles as she locks her car.

Overall responsibility for the Play is not her part of ship as Father used to say, and she has no intention of intruding on Miss Franklin's domain, or rather on Una Benchley's who does all the work. However she likes to put in an appearance, to show her interest and concern for the Staff and girls who are giving up a whole Saturday. And the men too. Miss Tamp is always overly grateful to the men when they turn up at School Dances, Fund Raisings or to help with the Leavers' Play. Miss Franklin regards this as yet more evidence of inanity. —After all, as she says to Una Benchley, —if they haven't already sired daughters they are quite likely to do so at any moment. Nobody falls about when women help.

As she stumps up the path Miss Tamp wonders what the situation is between Una Benchley and her ex-husband, but it is nothing to do with her and she dismisses the thought.

Margory Stillburn greets her at the Main Door of the Administration Block. —Good morning, she says. —Have you seen Marcia Hobbs?

—Good morning. No.

—Oh there she is. Margory waves at Marcia who has just appeared from the carpark.

—Hurray! she cries, and hurtles down the path to greet the lost sheep.

Miss Tamp continues on across the open space of the Entrance Hall of Admin, past the Main Notice Board with its paper messages which move gently in the breeze from the Science Block. Miss Tamp stops to check for vulgarity, obscenity even. She has to keep a sharp eye on the Notice Board. She marches past the Library which is closed. *Libraries are for Life* is visible through the glass door.

She turns the corner which leads to the hall and almost bangs into a scurrying figure with a clipboard. —What are you doing here? demands Miss Franklin, her head high.

Miss Tamp is not having any of that nonsense. She is silent.

Carmen's voice calls behind the swing doors. —OK gang. Once more. One and move and one and . . . Use your hoops. You're pulling remember!

Miss Franklin stands very straight. —I left in a rage last Tuesday afternoon . . .

Miss Tamp says nothing. She watches Miss Franklin with interest. Goodness me, she thinks.

—I shouldn't have done that, continues Miss Franklin.

Miss Tamp's face is now blank.

—I should have stayed, says Miss Franklin quietly. —I should have stayed and told you that if you think you can blackmail me or attempt to exert some sort of pressure over me because of my love for the finest woman who ever lived, you are mistaken.

Miss Tamp nods. —I realise that.

Miss Franklin's head shoves forward. Her white plume is a banner, an invincible standard to be carried to the jaws of death and beyond. —Then why did you do it!

—I'll tell you, says Miss Tamp. —Come with me.

—I'm not going in there, says Miss Franklin as Miss Tamp ushers her into the Staff toilets.

—Please sit down, says Miss Tamp indicating one of the plastic covered stools either side of the large flip-top rubbish bin beneath the paper towel dispenser. —I once attended a management course, she says.

Miss Franklin is on her feet. —God in Heaven!

Miss Tamp lays a hand on her shoulder. Mother's garnet exerts gentle pressure on Miss Franklin's rage. She sits.

—One of the things I remember most clearly, says Miss Tamp, —a lot of it was very boring, was one intelligent man, the Chairman of one of our biggest companies. Oil, I think he was. He said that one of the most important things he'd learnt in his entire career . . . Miss Tamp leans forward, every fibre of her body impacting. —Is that resolution cannot be achieved without conflict.

Miss Franklin is listening. —That is not received thinking.

—Not what we were taught. No.

—Resolution is achieved by one side giving way, being defeated, and the other side winning, says Miss Franklin. —Or by turning the other cheek and I have no intention of doing that. One balled hand punches the top of the rubbish bin which flips back and forward.

—Nor I! We are talking about conflict between equals.

Miss Franklin snorts. —Hhh!

—The man said, I can't remember his name, I wish I could, he was very impressive, he said skill was required to bring both sides to conflict. He said that then and only then do both sides back off. Learn to accept what they can live with. Agree on what I think he called their bottom lines.

Miss Franklin stares at the top of the rubbish bin. It has stopped moving. She lifts her eyes to Miss Tamp's face which is mottled red and white. —And that is what you propose we do?

Miss Tamp's hands tug at her taupe. —Yes, she says. —Achieve a *modus vivendi*.

—Hh, says Miss Franklin and walks out.

Miss Tamp runs the cold water tap for some time. She usually removes her ring before washing her hands but liquid soap is different. She dries her hands on a paper towel and feeds it to the rubbish bin. She glances at her face in the mirror above the hand basins, expells her breath once and walks out the door.

She pushes open the swing door to the hall. Miss Franklin is not visible. Everyone else is seated in small groups eating their lunches. The girls all sit together, the staff and friends sit about in scattered harmony. Miss Tamp can smell hard-boiled egg. She feels exhausted. She might even have a Flor Fino when she gets home.

She waves at the seated chewing faces. Jenni Murphy, her feet encased in Salvation Army cowgirl boots, waves back.

—Good afternoon ladies and gentlemen, says Miss Tamp. —I just popped in to thank you all, and especially those of you who are not directly connected with the school, for giving up your precious Saturday. And to see if I can do anything to help.

Heads shake sadly. Some smile. —Give my love to Faraday, calls Jenni. Cam's head does not lift.

Miss Tamp leaves and drives home to Faraday whom she is very pleased to see. She clasps him to her. —I've bought you a treat, she whispers. His meow is a harsh rasping sound as he twists in her arms. —Groper, says Miss Tamp. —Not now. Tonight.

Margory Stillburn lies in bed beside Derek who is sound asleep. She has placed her leather bookmark, a present from Betsy's eldest, in her copy of Thomas Merton's *Elected Silence,* which she reads and rereads because she finds his spiritual pilgrimage from atheist to Trappist monk the most exciting story she knows.

> Elected silence sing to me,
> And beat upon my whorlèd ear.
> Pipe me to pastures still and be
> The music that I care to hear.

The room is very dark. Sometimes if she has not pulled the curtains carefully enough there is a strip of light down one edge.

Margory lies on her back and gives thanks once again for the God-given message on Darren's old bomb. Don't worry. Be happy. Her eyes are damp with gratitude. She will continue to do what she can, but not destroy her sanity. Derek moans gently and turns from her in his sleep. —Derek? murmurs Margory. It has been a long day. Her hand strokes his back. —Derek. Her eyes close.

The northerly died down at midday, the southerly is not forecast until tomorrow. The harbour lies still, a gift laid out as Sooze and Bryce drop down the Ngaio Gorge having parked Jared and all the gears with his grandparents for the night of the Leavers' Play. Sooze's mother is a small, nimble woman dazed with the wonder of her grandson's first steps. —Come on then, she says, her knees on the Berber, her arms outstretched. —Come to Nana. There's a boy. Look! Henry, look! and her husband joins her pride.

—If this was Switzerland or wherever, people'd come for miles, says Sooze, her eyes on the white and red valerian falling down the sides of the gorge, the flopping rambler roses, the occasional flaunt of purple or blue cinerarias.

—What?

—The Garden Escapes. Wild flowers.

Bryce's mind is on the curves. —Hh.

Oriental Bay is dusty and golden at the end of the day, the traffic is heavy as they wait for the lights. A man heaves himself up from the sea and sits on the platform of the fountain which lies offshore. It is not operating at the moment although the night is still. They don't turn it on in the northerly because of the spray. Bryce says it's because the spray mucks up the rich windows of the high-rises. Maybe it will be turned on soon. —Ah, people will say as the vast plume of water grabs at the sky. —Look at the fountain. Grandmothers will point. —See? See the fountain!

—I always hope the thing'll start under some wanker's arse, says Bryce.

Sooze's laugh is half grunt. —Typical, she says. Her eyes are down as she buttons the red jacket of Jared's bear which she forgot to leave with him. Jared will not miss Bare Bum, as Bryce calls him. Sooze knows this, but providing him on all occasions comforts her. It makes her feel a proper mother, not the sort who rolls about on duckboards behind her son's back. Sooze's hands move quickly as she turns the bear face downwards on her lap.

The man dives off the still motionless fountain and motors back through the water with wide swinging arms.

Sooze and Bryce's car crawls away from the pedestrian crossing, its exhaust a series of muffled bangs. Bryce sold his Mitsubishi after the crash and Gutless, the old heap with which he replaced it, is getting worse.

—He can't swim either, says Bryce.

Sooze glances at him. He catches her eye and stares straight ahead. Sooze switches her gaze to the rear vision mirror. Three headless figures in chef's white uniforms sit side-by-side on the front seat of the van behind them. The middle jacket is open at the top button. Sooze twists and ducks her head, hoping for high hats as well but can see nothing more. The van shoots past. *Fisher's Catering. Functions division.*

Brock and Una sit on the bench outside the Main Entrance to the Assembly Hall. They have snatched a couple of spring rolls each, or rather four spring rolls have been snatched for them from the takeaway at the gate by Tracey Edwards and Ella Taheri who are Mrs Benchley's runners during the production of the Leavers' Play. There is no time for a snack in town and Eastbourne is out of the question. Una is elated and nervous, not nervous, of course she's not nervous. —Remember *The Importance of Being Earnest*? she says.

Brock nods, his mouth full.

Una pulls off her fawn cardigan. —What a night, she says, meaning this one. —You don't often get them here. Not your genuine fully paid-up balmy night.

Brock has stopped chewing. His voice is deep and sonorous as he declaims:

In such a night as this,
When the sweet wind did gently kiss the trees
And they did make no noise, in such a night
Troilus methinks mounted the Trojan walls,
And sigh'd his soul toward the Grecian tents,
Where Cressid lay that night
In such a night . . .

Una's frisson starts deep in her pelvis. She shivers and pulls her cardigan around her shoulders. —I must thank you, she says, —for all your help. It's made a tremendous difference.

Brock scrubs his beard with the napkin provided then pulls his fingers quickly through it checking for spills. —I've enjoyed it. Especially Tess. What a girl.

They talk about the excitement of Tess, her control, her timing which is extraordinary in someone of sixteen. Her voice. She has star quality, she is hypnotic as she strides around the stage in reconstituted ex-curtains.

Brock pats Una's knee. —You'll be famous. 'Discovered by Una Benchley.'

—It's very exciting, says Una, her eyes on his beautiful brown hand. Beautiful hands are rare. 'Have nothing in your houses that you do not know to be useful or believe to be beautiful.' What is she doing sitting here anyway. There's something about Charlotte Hopere and extra chairs. Una heaves herself from the bench and holds her hand out for his rubbish.

Brock stares up at her. Nobody could call her beautiful but she is a good sort. —Do you ever wake in the night knowing you're going to die? he asks.

Una flops back on the bench, her face anxious. —No.

Brock runs his hand over the curls on the left side of his head. When he combs his hair he runs it over his bald brown scalp as well which seems odd but presumably you would keep going through the motions. —It's terrifying! I've had it for years. It's worse, he says, —since Clive went. I wake in a muck sweat and it's so *real*.

There's something I've got to take otherwise I'll die and I haven't taken it. Some pill, something. Sometimes I find myself right out in the bathroom looking for it, shaking like a bloody . . . His hands fling apart.

—Leaf, says Una gently.

—Are you sure you haven't had it? he asks. —The feeling?

But Una cannot lie. She shakes her head. —No.

Brock sighs. —I must get back to LA. I've been away five months for Chrissake.

Una sits very still, a hand planted on each knee. She can see the inter-island ferry through a gap in the buildings. —Yes, she says.

Brock's voice drops. —We had been going to stay, you know. Clive and I. Come home.

—Had you? She hadn't noticed that glimpse of the harbour before. —Something must have been pulled down, she says.

—Hunh?

—There's a glimpse of the harbour.

—It's too small though, says Brock after a pause. —I can see that now. I had hoped for a cultural matrix, a bi-cultural matrix if you like, an indigenous theatre with guts. I haven't found that. He leans back. —I've found a bunch of dimbo loonies who think they're Baby Jane on wheels. A pack of prima donnas who just don't want to know.

Una stares at him. In such a night as this when the sweet wind did gently kiss the trees.

—Theatre guys here used to have tons of balls. It's like somebody's bitched it up, says Brock sadly. —I'd get locked in.

—What a load of crap! cries Una leaping to her feet. She strides into the Assembly Hall. —Charlotte, she calls to Mrs Hopere. —What's this about being short of chairs?

Mrs Hopere glances up, her face shiny. The chairs are a big job and last year's 4F, now 5C, are not really reliable, though they are amiably disposed as they fling the things about. Heavy wooden chairs are all very well and it's nice for the girls to be able to donate something when they leave, but they are an enormous amount of work. And anyway it's only the girls with well-heeled parents who get a look in as usual. Mrs Hopere longs for moulded plastic which stack.

—It's all right, she says. —Merryl found some behind the horse in the old gym.

—Stephanie! she calls.

Stephanie, the horns of whose chair have been lunging at the matador red tea towel wielded by Christine Goedhart, replaces the chair. —Yes, Mrs Hopere?

—Just get on please. *Twenty* in each row, Christine, and the aisle in the middle.

Miss Franklin appears. She wears her gown over russet-coloured rayon. Her shoes are polished. She still has her clipboard. —What's all this about chairs? she asks.

Mrs Hopere's hand touches her forehead briefly. —It's all right now, thanks, she says.

—There are some behind the old horse. The old gym I mean, says Miss Franklin striding off to her next checkpoint.

Mrs Hopere smiles briefly. Una's hand touches her shoulder and departs.

—*Christine!* shouts Mrs Hopere.

Christine's face is innocent, hurt almost, as she rights a chair.

—Can I give you a hand? Cam asks Mrs Hopere as he appears through the main door. 5C spring to merrily. The job is finished in no time.

—It's lovely, says Miss Franklin to Rita Vaughan who is doing her arrangement on the stage. —Will you be much longer?

Rita glances briefly at her watch. —There's plenty of time. She reverses with quick running steps to the edge of the stage, a large spike of deep blue delphinium clasped in her left hand as she gazes at her arrangement with pursed lips. Satisfied, she darts at the huge pottery vase which sits on a long-legged stand downstage right and shoves the spike into the Oasis foam. She stares again, her hand at her mouth.

—Time's getting on, says Miss Franklin. But Rita is lost to the world, surrounded by Christmas lilies, Paul's Scarlet roses and delphiniums from Marcia Hobbs' garden because Eastbourne is so much warmer and Marcia is green-fingered. Rita's selection never varies. Generations of Leavers will remember Mrs Vaughan's arrangements long after they have forgotten which play was which. The drenching heavy scent of lilies will swing them back to the best friend who nudged and giggled beside them at Leavers' Play and Break Up. They will know that the golden pollen of the stamens is an irremovable dye which must not be brushed against. If they were ever on Chairs they will know that Mrs Vaughan always put her background greenery in first, then her back-anchor delphinium, then her two lateral spikes and carried on from there.

Miss Hobbs is happy to provide the flowers but she herself prefers ikebana.

—My friend Fleur sent me a book on it once, Rita said years ago when Marcia first mentioned it. —But I couldn't get into it, you know what I mean.

—It does require a certain attitude of mind, agreed Marcia. —A discipline perhaps. A restraint.

—I like lots myself, said Rita, her hands reaching for the flower-laden buckets from Eastbourne. She sighed with pleasure. —Sometimes I think they look happiest of all like that, just flung together in a bucket for a good soak.

—Then why don't you just fling them in a vase?

—Oh no, said Rita, shocked. —They take hours to arrange properly.

She doesn't say a word against ikebana to Marcia of course, but she dislikes it intensely. She regards it as only one step removed from bonsai which is cruel. —Personally, she said that morning to Molly who is down from the King Country for the Leavers Play and Break Up, —I'd rather have daisies in a jam jar.

—You'd still arrange them though, Reet, said Molly, lighting her after-breakfast smoke.

Rita's hands moved on the checked cotton cloth. —No word from Fleur, I suppose?

Molly squinted at the match flame. —What do you think.

Una Benchley's ex-husband stops short in front of the stage, his arms akimbo as he stares at Rita's arrangement. Rita is scuttling around the base of the stand, her hands snatching discarded bits of greenery, stalks, overblown roses and dead lilies from the floor. She sweeps up the last fragments with Mr Gilchrist's broom and long-handled dust-pan and stands back, smiling at Brock.

Brock points an outraged hand. —You can't have that thing there!

Rita's expectant face falls. —What?

—That! That . . . Brock is almost gibbering.

—We always have a large mixed bowl on the edge of the stage. Rita is certain. —Paul's Scarlet, lilies and delphs. Always!

—Well you can't tonight!

—Why ever not?

—Because, because . . . this is *Mother Courage*!

Rita stands very straight. —So?

—Well, think woman, think!

Rita is now cross. —It's in front of the curtain, she snaps.

Brock is almost incoherent. —Yes, and when the curtain opens you'll have a huge red white and blue thing in the middle of the Thirty Years War for Chrissake!

—Don't you swear at me. We always have my arrangement! Always.

Miss Franklin appears, swinging out from the door beside the stage, her face eager. —What is the problem? she asks.

—He says . . . !

—She says . . . !

Miss Franklin is in her element. —I think, she says happily, that you'll have to consult a higher authority on this one. Has anyone seen the Headmistress?

★

Mrs Hopere has now switched from Chairs to help Mrs Toon with Tickets. Mrs Toon sits at a small table with her gear and tackle and trim, her float in a small locked drawer beneath her right hand. Mrs Hopere and Ella sit beside her. Ella has been detailed to this position by Mrs Benchley who knows that at this stage liaison with Front of House is essential.

Ella would rather be backstage where Tracey is with Mrs Benchley and the big kids. Ella is hacked off. Her lips pout, she looks restless and troubling. Mrs Benchley comes out from the door by the stage and walks straight past the altercation on and below stage to Mrs Toon and Mrs Hopere. —Where's Tess? she says. They have no idea. Ella is on her feet. —I'll have a look eh?

—Yes please, Ella. Una Benchley glances at her watch. —Cloakrooms first. If you haven't found her in fifteen minutes come to me backstage.

Ella springs away; the door bangs.

—It'll be all right, says Mrs Hopere, her eyes on Una's face, both hands clasping a maroon ticket roll.

—Of course, but they've started make-up. Mrs Benchley departs.

Mrs Toon chews her lower lip. She can't move obviously but it's another worry. Margory Stillburn lopes in the front door. —Margory! calls Mrs Toon and explains all. Mrs Stillburn departs quickly, her face resembling more than ever that of an endangered species of sharp-nosed marsupial.

Things are hotting up at Girls High. Not as regards temperature although the lights have been turned on. The air is sparking. Something is going to happen. Through the hall windows Mrs Toon can see the first of the parents hovering outside; the ones who arrive an hour early for everything and spend some time standing around in the hall when they are admitted, pointing and deciding which are the best seats of all. They will change places several times. They always bring neat fabric-covered cushions with handles and gaze with mild interest at the parents who scramble in at the last moment and sit or stand panting at the back of the hall.

Mrs Toon gazes at Cliff's gouache of Mother Courage and her waggon which is pinned on the wall beside her table. It is the original of the posters which Carmen, Cliff, Una and Brock plastered all over the city a month ago; even on illegal places like lamp posts because the authorities are usually lenient about minor infringements by Girls High. The painting fascinates Mrs Toon. She cannot understand how Cliff could have put both eyes on the profile side of the face, shown the full face as well and yet produced a strong likeness of Tess. More than a likeness, a portrait. The cart is good too. The black lines tug across the paper. The painting gives Mrs Toon a mad idea. Perhaps Cliff could paint Cissie and show what she is really like, underneath. But Scotty wouldn't like it. Not all those eyes.

Mrs Toon squares her shoulders, snaps out of it. Her eyes avoid those of the early parents who are not allowed in yet. One looks very like a previous Prime Minister. Perhaps he is a look-alike. He must be.

Mr Gilchrist, who comes up to Cam's shoulder, is talking to him earnestly. Mr Gilchrist has two pairs of walk shorts, one blue and grey checked polyester, the other a hot brown which Bryce is rude about. Mr Gilchrist alternates them throughout the year. No one has ever seen him in anything else. Mr Gilchrist's hand moves continually as he talks, tugging and twitching at the left side of his pants as he discusses the problem of the blue spot. Mr Gilchrist is knowledgeable and helpful and can't help being shy. Cam nods. —Yeah, he says, yeah. Sure.

Margot bounces out from backstage where she is Wardrobe and Carmen is Make-up.

—Has anyone seen her?

Cam and Mr Gilchrist try. —Who?

Margot shakes her head. —Tess. She sneezes violently. —And where's Sooze?

—I don't know, says Cam.

Margot sneezes again. An infuriating explosion of sound.

—The lilies, she gasps. Her eyes stream. She dabs them with a clutch of tissues from a box handed to her by Marcia Hobbs.

—Thanks, she gasps, retreating. —Thanks.

Marcia is all ready. This year's orchestra is not brilliant but they have worked hard. The leader, Beverley Ironside, is early. She sits tearing her nails to the quick, her hair a bush, her white face tense. —Relax, Beverley, says Marcia gently. She wears a long black frock with a rounded neckline and long sleeves. Her fluffy hair is piled on top of her head.

—Marcia suits her, doesn't it? hisses Beverley to her second fiddle Leonie when she arrives. Leonie glances up from her case. —Yeah. But so would Valerie. She squints higher. —Or Angela. She pauses. —Beverley even.

Beverley is not pleased.

Ella doesn't know what to do next. She has run at speed all through the school, or all the bits she can think of where Tess might be.

From the outside the school now looks like a ship ablaze with lights which, after a rattle of anchor chains and a few mournful bellows, will detach itself and sail into the harbour, an island of light broken off from the mainland.

Ella runs round the corner of the Main Lab and bangs into her friends from 3C; Sharon, Janine and Felicity. Sharon's hand leaps behind her gym. —Give us a drag, says Ella. —I could smell it a mile off, she lies. Her puff is furtive and not much fun. Coughing slightly she runs on to the Staff Toilets. She enters. Not a soul. Only the Men's opposite remains unsearched but Ella can't go in there because she is a girl. But Tess would. Tess wouldn't give a stuff. Ella opens the door cautiously. Someone is being sick, very sick. The noises are awful.

Tess Nation's face appears from the cubicle. —Get out of here! Her hands flap. —Out! Out!

Ella is terrified. Everyone knows that Tess eats third formers. Ella's dark eyes are wide. She stands her ground. —Mrs Benchley, she gasps.

Tess's face is scarlet. —Tell her I'm coming. And get out! *Out!*
Ella turns to flee. Tess grabs her arm. Someone moans somewhere. —If you tell, says Tess, —if you say one fucken word, I'll
kill you, you little bitch. The fingers clamp tight on Ella's brown
arm. —I mean it.

Ella is a brave messenger. She gulps. —I'll just say, I'll just say
you're coming, eh.

Tess drops Ella's arm and looks her in the eyes. —Yeah. She
nods slowly. —Yeah.

She opens the door, shoves Ella out and returns to the cubicle.
Annabelle is draped on the floor of the Men's toilet, her head
leans against the shiny white bowl. Tess presses the flush and lowers
the wooden seat. She lifts, almost drags Annabelle up from the vinyl
and cradles her in her arms. She leans her against the wall, she wets
paper towels and mops her face. She pushes back the tangled golden
hair and mops and mops, then dries. —You dumb little bitch, she
croons.

Annabelle's blue eyes are desperate. Her face is chalk white.
—He said . . . she gasps. —He said.

—Jesus Christ, sighs Tess, and takes her sister in her arms once
more.

—Where on earth have you been? Margot asks Sooze, glancing up
from running repairs to Swiss Cheese's trousers. Swiss Cheese
stands in the wide corridor which is Wardrobe, Make-Up and
Backstage, waiting in his/her shirt and bikini knickers, moon-like
face dark with numbers 5 and 9. The place reeks of greasepaint and
is very hot.

Sooze stares down at Margot. Since the incident in the Sports
Pavilion she has gone off Margot which she knows is totally
irrational and grossly unfair. When Margot is older she will talk
about menfolk.

—Did you like *Jonathan Livingstone Seagull?* she asks the pink
harried face.

—Where've you been!

—The car broke down. And we had a domestic, says Sooze.

Swiss Cheese is fascinated. So is Margot though she snaps on her not-in-front-of-the-children face. —All right, Madeline, she says, handing the mended pants to Swiss Cheese. —You're OK now.

—Thanks, Ms Murchison, says Swiss Cheese and departs reluctantly. —Tell, says Margot subsiding onto a chair, her knees clutched in boyish enthusiasm.

—Only if you tell me if you liked *Jonathan Livingstone Seagull*, says Sooze picking up the Chaplain's battered soutane and rehanging it. —When you were a kid.

—Of course I did, says Margot. —We all did.

—Mmn, says Sooze.

—Did you have a fight? begs Margot.

Sooze's hands are now busy rewinding the Cook's foot clothes.

—Just your average run of the mill up-and-downer. Bryce doesn't like it when the car goes phut.

—Men don't, says Margot, her face solemn.

—Is that right? says Sooze.

—How's the corporate wardrobe? says Carmen appearing from the make-up end. —Still no sign of Tess?

Margot looks around vaguely. —No.

Carmen shrugs and picks up the *Evening Post*. —'Lovely heavy cottons in full-blown stripes and reworked checks at sale prices,' she reads. —How about that?

Sooze could hug her.

Miss Franklin, Rita Vaughan and Brock burst in upon Miss Tamp in her study while she is adjusting the hang of her gown in front of the full-length mirror sniffed at by Miss Franklin. She did knock but the impetus of the group's arrival is such that they seem to storm in scattering pieces of broken barricades. They are all talking at once.

Miss Tamp holds up both hands, palm outwards. —Ladies. Ladies. And gentleman. Please. What is the problem?

Brock tells her that he is not going to see months, *months* of voluntary work (and he is about the highest paid dramaturg in LA not that he's mentioned it) go down the drain. —It is insane! Insane! He bangs his head between both hands.

Rita stands firm, a matronly guinea fowl in speckled black, white and grey. Her hands clasp and unclasp. Her damp lips move.

—I have always had my arrangement there! Always!

—But not this time. It'll wreck the whole input! Not only mine. I don't mean that. Brock's hand imitate Miss Tamp's palm outwards plea. —The whole flaming input. From everyone!

—I don't see why, huffs Rita. —It didn't wreck *Cradle Song* or *The Barretts of Wimpole Street*.

Brock tries. He really tries. He speaks slowly, carefully, straight at the elderly bimbo's red-veined cheeks. —Lady, he says gently, —This is theatre! This is Brecht! Not some *Fiddler on the Roof* wank.

Rita does not know what wank means, but she gets the drift. —Always! she insists.

Miss Franklin stands detached, a faint smile on her lips, her clipboard pressed to her russet bodice. She knows what will happen. And it does.

Miss Tamp sides with Brock. What else can she do. —You can't have flowers beside *Mother Courage*, she tells Rita gently. She takes her hand. Rita snatches it back. —Your flowers, your arrangements are a wonder, insists Miss Tamp. —We are all deeply grateful. Perhaps (oh joyful inspiration) they can go on top of the piano. That is the place!

—No one will see them, mutters Rita.

—They will. They will! Miss Tamp knows better than to appeal to Miss Franklin. —Won't they, Mr Benchley?

Brock is magnamimous in victory. —Sure, he says. —Sure. He lifts one hand to Miss Tamp as he departs and holds the door open for Rita who totters out, her face working.

Miss Franklin stands at the door and stares at Miss Tamp. Her lip curls, literally curls up the left side of her face. She leaves in silence.

Miss Tamp is oddly upset. She could have done nothing else. What else could she have done. The man was quite right. Flowers beside the Thirty Years War, let alone one of Rita Vaughan's spiked things, would wreck the most enthusiastic theatre-goer's perception of the play. Illusion recognised as illusion is one thing. Absurdity is another. But yet. But yet. Loyalty, loyalty, beats the pulse in her head. Miss Tamp moves to a long cupboard, hunts out a glass and pours herself a Flor Fino from the bottle she keeps for the Chairman of the Board of Trustees. She flings it back in one gulp. Her eyes meet the calm acceptance in those of the *Madonna del Parto*. Miss Tamp feels worse. Much worse.

Cam and Cliff are having a final check of Mother Courage's waggon in the quadrangle outside the Clothing Room. Cam pushes it from behind, pulls it from in front. It moves easily, smooth as silk it slinks across the asphalt looking great. Jenni Murphy's authentic looking artifacts rattle and clang. Cam and Cliff smile shyly at each other. Not bad eh, their eyes agree. They nod. Cliff starts pushing it towards the Administration Block past the boiler room and the line of tall silver rubbish tins.

Sooze runs around the corner heading for the Clothing Room. Someone has forgotten the sheet to cover Swiss Cheese's dead body at the end of Scene III. Sooze stops short, her hands are clasped, she is poised for flight. When Cam is old he will see her like this.

—Hi, he says.

—Hi.

They smile at each other. They stand very still.

—I thought I was pregnant, she says. —That's why I've kept away from the other work days. I was such a mess. . . . I didn't know what to do.

—I love you, says Cam.

—No.

—If you had been . . . he says some time later.

She shakes her head. —I'm not, she says. —Have you seen Bryce?

—No.

—He seems to have disappeared too. Her hand moves on Cam's face, tracing it as though she were blind. —He's talking about going back to University.

—What the hell for?

—He's got to do something. I can pay it, the fees. BCA. She looks him in the eye. —I'm OK now.

Cam takes her wandering hand and hides it in his. He takes a deep breath. —I could try and get him a job maybe. Put in a word with Mac at the site.

—Oh Cam. There is nothing to say but she tries. —He can't hammer, she says. She stands on her toes to kiss him once more. The tip of her tongue meets his, withdraws, meets again.

—It wouldn't work, she says eventually. —And anyway how could we. The sheet, she gasps, and runs for it.

Ella has blurted out her message to Una. —She's just coming, Mrs Benchley. Right now, she's coming.

—I'll go and get her.

—No, no. Ella dances about in front of Una's bulk, a mother bird attempting diversion from the nest. —She's just coming. Fair go.

Una pushes her to one side and strides out of the hall door. Rita Vaughan, Miss Franklin and Brock progress down the stairs in single file. Brock is very cheerful.

—Hi, he says on the bottom step. —What news on the Rialto?

—Oh shut up, snaps Una and surges on.

She meets Tess and Annabelle around the corner. Tess has her arm round Annabelle.

—Annabelle! says Una, —What's wrong?

—She's a bit sick, says Tess. —I'm taking her to the sick room.

—There's no one there, says Una. —Matron's not on duty.

Tess's head lifts. —Then I'll stay with her. She will too. Una can see that. —Come along, she says and escorts them to the Sick Bay. —Lie down Annabelle, she says, folding the blue bed cover briskly and pulling the inadequate curtain.

Annabelle collapses onto the narrow bed and puts one arm across her face. Tess tips the water out of Matron's wide-necked vase of Iceberg roses, dumps them in the sink and puts the vase on the floor beside Annabelle. She sits beside her and holds her hand.

Una chews her lip. —Tess, she says, —Annabelle. If I get Mrs Stillburn to mind Annabelle, Tess, will you come and be made up? She glances at her watch. —It's getting late.

Tess says nothing. She looks at Annabelle who moves her arm and gives Tess the faintest possible nod. Her forehead is sweating. —I'm OK now, she says.

—OK, says Tess. She glares up at Una. —But I'm not leaving till she comes.

Una almost runs out the door.

Margory Stillburn has bathed Annabelle's face again, made her tea and wrapped her in an Air Cell blanket. It is too hot for a hot water bottle. She turns off the main light. There is a small light with a red shade by the bed. She sits beside Annabelle in Matron's cane chair. —Don't talk Annabelle, she says. —Try to go to sleep. It's all right. I'll take you both home.

—I think I'm going to have a baby, whispers Annabelle who is fourteen.

Margory's hands clench. She says nothing.

—He said it was all right, see.

—Yes, says Margory.

Annabelle grabs for the vase and retches green bile. —I've got a real shitty pain, Mrs Stillburn, she gasps.

Margory's hand is on the telephone.

Annabelle sits bolt upright. —Where's Tess? Tess, she screams.

—I'm here Annabelle, I'm here, says Margory.

The lights of the parking cars search around the room.

—Tess, moans Annabelle. —Jesus, Tess.

*

Gutless had died in the middle of Oriental Bay. It died slowly, drifting to a halt outside the Teps.

—Sod the thing, muttered Bryce.

Sooze leant forward. —Petrol, she said.

Bryce swung at her. —What d'you mean, petrol?

—Just what I said. Petrol. Look. Her finger demonstrated.

—I filled it just the other day!

—OK OK. You filled it just the other day. She paused. —When?

His face was outraged. —Don't you believe me!

—Sure, sure. I believe you. I believe you! It's sprung a leak. It's sprung a great big thundering leak and all the lovely lovely petrol's gone way way leakies.

—Very funny. Bryce flung himself about, arms flailing. —Ha ha ha!

Her face changed. —I don't believe you. Why should I pretend I do! She swung around, leapt onto her knees and stretched her arm down to the floor behind her seat for the orange petrol can, an essential part of Gutless's survival kit. She dragged it back, narrowly missing Bryce's left ear, and slid back into her seat. She waved the thing in front of him. —Here you are, she said.

—What do you want me to do with it?

Her hands tightened on the handle. —I want you to take this can and walk to the nearest garage and get it filled with petrol and walk back here and put it in the tank so that you can drive this, this *thing* to school. She snatched at her watch. —We're late already.

—What's the point if there's a leak?

—There isn't a fucking leak, she shouted. She waved the can in rage. It cracked her knee bone. Tears of pain leapt to her eyes. She shoved the thing at him gasping. —Petrol.

He looked around, his eyes vague behind his glasses. — Where's the nearest garage?

Her head was high. —I don't know. I'm a woman. Boys get petrol for car cars.

He stared at her. Her eyes were wild, her face flushed. —I'll kill you, he said quietly.

She nodded. —OK, she said. —OK. Do that.

They drive in rigid silence to the Main Door of the Assembly Hall. Sooze scrambles out. —Use the Staff Car Park, she says.

—Too kind, snarls Bryce and drives on. He parks the car in the Car Park, turns off the ignition and sits silent, staring at the cyclone netting fence, his driving glasses still on. After about five minutes he replaces the key which is still clenched in his hand, starts up, backs out past Carmen's red Nifty Fifty and drives down the main drive. Jenni Murphy waves to him as she walks up the left-hand side past the oleanders but he doesn't recognise her. Her hair is now electric blue, rather effective. She carries the portable vidcam slung over her shoulder. Bryce drives to the nearest pub to think.

He hasn't been here for years. It used to be brown, friendly but anonymous. Someone has tarted the place up. There are bright lights, stainless steel, black and grey plastic. The drinkers are exactly the same as before. They have not kept up.

Bryce leans against the bar and orders a whisky. Someone shoves a heavy Grants Whisky ashtray along the counter. It skids along the spilt beer on the stainless steel, streaking past his eyes. Bryce stares at the expanse of steel. His hands tighten on its rim. He never told Sooze why he left the morgue. She was glad at the time though, very glad. And now what, now what. Thunderguts murmurs in his ear. —I always knew you were a quitter.

There is a lot of noise. A great deal of noise. A small man next to Bryce wears a long yellow coat over his shorts. It comes well below his knees. Bryce's grandmother had one like it. Her duster coat, she called it. The man is telling a story with much emphasis. —He said, he said to me the other day, he said, You're getting bald. I said, Not as bald as you are. He said, My daughter was married the other day. I said, No! The small man hitches at his yellow coat and drinks deeply. —The older you are the quicker they grow, he says.

His companion nods into his beer. —You're right there, he says sadly. —It catches up with you.

Bryce shoves out his arm with the empty glass. —'Nother whisky, he says. —Hey Jack. Another whisky, please.

Bryce is a cheap drunk. He has no head at all which is why he seldom drinks.

He stands in the Men's at Girls High and slaps cold water from the hand basin over his face. He peers at himself with interest; dark eyes, dark curly hair, a lot of hair. He is hairy, Bryce. Sooze has never expressed any objection though she gets sick of them in the bathroom but Bryce does the cleaning now. Bryce's mouth is slightly open as he pulls down the lower eyelid of his left eye. Cliff walks in.

—Hi, says Bryce.

Cliff walks in silence to the cubicle and gushes forth.

Bryce reverts to Standard Four body language for insult. He jigs from one foot to the other. He sniggers. —Not playing speaks then?

Cliff comes out, all zipped up and ready to go. He rinses his hands in silence, dries them on a paper towel and throws it on the floor.

—Pick that up, orders Bryce. He points to the rubbish bin. —Put it in there.

—Get stuffed, says Cliff, heading for the door.

Bryce reaches out an arm and grabs his shoulder. —Talking of which, he says. —Is Carmen a good fuck?

Cliff swings in amazement. —I've often wondered, says Bryce.

Cliff lays in. He really lays in. His strength is as the strength of ten. He has never punched anyone in his life. He regards violence as the pits. He is a pacifist. His arms flail about. His fists are balled. A blow cracks against Bryce's jaw. Cliff is even more astonished. The knuckles of his left hand smart. Bryce crashes against the swing door of the Men's and collapses on the polished vinyl corridor. His hand touches his jaw. He looks stoned. Carmen, who has been sent by Una to find Sooze and Swiss Cheese's sheet pronto, nearly falls over him.

—What's going on! She is furious. Absolutely livid. She drags Bryce up from the floor. He nearly falls over. —You stink, says Carmen.

Cliff leans against the opposite wall of the corridor panting. How amazing. He beams at his lady. He smiles at his love.

Carmen looks from one to the other. —What the hell've you been doing! she says.

There is silence. Bryce's hands which have been supporting his face, open. He peers at her. —I asked him if you were a good fuck, he says. His head moves from side to side. —Shouldn't've done that. He blows air slowly out through his mouth and looks at Cliff. —Apologise. Ttt. Apologise . . . profusely.

Carmen's silence lasts only a second. —Why didn't you ask *me*! Her head lifts. Her eyes blaze. —I could've told you. I've never had any complaints.

She rounds on Cliff. —What the hell do you think I am! Some sort of bloody *damsel*. I will not, I will not be *fought* over. I can look after myself! It's bad enough, it's bad enough, she says, her face pink, her hands moving, —not being able to take my clothes off without you sketching or painting or mooning about staring at me as though I'm some sort of freak! I'm me! I'm me! Her hands slam the front of her T-shirt. —Not some bloody trophy. Not some art thing. What's happened to your painting of Sooze? Why've you never finished that!

—Sooze, says Bryce thoughtfully. He turns and walks up the corridor towards the Assembly Hall. One hand pats the wall occasionally. —Sooze, he says.

Una stands backstage watching Tess who sits silent; made up, dressed, waiting. She could wait for ever. The other members of the cast jiggle and prance about her. They preen themselves constantly in front of the spotty mirrors. They are enchanted with their make-up, their pretend clothes, their own special props. They fuss and fidget and sweat with first night nerves. Their hearts beat fast. —Shit, they mutter to each other with sweaty palms. —I'm terrified. —Me too, they gasp. Nothing will ever be quite as good, in this particular way, ever again.

Tracey the backstage runner tugs Una's sleeve. —Telephone, Mrs Benchley. It's Mrs Stillburn.

Una looks away quickly from Tess whose head lifts. —Thank you Tracey, she says and walks to the far end of Wardrobe where the phone hangs on the wall.

Margory's voice is a whisper. —I've rung the ambulance, she says. —I thought she might be having a miscarriage . . .

—What! gasps Una.

—. . . but she's asleep now, continues Margory. There is a long pause. —She wanted Tess.

Una says nothing. She concentrates on not looking at Tess.

—What'll we do? says Margory. —I'll go with her of course if, if she has to, but . . .

—Keep in touch, says Una. —Let me know what they say.

Rita's arrangement on the piano is a dead bore but what can Marcia do. She has to duck around the thing as she conducts the orchestra through the *allegretto* from a *Divertimento* by Mozart which they do really well except for a slight dragging in the strings. She is not sure whether the pianist Phoebe Saltburn can see her at all. It really is a bit much. Marcia smiles approvingly at the girls in the orchestra and sits again. The applause is considerable. —Lovely, murmur the parents of the musical.

The hall is full. The usual panting latecomers pile in the back looking both hunted and relieved. They are not allowed to stand because of fire regulations but there is no way they can disperse to the scattered empty seats throughout the hall at this stage. Mrs Toon and Mrs Hopere will help them at the end of Scene One.

Marcia sits with her hands in her lap. The silent foxtrotters in the Shinto temple flash upon her inward eye which is the hell of solitude.

A ripple of interest follows the Video Team as they move down from the back of the hall to begin filming. Jenni is director, three flushed seventh formers operate the camera, the lights and the boom mike. Everyone is impressed, even the Back to Basics members of the audience.

There is a hush as Miss Tamp, Miss Franklin, Mr Smythe, Mrs Smythe, the members of the Board of Trustees and their partners file into their reserved seats four rows from the front. Thea Sinclair in the row behind looks at Miss Tamp's pale face. What on earth's the matter with her?

As Miss Tamp replaced her unwashed sherry glass in the back of the cupboard there had been a knock on her door. —Come in, she called.

Miss Franklin entered and closed the door. —I have been giving serious consideration to the proposal you made, she said.

Miss Tamp says nothing. Can it be, can it possibly be.

—I thought it a sincere proposal, one made genuinely for the good of the school.

—It was.

—I was of a mind to accept it. To attempt some sort of working compromise.

Miss Tamp's heart beats faster. —Good, she says quietly.

Miss Franklin slams it straight across the room at her. —But your behaviour tonight! To side with that, that *man*, against someone like Rita Vaughan! A member of your own staff. A long-time hard-working devoted staff member like Rita. No! storms Miss Franklin, both hands tugging at the front of her MA gown. —I will not attempt what you please to call a *modus vivendi* with someone without an ounce of loyalty. Not one ounce of loyalty! I shall take *my* 'dossier', as you call it, to the Board of Trustees.

Miss Franklin's back is ramrod straight. —I thought, she says, —that I should let you know.

The door opens following a perfunctory tap. —Ah, Miss Franklin, beams Mr Smythe, —you're here before us. Beaten us to the draw, eh. Grace? he says to his caftanned spouse. —You remember Miss Franklin, our First Assistant? His arm waves. —Miss Tamp of course you know.

Miss Franklin and Miss Tamp bow. Mrs Smythe smiles her golden smile.

—Would you care for a glass of sherry? murmurs Miss Tamp.

Marcia puts down her baton at the end of the second *passepied* from a Bach Suite. —Well *done*, she mouths at the orchestra.

The curtain parts, assisted at the edges by Ella and Tracey. The audience leans forward. The Leavers' Play has begun.

On the bare stage a Sergeant and a Recruiter stand shivering.

—How can you muster a unit in a place like this? asks the Recruiter.

They discuss problems of war and peace. The Sergeant explains that it takes a war to restore order. That in peace time the human race runs wild. That it's a job to get a war going but that once it's blossomed there is no holding it.

A jew's-harp is heard.

The cart rolls on pulled by Eilif and Swiss Cheese. On it sit Mother Courage and her daughter Kattrin, who is dumb.

Also available in Vintage

Barbara Anderson

PORTRAIT OF THE ARTIST'S WIFE

'Acutely observed, furiously gleeful, compulsively readable
...the work of a natural writer'
Janet Frame

'Extraordinary: an engaging narrative on Art v Love, sweeping across continents and cultures with visionary under-
standing of emotions and the games people play. It's the
story of Sarah Tandy, a New Zealand painter, and her
marriage to Jack, a brilliant novelist if hopeless person.
From her childhood in the Bay, through wedded bliss,
cultural odysseys in Europe and life on the homestead, this
novel spans forty years of love and misunderstanding,
unhappy families and artistic licence...This is a moving,
universal novel, a pleasure to read'
Time Out

'Barbara Anderson's novel is a rarity; an unadulterated,
unpretentious, enjoyable read...the voice that emerges
strongly from the book is intelligent and thoughtful and
vibrantly alive'
The Herald

VINTAGE

Also available in Vintage

Alice Hoffman

HERE ON EARTH

'Hoffman is shrewd and witty about the networks of gossip and affection in town, and she evokes place superbly... spellbinding'
Sunday Times

'When March returns to her childhood home to attend a funeral with her teenage daughter, she revisits the raw passion of an unrequited love. Abandoning her marriage and her own interests to resume an affair, she discovers that her former lover is a collector, a modern Bluebeard with violent tendencies. A gripping novel that evokes the tensions of small-town life'
Elle

'There is something irresistible about the novels of Alice Hoffman...Her stories have a quality of mystery and even darkness that puts a fresh spin on the commonplace, and at its very best can make the reader look at life from a fresh angle. If I could see things through Hoffman's eyes, I'm convinced life would be richer and more interesting...*Here on Earth* is a wonderful piece of storytelling'
Literary Review

VINTAGE

Also available in Vintage

Erik Fosnes Hansen

PSALM AT JOURNEY'S END

'The stories of the *Titanic*'s seven musicians, the famous
band that played as the ship went down'
The Times

'A great classical tale of experience and coming of age, of
friendship and love, of growth and demise. With its carefully researched exactitude, it is also a thoroughly modern
depiction of the beauty and self-destructiveness of European
culture'
Peter Høeg, author of
Miss Smilla's Feeling for Snow

'A rich, intricate narrative...With clear, balanced, at times
poetic prose, and a feeling for historical detail and psycho-
logical complexity, Hansen offers...an ensemble of com-
pelling character studies'
Time Out, New York

'A masterfully composed novel'
Jostein Gaarder, author of *Sophie's World*

VINTAGE

A SELECTED LIST OF CONTEMPORARY FICTION
AVAILABLE IN VINTAGE

☐ THE FERMATA	Nicholson Baker	£5.99
☐ GIRLS HIGH	Barbara Anderson	£5.99
☐ PORTRAIT OF THE ARTIST'S WIFE	Barbara Anderson	£5.99
☐ FALL ON YOUR KNEES	Ann-Marie MacDonald	£6.99
☐ I WAS AMELIA EARHART	Jane Mendelsohn	£5.99
☐ BIRDSONG	Sebastian Faulks	£6.99
☐ PSALM AT JOURNEY'S END	Erik Fosnes Hansen	£6.99
☐ HERE ON EARTH	Alice Hoffman	£6.99
☐ THE EBONY TOWER	John Fowles	£6.99
☐ THE MAGUS	John Fowles	£7.99
☐ THE PRINCE OF WEST END AVENUE	Alan Isler	£5.99
☐ THE CONVERSATIONS AT CURLOW CREEK	David Malouf	£5.99
☐ REMEMBERING BABYLON	David Malouf	£6.99
☐ THE GIANT'S HOUSE	Elizabeth McCracken	£5.99
☐ BELOVED	Toni Morrison	£6.99
☐ TAR BABY	Toni Morrison	£6.99
☐ THE WAY I FOUND HER	Rose Tremain	£6.99

- All Vintage books are available through mail order or from your local bookshop.

- Please send cheque/eurocheque/postal order (sterling only), Access, Visa, Mastercard, Diners Card, Switch or Amex:

☐☐☐☐☐☐☐☐☐☐☐☐☐☐☐☐

Expiry Date:_____ Signature:_____

Please allow 75 pence per book for post and packing U.K.
Overseas customers please allow £1.00 per copy for post and packing.

ALL ORDERS TO:
Vintage Books, Books by Post, TBS Limited, The Book Service,
Colchester Road, Frating Green, Colchester, Essex CO7 7DW

NAME:_____

ADDRESS:_____

_____

_____

Please allow 28 days for delivery. Please tick box if you do not
wish to receive any additional information   ☐
Prices and availability subject to change without notice.